AS236182

Praise for the Lily Bard Mysteries

'Ex ptionally well-plotted . . . an extremely compelling
Romantic Times

d, clever and quick' *Library Journal*

'L is a terrific character with dark shadings and stark fe but learning strength and cleaving to it. A supporting ca of quirky characters fully rendered in quick strokes w old readers as surely as the complex resolution in this c on the bleeding edge of noir' *Booklist*

ing . . . Lily's triumphant progress from scarred to fierce fighter is very rewarding. Bravo, Ms Harris!'
Pen & Dagger

test engaging outing . . . indeed, Lily has such an e ng voice, full of pain and redemption, that the c ng of clues and the unfolding of the crime take a b at to her personal story' *Publishers Weekly*

er, more unusual, than any other mystery I've read This novel is the third in the series; the other two tter be waiting for me under the Christmas tree'
Washington Post Sunday Book World

D0321236

Charlaine Harris is the bestselling author of the *Sookie Stackhouse* series, adapted for HBO as *True Blood*, as well as three other exceptional series – *The Aurora Teagarden Mysteries*, *The Lily Bard Mysteries* and *The Harper Connelly Series*. She is married, with children, and lives in central Texas.

By Charlaine Harris

STANDALONE NOVELS

Sweet and Deadly
A Secret Rage

THE AURORA TEAGARDEN MYSTERIES

Real Murders
A Bone to Pick
Three Bedrooms, One Corpse
The Julius House
Dead Over Heels
A Fool and His Honey
Last Scene Alive
Poppy Done to Death

THE LILY BARD MYSTERIES

Shakespeare's Landlord
Shakespeare's Champion
Shakespeare's Christmas
Shakespeare's Trollop
Shakespeare's Counselor

THE SOOKIE STACKHOUSE NOVELS

Dead Until Dark
Living Dead in Dallas
Club Dead
Dead to the World
Dead as a Doornail
Definitely Dead
All Together Dead
From Dead to Worse
Dead and Gone
Dead in the Family
Dead Reckoning
Deadlocked
Dead Ever After
A Touch of Dead
The Sookie Stackhouse Companion
After Dead

THE HARPER CONNELLY SERIES

Grave Sight
Grave Surprise
An Ice Cold Grave
Grave Secret

SHAKESPEARE'S COUNSELOR

A LILY BARD MYSTERY

CHARLAINE HARRIS

An Orion paperback

First published in Great Britain in 2011
by Gollancz
This paperback edition published in 2013
by Orion Books,
an imprint of The Orion Publishing Group Ltd,
Orion House, 5 Upper St Martin's Lane,
London WC2H 9EA

An Hachette UK company

1 3 5 7 9 10 8 6 4 2

Copyright © Charlaine Harris 2001

The moral right of Charlaine Harris to be identified as the author
of this work has been asserted in accordance with
the Copyright, Designs and Patents Act 1988.

All rights reserved. No part of this publication may be
reproduced, stored in a retrieval system, or transmitted,
in any form or by any means, electronic, mechanical,
photocopying, recording or otherwise, without the prior
permission of the copyright owner.

All the characters in this book are fictitious,
and any resemblance to actual persons, living
or dead, is purely coincidental.

A CIP catalogue record for this book
is available from the British Library.

ISBN 978-1-4091-4732-9

Typeset at The Spartan Press Ltd,
Lymington, Hants

Printed and bound in Great Britain by
Clays Ltd, St Ives plc

The Orion Publishing Group's policy is to use papers
that are natural, renewable and recyclable products and
made from wood grown in sustainable forests. The logging
and manufacturing processes are expected to conform to
the environmental regulations of the country of origin.

www.charlaineharris.com
www.orionbooks.co.uk

This book is dedicated to the memory of
Elizabeth Daniels Squire,
who was many things – all of them good.

DUMFRIES & GALLOWAY LIBRARIES	
AS236182	
Askews & Holts	Jan-2014
AF	£7.99

Chapter One

I connected with a hard blow to the nose, rolled on top of him, gripped his neck, and started to squeeze. After the pain, the unfathomable humiliation, this rage was completely pure and good. His hands gripped my wrists, struggled to pull my fingers away. He was making noises, hoarse and pleading, and I gradually realized he was saying my name.

That wasn't part of the memory.

And I wasn't back in that shack in the cotton fields. I was on a firm wide bed, not a sagging cot.

'Lily! Stop!' The grip on my wrists increased.

I wasn't in the right place – or rather, the wrong place.

'Lily!'

This wasn't the right man . . . the wrong man.

I released my grip and scrambled off the bed, backing into a corner of the bedroom. My breath was coming in ragged pants, and my heart thudded way too close to my ears.

A light came on, blinding me for the moment. When I got used to the radiance, I realized with agonizing slowness that I was looking at Jack. Jack Leeds. Jack had blood streaming from his nose and red marks on his neck.

I'd done that to him.

I'd done my best to kill the man I loved.

'I know you don't want to do this, but maybe it'll help,' Jack was telling me, his voice altered by the swelling of his nose and throat.

I tried very hard not to look sullen. I didn't want to go to any damn therapy group. I didn't like to talk about myself, and wasn't that what therapy was for? On the other hand, and this was the decisive hand, I didn't want to hit Jack again, either.

For one thing, hitting was a terrible insult to the one you loved.

For another thing, eventually Jack would hit me back. Considering how strong he was, that was not an unimportant factor.

So, later that morning, after Jack left to drive to Little Rock to talk to a client, I called the number on the flyer we'd seen at the grocery store. Printed on bright green paper, it had caught Jack's eye while I was buying stamps at the office booth at the front of the store.

It read:

HAVE YOU BEEN SEXUALLY ASSAULTED?

ARE YOU FEELING ALONE?

CALL TODAY 237-7777

ATTEND OUR THERAPY GROUP

ALONE NO MORE!

'Hartsfield County Health Center,' said a woman's voice.

I cleared my throat. 'I'd like to find out about the therapy group for rape survivors,' I said, in as level a voice as I could manage.

'Of course,' said the woman, her voice scrupulously neutral and so consciously nonjudgmental it made my teeth hurt. 'The group meets Tuesday nights at eight, here at the center. You don't have to give me your name at this time. Just come in the end door, you know, the door that opens on the staff parking lot? You can park there, too.'

'All right,' I said. I hesitated, then asked a crucial question. 'How much is it?'

'We got a grant to do this,' she said. 'It's free.'

My tax dollars at work. Somehow that made me feel better.

'Can I tell Tamsin you'll be coming?' the woman asked. Definitely a local; I could tell by the number of syllables in 'tell.'

'Let me think about it,' I told her, suddenly frightened of taking a step that would undoubtedly add to my pain.

Carol Althaus lived in the middle of chaos. I had dropped all but three of my customers, and I wished Carol had been one of them, but I'd had one of my rare moments of pity and kept her on. I was only cleaning Carol, the Winthrops, and the Drinkwaters, and Monday was the day I did all three. I went back to the Winthrops on Thursday, and I remained open for the odd errand or special cleaning job other days, but I was also working for Jack, so my schedule was complicated.

Carol's chaos was of her own making, the way I saw it, but it was still chaos, and I like order.

Carol's life had gone out of control when she'd married Jay Althaus, a divorced salesman with two sons. To Jay's credit, he had custody of his sons. To Jay's debit, he was on the road all the time, and though he may have loved Carol, who was anemically attractive, religious, and stupid, he also needed a live-in baby-sitter. So he married Carol, and despite all their previous experiences with the two boys, they had their own babies, two girls. I'd begun working for Carol when she was pregnant with the second girl, throwing up intermittently every day and sitting limply in a recliner the rest of the time. I'd kept all of the children for a day and a half, only once, when Jay had had a car wreck out of town.

Probably these children were not demonic. Possibly, they were quite typical. But collectively, they were hell.

And hard on a house, too.

Carol needed me to come at least twice a week, for maybe six hours at a stretch. She could afford four hours a week, just barely. I gave Carol Althaus the best value for her money she would find anywhere.

During the school year, it was nearly possible for Carol to cope. Heather and Dawn were still at home, only five and three years old, but the boys (Cody and Tyler) were in school. Summers were another kettle of fish.

It was late June, so the kids had all been home for about three weeks. Carol had enrolled them in four Bible schools. The First Baptists and the Central Methodists had already completed their summer programs, and the house was even more littered with paper fish and bread glued to paper plates, sheep made from cotton balls and Popsicle sticks, and lopsided drawings of fishermen pulling in nets filled with people. Shakespeare Combined Church (a fundamentalist coalition) and the joint Episcopalian/Catholic Bible schools were yet to come.

I entered with my own key to find Carol standing in the middle of the kitchen, trying to get the snarls out of Dawn's long curls. The little girl was wailing. She had on a nightgown with Winnie the Pooh on the front. She was wearing toy plastic high heels and she'd gotten into her mother's makeup.

I surveyed the kitchen and began to gather dishes. When I reentered the kitchen a minute later, laden with dirty glasses and two plates that had been on the floor in the den, Carol was still standing in the middle of the floor, a quizzical expression on her face.

'Good morning, Lily,' she said, in a pointed way.

'Hello, Carol.'

'Is something wrong?'

'No.' Why tell Carol? Would she be reassured about my well-being if I told her I'd tried to kill Jack the night before?

'You could say hello when you come in,' Carol said, that little smile still playing across her face. Dawn looked up at me with as much fascination as if I'd been a cobra. Her hair was still a mess. I could solve that with a pair of scissors and a brush in about five minutes, and I found the idea very tempting.

'I'm sorry, I was thinking of other things,' I told Carol politely. 'Was there anything special you needed done today?'

Carol shook her head, that faint smile still on her face. 'Just the usual magic,' she said wryly, and bent to Dawn's head again. As she worked the brush through the little girl's thick hair, the oldest boy dashed into the kitchen in his swimming trunks.

'Mom, can I go swimming?' Carol's fair complexion and brown hair had been passed on to both the girls, but the boys favored, I supposed, their own mother: they were both freckle-faced and redheaded.

'Where?' Carol asked, using a yellow elastic band to pull Dawn's hair up into a ponytail.

'Tommy Sutton's. I was invited,' Cody assured her. 'I can walk there by myself, remember?' Cody was ten and Carol had given him a range of streets he could take by himself.

'Okay. Be back in two hours.'

Tyler erupted into the kitchen roaring with rage. 'That's not fair! I want to go swimming!'

'Weren't invited,' Cody sneered. 'I was.'

'I know Tommy's brother! I could go!'

As Carol laid down the law I loaded the dishwasher and cleaned the kitchen counters. Tyler retreated to his room with a lot of door slamming and fuming. Dawn trotted off to play with her Duplos, and Carol left the room in such a hurry I wondered if she was ill. Heather appeared at my elbow to watch my every move.

I am not much of a kid person. I don't like, or dislike, all children. I take it on an individual basis, as I do with adults. I very nearly liked Heather Althaus. She would be old enough for kindergarten in the fall, she had short, easy-to-deal-with hair since a drastic self-barbering job that had driven Carol to tears, and she tried to take care of herself. Heather eyed me solemnly, said 'Hey, Miss Lily,' and extricated a frozen waffle from the side-by-side. After popping it in the toaster, Heather got her own plate, fork, and knife and set them on the counter. Heather had on lime green shorts and a kingfisher blue shirt, not a happy combination, but she'd gotten dressed herself and I could respect that. In acknowledgment, I poured a glass of orange juice for her and set it on the table. Tyler and Dawn trotted through on their way out to the fenced-in backyard.

For a comfortable time, Heather and I shared the kitchen silently. As she ate her waffle, Heather raised her feet one at a time when I swept, and moved her own chair when I mopped.

When there was only a puddle of syrup on the plate, Heather said, 'My mama's gonna have a baby. She says God will give us a little brother or a sister. She says we don't get to pick.'

I leaned on my mop for a moment and considered this news. It explained the unpleasant noises coming from the bathroom. I could not think of one single thing to say, so I nodded. Heather wriggled off the chair and ran to the switch to turn on the overhead fan to dry the floor quickly, as I always did.

'It's true the baby won't come for a long time?' the little girl asked me.

'That's true,' I said.

'Tyler says Mama's tummy will get real big like a watermelon.'

'That's true, too.'

'Will they have to cut her open with a knife, like Daddy does the watermelon?'

'No.' I hoped I wasn't lying. 'She won't pop, either,' I added, just to cover another anxiety.

'How will the baby get out?'

'Moms like to explain that in their own way,' I said, after I'd thought a little. I would rather have answered her matter-of-factly, but I didn't want to usurp Carol's role.

Through the sliding glass doors to the backyard (doors that were perpetually decorated with handprints) I could see that Dawn had carried her Duplos into the sandbox. They'd have to be washed off. Tyler was firing the soft projectiles of some Nerf weapon in the general direction of a discarded plastic soda bottle he'd filled with water. The two seemed to be fine, and I couldn't see any danger actually lurking. I reminded myself to check again in five minutes, since Carol was definitely indisposed.

With Heather at my heels, I went to the room she shared with her sister and began to change the sheets. I figured that any second, Heather would exhaust her attention span and go find something else to do. But instead, Heather sat on a child-sized Fisher Price chair and observed me with close attention.

'You don't *look* crazy,' she told me.

I stopped pulling the flat sheet straight and glanced over my shoulder at the little girl.

'I'm not,' I said, my voice flat and final.

It would be hard to pin down exactly why this hurt me, but it did. What a senseless thing to waste emotion on, the repetition by a child of something she'd apparently heard adults say.

'So why do you walk by yourself at night? Isn't that a scary thing to do? Only ghosts and monsters are out at night.'

My first response was that I myself was scarier than any ghost or monster. But that would hardly be reassuring to a little girl, and already other ideas were flickering through my head.

'I'm not afraid at night,' I said, which was close to the truth. I was not any more afraid at night than I was in the daytime, for sure.

'So you do it to show them you're not afraid?' Heather asked.

The same wrenching pain filled me that I'd felt when I saw Jack's bloody nose. I straightened, dirty sheets in a bundle in my arms, and looked down at the little girl for a long moment.

'Yes,' I said. 'That's exactly why I do it.'

I knew then and there that I would be at the therapy session the next night. It was time.

For now, I taught Heather how to make hospital folds.

Chapter Two

I slid through the designated door the next night as though I'd come to steal some help, not to get it for free.

There were four cars in the parking lot, which was only partially visible from the street. I recognized two of them.

The side door we were to use was a heavy metal door. It slid shut behind me with a heavy thud, and I walked toward the only two rooms that were well lit. All the other doors up and down the corridor were shut, and I was willing to bet they were probably locked as well.

A woman appeared in the first open doorway and called, 'Come on in! We're ready to get started!' As I got closer I could see she was as dark as I was blond, she was as soft as I am hard, and I was to find she talked twice as much as I'd ever thought about doing. 'I'm Tamsin Lynd,' she said, extending her hand.

'Lily Bard,' I said, taking the hand and giving it a good shake.

She winced. 'Lily? . . .'

'Bard,' I supplied, resigned to what was to come.

Her eyes got round behind their glasses, which were wire framed and small. Tamsin Lynd clearly recognized my name, which was a famous one if you read a lot of true crime.

'Before you go in the therapy room, Lily, let me tell you the rules.' She stepped back and gestured, and I went into what was clearly her office. The desk and its chair were arranged facing the door, and there were books and papers everywhere. The room was pretty small, and there wasn't space for much after the desk and chair and two bookcases and a filing cabinet. The wall behind the desk was covered with what looked like carpeting, dark gray with pink flecks to match the carpet on the floor. I decided it had been designed for use as a bulletin board of sorts. Tamsin Lynd had fixed newspaper and magazine clippings to it with push-pins, and the effect was at least a little cheerful. The therapist didn't invite me to sit, but stood right in front of me examining me closely. I wondered if she imagined herself a mind reader.

I waited. When she saw I wasn't going to speak, Tamsin began, 'Every woman in this group has been through a lot, and this therapy group is designed to help each and every one get used to being in social situations and work situations and alone situations, without being overwhelmed with fear. So what we say here is confidential, and we have to have your word that the stories you hear in this room stop in your head. That's the most important rule. Do you agree to this?'

I nodded. I sometimes felt the whole world had heard my story. But if I'd had a chance to prevent it, not a soul would've known.

'I've never had a group like this here in Shakespeare, but I've run them before. Women start coming to this group when they can stand talking about what happened to them – or when they can't stand their lives as they are. Women leave the group when they feel better about themselves. You can come as long as I run it, if you need to. Now, let's go to the therapy room and you can meet the others.'

But before we could move, the phone rang.

Tamsin Lynd's reaction was extraordinary. She jerked

and turned to face her desk. Her hand shot out and rested on top of the receiver. When it rang again, her fingers tightened around the phone, but she still didn't lift it. I decided it would be tactful to step around the desk and look at the clippings on the wall. Predictably, most were about rape, stalking, and the workings of the court system. Some were about brave women. The counselor's graduate and postgraduate degrees were framed and displayed, and I was duly impressed.

The manifestly intelligent Tamsin had picked up the phone and said, 'Hello?' as though she was scared to death.

The next thing I knew, she'd gasped and sunk down into the client chair in front of the desk. I abandoned my attempt to look like I wasn't there.

'Stop this,' the therapist hissed into the phone. 'You have to stop this! No, I won't listen!' And she smashed the receiver into its cradle as though she was bashing in someone's head. Tamsin took several deep breaths, almost sobbing. Then she was enough under control to speak to me.

'If you'll go on next door,' she said, in a voice creditably even, 'I'll be there in a minute. I just need to collect a few things.'

Like her wits and her composure. I hesitated, about to offer help, then realizing that was ludicrous under the circumstances. I eased out from behind Tamsin's desk and out the door, took two steps to the left, and went into another.

The room next door was probably a lot of things besides the therapy room. There was a large institutional table, surrounded by the usual butt-numbing institutional chairs. The room was windowless and had a couple of insipid landscapes on the walls as a gesture toward decoration.

There were women already waiting, some with canned drinks and notepads in front of them.

My almost-friend Janet Shook was there, and a woman whose face was familiar in an unpleasant way. For a moment, I had to think of her name, and then I realized the formally dressed, fortyish big-haired woman was Sandy McCorkindale, wife of the minister of Shakespeare Combined Church, known locally as SCC. Sandy and I had clashed a couple of times when I'd been hired by the church to serve refreshments at board meetings of the SCC preschool, and we'd had a difference of opinion at the Ladies' Luncheon, an annual church wingding.

Sandy was about as pleased to see me as I was to see her. On the other hand, Janet smiled broadly. Janet, in her midtwenties, was as fit as I was, which is pretty damn muscular. She has dark brown hair that swings forward to touch her cheeks, and bangs that have a tendency to get in her eyes. Janet and I sometimes exercise together, and we are members of the same karate class. I sat down by her and we said hello to each other, and then Tamsin bustled into the room, a clipboard and a bunch of papers clutched to her big bouncy chest. She had recovered quite well, to my eyes.

'Ladies, have you all met each other?'

'All but the latest entry,' drawled one of the women across the table.

She was one of three women I didn't recall having met before. Tamsin performed the honors.

'This is Carla, and this is Melanie.' Tamsin indicated the woman who'd spoken up, a short, thin, incredibly wrinkled woman with a smoker's cough. The younger woman beside her, Melanie, was a plump blonde with sharp eyes and an angry cast to her features. The other woman, introduced to me as Firella, was the only African American in the group.

She had a haircut that made the top of her head look like the top of a battery, and she wore very serious glasses. She was wearing an African-print sleeveless dress, which looked loose and comfortable.

'Ladies, this is Lily,' Tamsin said with a flourish, completing the introductions.

I got as comfortable as the chair would permit, and crossed my arms over my chest, waiting to see what would happen. Tamsin seemed to be counting us. She looked out the door and down the hall as if she expected someone else to come, frowned, and said, 'All right, let's get started. Everyone got coffee, or whatever you wanted to drink? Okay, good job!' Tamsin Lynd took a deep breath. 'Some of you just got raped. Some of you got raped years ago. Sometimes, people just need to know others have been through the same thing. So would each one of you tell us a little about what has happened to you?'

I cringed inside, wishing very strongly that I could evaporate and wake up at my little house, not much over a mile from here.

Somehow I knew Sandy McCorkindale would be the first to speak, and I was right.

'Ladies,' she began, her voice almost as professionally warm and welcoming as her husband's was from the pulpit, 'I'm Sandy McCorkindale, and my husband is the pastor of Shakespeare Combined Church.'

We all nodded. Everyone knew that church.

'Well, I was hurt a long, long time ago,' Sandy said with a social smile. In a galaxy far, far, away? 'When I had just started college.'

We waited, but Sandy didn't say anything else. She kept up the smile. Tamsin didn't act as though she was going to demand Sandy be any more forthcoming. Instead, she turned to Janet, who was sitting next to her.

'Lily and I are workout buddies,' Janet told Tamsin.

'Oh, really? That's great!' Tamsin beamed.

'She knows I got raped, but not anything else,' Janet said slowly. She looked at me out of the corner of her eye. She appeared to be concerned about the effect her story would have on me. Ridiculous. 'I was attacked about three years ago, while I was on a date with a guy I'd known my whole life. We went out parking in the fields, you know how kids do. All of a sudden, he just wouldn't stop. He just . . . I never told the police. He said he'd tell them I was willing, and I didn't have a mark on me. So I never prosecuted.'

'Next, ah, Carla?'

'I was shooting pool at Velvet Tables,' she said hoarsely. I estimated she was approaching fifty, and the years had been hard. 'I was winning some money, too. I guess one of them good ole boys didn't like me beating the pants off of 'em, put something in my drink. Next thing I know, I'm in my car buck naked without a dime, my keys stuck up my privates. They'd had sex with me while I was out. I know all of 'em.'

'Did you report?' Tamsin asked.

'Nope, I know where they live,' Carla said.

There was a long silence while we chewed that over. 'That feeling, the need for vengeance, is something we'll talk about later,' Tamsin said finally. 'Melanie, would you tell us what happened to you?'

I decided that Tamsin didn't know Melanie that well, just from the timbre of her voice.

'I'm new to anything like this, so please just bear with me.' Melanie gave a nervous and inappropriate giggle that may have agreed with the plump cheeks and pink coloring, but clashed with the anger in her dark eyes. Melanie was even younger than Janet, I figured.

'Why are you here, Melanie?' Tamsin was in full therapist mode now, sitting with her clothes arranged over her round form in the most advantageous way. She crossed her ankles, covered with thick beige stockings, and tried not to fiddle with the pencil in her clipboard.

'You mean, what incident?' Melanie asked.

'Yes,' Tamsin said patiently.

'Well, my brother-in-law done raped me, that's why! He come to my trailer all liquored up, and he busted in my door, and then he was on me. I didn't have time to get my .357 Magnum, I didn't have time to call the cops. It was so fast you wouldn't believe it.'

'Did the police arrest him?'

'Sure they did. I wouldn't leave the police station until he was in it, behind bars. The police tried to talk me out of it, said it was a family feud gone wrong, but I knew what I was doing and I know what he was doing, which was nothing I wanted him to do. His wife had told me he made her do it, too, when she was sick and didn't want to. They was married, so I guess she didn't feel like she could complain, but I sure could.'

'Good for you, Melanie,' Tamsin said, and I mentally echoed that. 'It can be hard to stand up for what you know is right. Firella?'

'Oh. Well . . . I moved here from New Orleans about a year ago,' Firella said. 'I'm an assistant principal at the junior high school here in Shakespeare, and I had a similar job in Louisiana.' I revised my estimate of her age upward. Firella was probably closer to fifty than to the thirty-five I'd originally assumed. 'When I lived in New Orleans, I got raped at the school, by a student.' Then Firella's lips clamped shut on the rest of her story, as if she'd given me enough to think about, and she was right. I remembered the smell of school, chalk and lockers and dirty industrial carpeting, and the silence of the building after the children had gone home. I thought of someone, some predator, moving silently through that building . . .

'He broke my arm, too,' Firella said. She moved her left arm a little as if testing its usability. 'He knocked out some of my teeth. He gave me herpes.'

She said all this quite matter-of-factly.

She shrugged, and was silent.

'And they caught him?'

'Yeah,' the woman said wearily. 'They caught him. He told them I'd been having sex with him for months, that it was consensual. It got really ugly. It was in all the papers. But the broken arm and the missing teeth were powerful testimony, yes indeed.'

Tamsin cut a glance toward me to make sure I was absorbing the fact that I wasn't the only victim in the world who'd gone through an extraordinary ordeal. I've never been that egotistical.

'Lily, do you feel able to tell us your story tonight?' the therapist asked.

Fighting a nearly overwhelming impulse to get up and walk out, I forced myself to sit and consider. I thought about Jack's nose, and I thought about the trust the other women had extended to me. If I had to do this, it might as well be now as any other time.

I focused on the doorknob a few feet past Tamsin's ear. I wished that some time in the past, I'd made a tape recording of this. 'Some years ago, I lived in Memphis,' I said flatly. 'On my way home from work one day, my car broke down. I was walking to a gas station when I was abducted at gunpoint by a man. He rented me to a small group of bikers for the weekend. That was what he did for a living. They took me to a – well, it was an old shack out in the fields, somewhere in rural Tennessee.' The fine trembling began, the nearly imperceptible shivering that I could feel all the way to the soles of my feet. 'There were about five of them, five men, and one or two women. I was blindfolded, so I never saw them. They chained me to a bed. They raped me, and they cut patterns on my chest and stomach with knives. When they were leaving, one of them gave me a gun. He was mad at the guy who'd rented me to them, I can't remember why.' That wasn't true, but I didn't want to explain further. 'So the gun had one bullet. I could have killed myself. I was a real mess by then. It was real hot out there.' My fists were clenched, and I was struggling to keep my breathing even. 'But when the man who'd kidnapped me came back – I shot him. And he died.'

It was so quiet in the room that I could hear my own breathing.

I waited for Tamsin to say something. But they were waiting on me. Janet said, 'Tell us how it ended.'

'Ah, well, a farmer, it was his land, he came by and found me. So, he called the police, and they took me to the hospital.' The condensed version.

'How long?' Tamsin asked.

'How long did they keep me? Well, let's see.' The shivering increased in intensity. I knew it must be visible by now. 'Friday afternoon and Friday night, and all day Saturday, and part of Sunday? I think.'

'How long before the farmer got there?'

'Oh! Oh, sorry. That was the rest of Sunday, and Monday, and most of Tuesday. Quite a while,' I said. I sat up straighter, made my fists unclench. Tried to force myself to be still.

'I remember that,' Melanie said. 'I was just a kid, then. But I remember when it was in all the papers. I remember wishing you had had a chance to shoot them all.'

I flicked a glance at her, surprised.

'I remember thinking that you were asking for it, walking after your car had broken down,' Firella said. We all looked at her. 'That was before I found out that women had a right to walk anywhere they wanted, with no one bothering 'em.'

'That's right, Firella,' Tamsin said firmly. 'What's the rule, people?'

We all waited.

'Don't blame the victim for the crime,' she said, almost chanting.

'Don't blame the victim for the crime,' we chorused raggedly. I thought some of us got the idea better than others, judging by their expressions.

'Baby-sitter accepts a ride home with the father of the kids, he rapes her. Is she at fault?' Tamsin asked us fiercely.

'Don't blame the victim for the crime!' we said. I have to admit this was an effort for me. I was about to decide Jack owed me big time when I remembered the blood running out of his nose.

'A woman's walking on a street alone at night, she gets grabbed and raped,' Tamsin said. 'Is it her fault?'

'Don't blame the victim for the crime!' we said firmly.

'A woman's wearing a tight skirt and no bra, goes to a bar in a bad part of town, gets drunk, takes a ride with a stranger, gets raped. Is it her fault?'

The chorus died out. This required more thought.

'What do you think, Lily?' Tamsin asked me directly.

'I think wanting to look attractive, even provocative,

doesn't mean you deserve to get raped. I think even the stupidity of getting drunk with people you don't know doesn't merit the punishment of being raped. At the same time, women should be responsible for their own safety . . .' I trailed off.

'And what does being responsible for your own safety mean?'

That was something I could answer. 'It means learning to fight,' I said with certainty. 'It means being cautious. It means taking care of your car so it won't break down, making sure your doors are locked, and evaluating the scene around you for danger.'

Some of the women looked dubious when I mentioned fighting, but the rest of my measures met with approval.

'How responsible for your own safety were you before you got raped?' the therapist asked. Her dark eyes were fixed on me intently. She leaned forward, and the blouse gaped slightly because she filled it up too much.

I tried to remember. 'Not very. I made sure I always had enough money to make a phone call. When I was going on a first date with someone I didn't know, I made sure a friend or two knew where I was going and who I was with.'

'So wouldn't you say that most of this wisdom is hindsight?'

'Yes.'

'Can you blame other women for not having the same sense?'

'No.'

The talk went on, and I confined myself to listening for the rest of the hour. The problem of responsibility was a knotty one. Women dress provocatively to attract sexual attention and admiration, because that's gratifying. I believed that very few women would wear a push-up bra, a low-cut blouse, high heels, tight skirts, if they were going to stay home working on the computer, for example. But sexual attention does not equate with rape. I knew of no woman who would walk out the door for an evening of barhopping with the idea that maybe she would enjoy being forced at knifepoint to give a blow job to a stranger. And very few women walked alone at night hoping a man would offer them a choice between sex and strangulation.

The fact remained that stupidity and/or poor judgment are not punishable by rape. And that was the bottom line, as far as I was concerned, and as far as Tamsin was, I thought, by the way she seemed to be steering the group.

What about the great-grandmothers and children who got raped? They were only sex objects to the eyes of the hopelessly warped. They could hardly be accused of 'asking for it'.

This pattern of thought was familiar to me, an old treadmill. Once I'd reconfirmed where we were going, I thought about the therapist herself. By her bearing and presence, Tamsin Lynd was forcing us to think about events and issues we found it hard to face. What a job – having to listen to all this! I wondered if she'd ever been raped herself, decided it was none of my business to ask since she was the natural – and neutral – leader of the group, at least ostensibly. Whether or not Tamsin had survived a rape, she definitely had problems to face now. That phone call had not been from a friend.

When the session was over, Tamsin ushered us out, remaining behind in the empty building to 'clear some things up,' she said. Once we were outside in the parking lot, the cocoon of mutual pain dissolved, and Melanie and Sandy scooted off immediately. Carla got in an old boat of a car and lit a cigarette before she turned the key in the ignition. Firella said, to no one in particular, 'I live right down the street.' She arranged her keys between her fingers in the approved face-ripping position and strode off into the dark.

Janet gave me a hug. This was not typical of our relationship and almost made me flinch. I held rigidly stiff and pressed my hands against her back in an attempt at reciprocation.

She took a step away and laughed. 'There, that better?'

I was embarrassed and showed it.

'You don't need to pretend with me,' she said.

'What's the story on Tamsin?' I asked, to get off the subject.

'She's had this job about a year,' Janet said, willing to go along with my drift. 'She and her husband have a little house over on Compton. They're both Yankees. He has a different last name.' Janet clearly saw that as evidence that the couple had a very untraditional marriage.

'Does that bother you?'

Janet shook her head. 'She can screw alligators, for all I care. Coming to this group is the most positive step I've taken since I got raped.'

'It doesn't seem like you, not reporting,' I said carefully.

'It's not like me now. It was like me then.'

'Do you ever think of reporting it, even now?'

'He's dead,' Janet said simply. 'It was in the paper last year. You may remember. Mart Weekins? He was trying to pass on a yellow line on that big curve outside of town on Route Six. Semi was coming the other way.'

'So,' I said. 'He wasn't taking responsibility for himself, I guess. Would you say his being there was – unwise?'

'I wonder if he was dressed provocatively,' Janet said, and we both laughed like maniacs.

As it happens so many times, once I'd met Tamsin Lynd, I saw and heard of her everywhere. I saw her at the post office, the grocery store, the gas station. Sometimes she was with a burly man with dark hair and a beard and mustache carefully shaved into a pattern. Each time, she gave me a friendly but impersonal nod, so I could acknowledge or ignore her as I chose.

As Jack and I drove to Little Rock the next week, after my second therapy session, I tried to describe her character and found I had no handle on it at all. Usually, I know right away if I like someone or not, but with Tamsin I just couldn't tell. Maybe it didn't make any difference, if the person was supposed to be helping you get your head straight. Maybe I had no business liking her or hating her.

'She's smart,' I said. 'She always gets us to talking about different sides to our experience.'

'Is she likable?' Jack smoothed his hair back with one hand while gripping the steering wheel with the other. His wiry black hair was escaping from its band this morning, a sure sign he'd been thinking of something else while he got dressed. I wondered if my job performance was the issue on his mind.

'Not really,' I said. 'She's got a strong character. I just don't know what it's made up of.'

'You usually make up your mind about someone faster than that.'

'She puzzles me. Maybe it's a part of being a counselor, but she doesn't seem to want to focus right now on how we feel about the attacker, just about the problems we have adjusting to being attacked.'

'Maybe she's assuming you all hate men?'

'Could be. Or maybe she's just waiting for us to say it. I guess none of us are in the "Men Are Wonderful" club, and

I think one or two in the group really hate all men, to some extent.'

Jack looked uncomfortable. I wasn't sure how much he wanted to hear about this new experience of mine, and I wasn't sure how much I was willing to share.

'You sure you're okay at this new job?' he asked, for maybe the hundredth time.

'Jack,' I said warningly.

'I know, I know, I just . . . feel responsible.'

'You *are* responsible. But I'm fine, and I'm even enjoying myself some.' Jack had this idea that I should be a private detective, like him. To achieve this, I had to work with an experienced investigator for two years. This job was my first step, and the experienced investigator was Jack.

We pulled up in the parking lot of a strip mall in the western part of Little Rock. This was the second Marvel Gym to open in the city, and it had taken over about three store widths in the strip mall. Mel Brentwood was risking a chunk of investment money in opening a second gym, especially since Marvel was no back-to-basics weightlifting place. Marvel was a deluxe gym, with different classes all day, a special room for aerobic equipment (treadmills and stair climbers), a sauna and tanning beds, a whirlpool, and lots of free weights for people who actually came to the gym to pump some iron.

I went in the women's changing room, which also contained the women's bathroom, and peeled off my shirt and shorts, folding them to stack in my tiny locker. Underneath, I wore what I considered a costume, since I wouldn't ever wear it otherwise: a Spandex unitard patterned in a leopard print. It came to mid-thigh and was sleeveless. Across the chest, MARVEL was printed in puffy letters, with the word 'gym' centered underneath in smaller type. Though this so-called garment was brief and showed every ounce I had on me, it covered the scars left from the knifing I'd taken. I wore heavy black socks and black Nikes to look a little more utilitarian. After a moment's thought, I left my purse out when I pushed my locker shut, then went out to the main floor to punch in my time clock. My job, the lowest paid as the newest employee, was to check 'guests' in, that being the gym's euphemism for people who'd paid for a year's membership. The rest of my job consisted of showing new guests how to use the equipment, spotting for someone who'd come without a buddy, pushing the drinks and clothes the gym sold, and answering the phone. There were always two people on duty, always a man and a woman. If the man who shared my shift wanted to go work out, I was supposed to watch the desk. He was supposed to do the same for me.

I had never shown quite so much of myself to so many strangers, on a day-to-day basis. Even before what I labeled my 'bad time', I'd been modest. But I had to blend in with the other employees, most of whom were younger. If any of them had had a body like mine they would have flaunted it much more than I was doing, Jack had assured me.

To minimize my self-consciousness about appearing in this getup, I kept my makeup to a minimum, avoided direct eye contact with the men, and tried to squelch any interest manifested by any of the guests.

Since the front door had been opened already, I knew the manager was there. Sure enough, the light in her office was on. Linda Doan didn't like me and was determined to get rid of me the first chance she got. But Linda couldn't fire me, though she didn't know that yet. She didn't know why I was really at Marvel.

I was *undercover*. The very term had a tendency to make

me snicker, but it was true. Since its opening seven months before, the gym had been plagued by a thief. Someone was sneaking into the changing rooms and stealing items – cash, jewelry, cell phones – from the guests. It wasn't impossible that the thief was a guest, but Jack thought the culprit was one of the staff, given the territory the thief had covered.

'The men's changing room, the ladies' changing room, the storage cubes outside the sauna,' Mel Brentwood had moaned. 'Drinks, watches, chains, cash. Never a lot, never anything awfully expensive, but it's just a matter of time. And the guests will hear about it and they won't come. If we don't find out who's responsible, I'll fire everyone working there and replace all of them, I swear I will.'

I was pretty sure such drastic action was illegal, but it wasn't my business to say so, and I noticed Jack glanced out the window and kept his face blank. Mel couldn't be the idiot he projected himself to be. He had started this string of gyms with money he'd begged and borrowed from skeptical friends of his parents, and he'd made the gyms prosper by thinking of ever-new ways to get them in the news without actually burning them down.

'Can we install a camera in the changing room?' Jack asked.

'Hell, no! How do you think these people, most of 'em trying to take off weight, would react to discovering they'd been on camera? There's no way to put one in there that no one would notice.' But I could tell the idea had caught Mel's interest. 'If I didn't want to take the thief to court . . . ,' he said slowly. 'If I just wanted to catch the bastard and fire him . . .'

'The camera would never come up,' Jack said. 'We could take it out, destroy the tape, no one the wiser. I can run by

Sneaky Pete's. I'm not crazy about the idea of filming people who don't know about it, but it would work.'

'So, do I need Lily?' Mel Brentwood eyed me like I was a gunslinger who might draw on him.

'Sure. There are things cameras won't catch,' Jack said. 'And we have yet to figure out a way to disguise them.'

'Okay, girl,' Mel said, whacking me on the shoulder to get me fired up for the big game. 'You start work as soon as you can get your tights on.'

I eyed him balefully. I wasn't happy about working for Mel, but I'd worked for plenty of people I hadn't liked. I told myself to ease up. Politically correct he wasn't, but Mel would pay Jack to do this, Jack would have another client who would call him when he got in a jam, and Jack's business would prosper.

So there I was, in Marvel Gym, in glorious leopard print Spandex, making sure guests swiped their green plastic cards as they came in so their presence would be recorded on the computer. I handed out small towels to the guests who'd forgotten theirs, I checked the supply of bath-sized towels in the locker rooms, and I sold the expensive 'health' drinks displayed in the cooler behind the counter. Those tasks were constants, but every day there was some specific problem to solve. In the first hour I worked today, I unstuck the weight-setting peg on a leg-extension device. Then I discreetly sprayed cleaner on a weightlifting bench after a particularly sweaty guest had used it, and got the vacuum out to suck up clods of dirt tracked in by a guest who'd been running in the mud yesterday.

Mostly, I grew angrier by the second at Byron, the twenty-four-year-old man who shared my shift. I watched Byron loaf his way through his workout, making himself friendly with every female in the place except me. Me, he tried to dodge.

Byron was sculpted. You could tell he thought of himself that way; sculpted as a Greek statue, sensuous, masculine. That is, if Byron knew any of those words. Byron was a waste of space, in my opinion. In my two weeks at Marvel, I couldn't count the times I had hoped he was the thief. Unless people would pay the high membership fee just to gaze upon Byron, he was a poor employee: pleasant to those people he liked, people he felt could help him, and rude to the guests who couldn't do anything for him, guests who expected him to actually work. And he'd fondle anything that stood still. Why Linda Doan had hired Byron was a mystery to me.

'I need to go put some more towels in the women's locker room,' I told him. 'Then I'm going to start my own workout.'

'Cool,' said Byron. Mr Articulate. He began doing another set of ab crunches.

I took the pile of towels into the tiled locker room. Someone was taking a shower when I walked in, which was surprising because it was a little early for the rush we got about ten, ten-thirty. The water cut off as I reached the shelves where I stacked the towels. I was walking lightly because I always do.

I caught a guest red-handed. She was going through my purse, which I'd left temptingly propped against an extra pair of shoes by my locker. It took me a minute to mentally leaf through the pictures I'd tried to commit to memory, and finally I came up with her name: Mandy Easley.

Mandy became aware of me after I'd watched her get a twenty out of my wallet and flip open the credit card compartment. Mandy was only in her twenties, but she looked like a hag when her eyes met mine. Her dark brown hair was still wet from the shower, her narrow face was bare of makeup, and her towel was wound around her modestly, but she still didn't look innocent. She looked guilty as hell.

'Oh! Ah, Lily, right? I was just getting some change for the Tampax machine,' she said, in a jittery voice. 'I hope you don't mind. I didn't have the right change, and your purse was just sitting here.'

'Machine takes twenties now?'

'Ah, I . . .' The twenty fluttered from her fingers as she stared down at the purse, exactly as if it had just materialized in her hands. 'Oh, that fell out! I'm sorry, let me just put it back in . . .' and she fumbled for the bill. She was one big twitch.

'Ms Easley,' I said, and by my voice she knew I wasn't going to smooth it over.

'Oh, shit,' she said, and covered her face with her hands as if she was overwhelmed with shame. 'Lily, honestly, I never did anything like this before.' She tried to squeeze out some tears, but couldn't quite manage. 'I just have such bad money problems, please don't call the cops! My mom would die if I had a record!'

'You already have a record,' I observed.

Her face flashed up from her hands and she glared at me. 'What?'

'You have a record. For shoplifting and passing bad checks.' The computer had told us what employees and guests had been present at Marvel during the time the various thefts had occurred, and twenty-three-year-old divorcee Mandy Easley's name had recurred. Jack had run a check on her.

'We'll be glad to refund your membership money by

mail after you hand us your card,' I said, as I'd been instructed to do. 'When I have your card in my hand, you can go.'

'You're not going to call the police?' she asked, unable to believe her good luck. I felt exactly the same way.

'If you return your card, then you can go.'

'All right, Robocop,' she said furiously, relief shoving her over the edge of caution. 'Take the damn card!' She turned to yank it out of the pocket on her shorts, which were draped over the bench behind her. She extricated the plastic card and threw it at me. Mandy didn't look like a well-groomed young matron any more as she yanked my twenty out of my purse and thrust it into the same pocket. She was sneering in my face.

I had seldom seen anyone look quite so ugly, male or female. I thought Mandy Easley was just as much a waste of space as Byron, and I wished her out the door. I was sick to death of her.

She read something in my face that stopped her manic rant. Yanking off the towel, she let it drop to the floor while she pulled on her shorts and a T-shirt and thrust her feet into sandals. She gathered up her purse, spitefully knocked over the stack of towels as her parting shot, and headed out the door to the hall leading to the main room. She spun on her heel to fire some comment my way, something that could be heard by everyone in the weights room, but I began moving toward her with all my disgust in my face. She hurried out of the gym for the last time.

I had to straighten up the locker room, of course, and though it made me sick to do so, I had to pick up the card Mandy had thrown at me. While I was refolding the towels and placing them in the resurrected rack, I pictured many gratifying ways to make Mandy pick up her own card. By the time I had to take my place beside Byron again, I was in at least an equitable mood.

'What happened to Mandy?' he asked casually, taking a moment away from his absorbed fascination with his own face reflected in the gleaming counter. 'She took outta here like a scalded cat.'

I couldn't tell him she'd been stealing. That would jettison the whole idea. But I could tell him something else. 'I had to take her membership card,' I said, even more seriously and quietly than normal.

He goggled with curiosity. 'What? Why?'

I was drawing a blank.

'Did she . . . make a pass at you?' Byron supplied his own scenario. I could practically see the steam coming out of his ears. 'Did she actually . . . was she actually *doing* something? In the shower?'

I wasn't supposed to disclose Jack's business arrangement with Mel Brentwood. I looked away, hoping to indicate embarrassment. 'I don't want to talk about it,' I said truthfully. 'It was really ugly.'

'Poor Lily,' Byron said, laying his hand on my shoulder and giving it a squeeze. 'You poor girl.'

Was he *blind?*

Biting the inside of my lips to keep from snarling, I managed to indicate to Byron that I wanted to go work out, and he let his hand trail off my shoulder while I went to the leg press. After I'd warmed up and put the first set of forty-fives on, I dropped down into the sleigh-type seat and placed my feet against the large metal plate. Pushing up a little to relieve the pressure, I flipped the prop bars outward, and let the plate push my knees to my chest. I pushed, and felt everything tighten in a surprisingly relaxing way as I exhaled. Legs to chest, inhale. Legs out straight, exhale. Over and over, until the set was done and I could add another pair of forty-fives.

Toward the end of my workout, I realized I should be feeling proud that I had successfully completed my first assignment as a private investigator. Somehow, television and the film industry had not prepared me for the mundane satisfaction of detecting a thief. I hadn't gotten to run after anyone waving a gun; the police hadn't threatened me; Mel Brentwood hadn't tried to sleep with me. Could it be I had been misled by the media?

As I pondered this, I noticed that Byron had been so anxious to start spreading the 'news' about Mandy that he'd actually gotten the glass spray out and begun cleaning some of the mirrors that lined the gym walls. This brought him into murmuring distance of some of his cronies and the many sideways glances at me were a clear indication that my brush with Mandy was being mythologized.

At least I'd gotten some good workouts, being on this job. I wondered how long Mel would want me to work after this; this might be the last time I'd have to come to Marvel Gym.

Jack picked me up at the end of my shift. I was so glad to see him it made me feel almost silly. Jack is about five foot ten, his hair is still all black, and his eyes are hazel. He has a scar, a very thin one – a razor scar – running from the hairline close to his right eye down to his jawline. It puckers a very little. He has a narrow, strong nose and straight eyebrows. He's been a private detective since he got urged to resign from the Memphis Police Department about five years ago.

'I like the outfit,' he said, as we walked to his car.

'In this heat, I feel like one big smell,' I said. 'I want to shower and put on something cotton and loose.'

'Yes, ma'am. You just happy to see me, or did something interesting happen at the gym?'

'A little bit of both.'

When we were in the car and on our way back to Shakespeare, the town where I've lived for five years, I began to tell Jack about my day. 'So it was Mandy Easley all along,' I concluded. 'I guess I found myself a little disappointed.'

'You just want to catch Byron doing something,' Jack said. I turned, huffing in exasperation, in time to catch the amused curl of his lips flatten out into a serious expression.

'Being a stupid jerk isn't a jailable offense,' I admitted.

'Jails wouldn't be big enough,' Jack agreed.

'What will happen now?'

'I'll call Mel when we get home.'

While Jack was on the phone, I peeled off the nasty unitard and dropped it in the hamper. The shower, in the privacy of my own bathroom, cramped as it was, was just as wonderful as I had anticipated. Drying off was sheer bliss. I fluffed up the wet blond curls that clung to my head, I checked to make sure I'd gotten my legs very smooth, and I put on a lot of deodorant and skin cream before I came out to join Jack. He was putting steaks in a marinade. We didn't eat much beef.

'Special occasion?'

'You caught your first thief.'

'And you're going to congratulate me with dead cow?'

He put down the pan and eyed me with some indignation. 'Can you think of a better way?'

'Ah . . . yes.'

'And that would be?'

'You're slow on the uptake today,' I said critically, and took off my robe.

He caught on right away.

We'd returned to Shakespeare too late to attend karate class, so later that night we took a walk. Jack had spent most of the day sitting down, and he wanted to stretch before bed.

'Mel says thanks,' Jack told me, after we'd been clipping along for maybe twenty minutes. 'I think he'll call us again if he has any problems. You did a good job.' He sounded proud, and that lit an unexpected glow somewhere in my chest.

'So, what next?' I asked.

'We've got a Workman's Comp. job I'm sure you can handle,' Jack said. 'I get a lot of that kind of case.'

'The person is claiming he can't work any more?'

'Yeah. In this case, it's a woman. She fell on a slippery floor at work, now she says she can't bend her back or lift anything. She lives in a small house in Conway. It can be hard watching a house in some neighborhoods, so you may have to be creative.'

That was not the adjective that sprang to my mind when I thought of my abilities, so I felt a little anxious.

'I'll need a camera, I'm assuming.'

'Yes, and lots of time fillers. A book or two, newspapers, snacks.'

'Okay.'

We paced along for a few more minutes. A familiar car went by, and I said, 'Jack, there's my counselor. And her husband, I think.'

We watched the beige sedan turn the corner onto Compton. That was the way we'd planned to go, too, and when we rounded the same corner, we saw the car had stopped in front of an older home. It was built in a style popular in the thirties and forties, boxy and low with a broad roofed porch supported by squat pillars. Tamsin and the man with her had already left their car, and he was at the front door. She was standing slightly behind him. Under the glare of the porch light, I could see he was partially bald, and big. The clink of keys carried across the small yard.

Tamsin screamed.

Jack was there before I was. He moved to one side as I caught up, and I saw that there was a puddle of blood on the gray-painted concrete of the porch. I cast my gaze from side to side, saw nothing that could have produced it.

'There,' Jack said, still one step ahead of me.

Following his pointing finger, I saw there was a squirrel hanging from a branch of the mimosa tree planted by the porch. The heavy scent of the mimosa twined with the hot-penny smell of blood.

Since I didn't have a bird feeder or fruit bushes, I happened to like squirrels. When I realized the squirrel's throat had been cut and the little animal had been hung on the tree like an out-of-season Christmas ornament, I began a slow burn.

I could hear Tamsin sobbing in the background and her husband saying, 'Oh, not here, too. Honey, maybe it was just some kids, or someone playing a sick joke . . .'

'You *know* it was him. You *know* that,' Tamsin said, choking and gasping. 'I told you about the phone calls. It's him, again. He followed me.'

Jack said, 'Excuse me, I'm Jack Leeds. This is Lily. We were just out walking. Sorry to intrude, but can we help?'

The man with his arm around Tamsin said, 'I'm sorry,

too. We can't believe . . . excuse me, I'm Cliff Eggers, and this is my wife, Tamsin Lynd.'

'Tamsin and I know each other,' I murmured politely, trying not to look at Tamsin's face while she was in such distress.

'Oh, Lily!' Tamsin took a long, shuddering breath, and she appeared to be trying to pull herself together in the presence of a client. 'I'm sorry,' she said, though damned if I could think for what. 'This is just very upsetting.'

'Sure it is,' Jack agreed. 'Don't you think we ought to call the police, Ms Lynd?'

'Oh, we'll call them. We always do. But they can't do anything,' her husband said, with sudden violence. He ran a big hand across his face. He had one of those neatly trimmed beards that frames the mouth. 'They couldn't do anything before. They won't do anything now.' Cliff Eggers's voice was choked and unsteady. He was fumbling with the keys to the door and he managed to open it.

They stepped in their hall, and Tamsin beckoned me in behind them. I caught a glimpse of a large, friendly room. There were pictures hung over an antique chest to the right of the door. In the framed grouping I saw a wedding picture with Tamsin in full white regalia, and her husband's business college diploma. There was a big brass bowl of potpourri on the chest, and my nose began to stop up almost instantly.

Tamsin said, 'We'll call them tomorrow morning.' Her husband nodded. Then he turned back to us. 'We appreciate your coming to help us. I'm sorry to involve you in something so unpleasant.'

'Excuse us, please,' Tamsin said. She was obviously just barely containing her anguish. I felt she knew she'd made a mistake asking us in, that she was just waiting for us to leave so she could drop that facade, crumble completely.

'Of course,' Jack said instantly. He looked at Cliff. 'Would you like us to . . .' and he nodded toward the squirrel.

'Yes,' Cliff said with great relief. 'That would be very kind. The garbage can is at the rear of the backyard, by the hedge.'

We stepped back out on the porch, and Cliff and Tamsin had closed the door before Jack and I chanced looking at each other.

'Huh?' I said, finally.

'Double huh,' Jack said. He fished a pocketknife out of his jeans and leaned over the waist-high railing to cut the string. Holding the little corpse at arm's length, he went down the steps and around the house to the garbage can. Cliff's telling Jack that the garbage can was 'by the hedge' was unnecessary, since everything in the Eggers-Lynd yard was 'by the hedge'. It was an older home, and the original owners had believed in planting. The front yard was open to the street, but the clipped thick growth followed the property line down both sides and across the back of the yard. The surrounding greenery gave the yard a feeling of enclosure. While I waited, I thought I heard voices, so I went around the house to look into the backyard. In the darkness by the hedge at the rear of the property, I saw two figures.

Jack came back after a few more seconds. 'Their neighbor was outside, wanted to know what had happened,' he explained. 'He's a town cop, so at least law enforcement will know something about this.' I could tell Jack had suspected Cliff Eggers wouldn't call about the incident.

I wondered belatedly if I should have tried to deduce something from the state of the squirrel's body. But I was clueless about squirrel metabolism, especially in this heat, and it would be way beyond me to try to estimate how long the poor critter had been dead. After a last glance at the blood, and a pang of regret that I had nothing with which to swab it up, I joined Jack on the driveway and we resumed our walk.

We didn't say anything else until we were a block away from the house, and then it wasn't much. Someone was stalking Tamsin Lynd, and from all the cues in the conversation we'd had with the couple, this persecution had been going on for some time. If Tamsin and her husband were unwilling to ask for help, what could be done?

'Nothing,' I concluded, straightening up after washing my face in the bathroom sink.

Jack picked up on that directly. 'I guess not,' he agreed. 'And you watch your step around her. I think this therapy group is good for you, but I don't want you catching some kind of collateral fallout when her situation implodes.'

As I composed myself for sleep thirty minutes later, I found myself thinking that it hardly seemed fair that Tamsin had to listen to the group's problems, while her own were kept swept under the rug of her marriage. I reminded myself that, after all, Tamsin was getting paid to do her job, and she had been trained to cope with the inevitable depression that must follow hearing so many tales of misery and evil.

Jack wasn't yet asleep, so I told him what I'd been thinking.

'She listens to a lot of bad stuff, yeah,' he said, his voice quiet, coming out of the darkness. 'But look at the courage, look at the toughness. The determination. She hears that, too. Look how brave you all are.'

I couldn't say anything at all. My throat clogged. I was glad it was dark. At last, I was able to pat Jack's shoulder;

and a minute later, I heard by his breathing that he was asleep. Before it could overcome me, too, I thought, *This is why Jack is here beside me. Because he can think of saying something like he just said.*

That was a fine reason.

Chapter Three

By my third therapy session, Tuesday night was no longer a time I dreaded.

I'd had hours sitting in a car, standing in a convenience store, and drifting around a mall – all in pursuit of the Worker's Comp. claimant – to analyze our counseling sessions. I had to admit I couldn't tell if Tamsin Lynd was following some kind of master plan in directing us along the path to recovery. It seemed to me that often we just talked at random; though from time to time I could discern Tamsin's fine hand directing us.

Not one of the women in the group was someone I would've picked for a friend, with the exception of Janet Shook. Sandy McCorkindale made me particularly edgy. She tried very hard to be the unflawed preacher's wife, and she very nearly succeeded. Her veneer of good modest clothes and good modest makeup, backed by an almost frenzied determination to keep the smooth surface intact, was maintained at a tremendous, secret cost. I had lived too close to the edge of despair and mental illness not to recognize it in others, and Sandy McCorkindale was a walking volcano. I was willing to bet her family was used to living on tiptoe, perhaps even quite unaware they were doing so.

The other women were OK. I'd gradually learned their personal histories. In a town the size of Shakespeare, keeping identities a secret was impossible. For example, not only did I know that Carla (of the croaking voice) was Carla Preston, I knew that her dad had retired from Shakespeare Drilling and Exploration, and her mom took the lunch money at the elementary school cafeteria. I knew Carla smoked like a chimney when she went out the back door of the Health Center, she'd been married three times, and she said everything she thought. She'd become a grandmother when she was thirty-five.

Melanie Kleinhoff no longer looked quite as sullen, and despite her youth and pale doughy looks, she set herself goals and met them (no matter how difficult) to the point of idiocy. She had never graduated from high school and she was still married to the man whose brother had raped her. Firella Bale, probably the most educated of all of us – with the exception of our counselor – seemed baffled sometimes by how to fit in; she was black, she was smart and deliberate, she had taught others, and she worked in a position of authority. She was a single mother and her son was in the army.

Sandy, Janet, and I had never doubted that we could share our problems with a woman of another race. Tamsin seemed a little more careful of Carla and Melanie. We would all have known right away if Carla was uncomfortable with Firella, since Carla had few thoughts she didn't set right out in front of us. Luckily, she seemed to have passed that particular rock in the road. Melanie hadn't, and we could watch her prejudice struggle with her good sense and her own kindness. Our common fate transcended our color or economic status or education, but that was easier for some of us to acknowledge than others.

I had neither witnessed any more incidents nor heard any rumors about Tamsin and her husband. I had not spoken a word about what Jack and I had seen that evening while we were out walking. As far as I could tell, no one in Shakespeare knew that someone was stalking our counselor.

Sandy McCorkindale was waiting outside when I arrived for our third evening together. While I knew more about Sandy's life than I knew about almost any of the others – I'd met her husband, seen her sons, worked in her church, walked by her home – I realized I understood her less than any member of our little group. Waiting in the heat with her was not a happy prospect.

In the two weeks since our first meeting, the season had ripened to full-blown summer. It was hotter than the six shades of hell standing on the asphalt, maybe the temperature was down to ninety-four from the hundred and four it had been that afternoon. At eight o'clock, the parking lot wasn't dark; there was still a glow from the nearly vanished sun. The bugs had started their intense nightly serenade. If I drove out of town right now and parked by the road in an isolated place and tried to talk to a companion, the volume of bug and frog noise would put a serious crimp in the conversation. Anyone expecting nature to be silent – especially in the South – was plain old nuts.

I got out of my car reluctantly. It had been a fruitless day on stakeout in Little Rock, and Jack was out of town on a missing-persons job, so I wasn't having the mild glow of accomplishment I usually enjoyed after a long day. When I went home after the therapy hour, I promised myself, I would take a cool shower and I would read. After a day spent dealing with others, television was just one more batch of voices to listen to; I'd rather have a book in my hands than the remote control.

'Evening, Sandy,' I called. At that moment, the pole-mounted security lights came on. With the residual daylight creating long shadows from behind the trees, I was walking across a visual chessboard to reach the woman standing by the side door we always used. As I drew closer, I could see the preacher's wife had sweat beaded on her forehead. She was wearing the current young matron uniform, a white T-shirt under a long sleeveless, shapeless khaki dress. Sandy's streaked hair was still in its slightly teased-with-bangs Junior League coiffure, and her makeup was all in place, but there was definitely something happening in her head. Her brown eyes, dark and discreetly made up, darted from my face to the cars to the bushes and back.

'Tamsin didn't leave the door open,' Sandy said furiously. She was carrying her straw shoulder bag in the usual way, but with an abrupt gesture she let the strap slide down her arm and she swung the bag, hard, against the side of her car. That made me jump, and I had to repress a snarl.

I wondered, for maybe the fifth or sixth time, why Sandy kept coming. She'd never talked in any more detail, or with any more feeling, about what had happened to her, but she kept showing up. She was making a real effort to keep herself separated from the common emotional ground. But every Tuesday night, there she was in her chair, listening.

I leaned against the wall to wait for Tamsin to unlock the door. I didn't feel up to any more emotional outbursts from Sandy McCorkindale.

Melanie and Carla arrived together. I had decided they'd known each other before coming to the therapy group. In conversation, I'd heard them refer to common acquaintances.

'Good! I got time for a cigarette,' Carla said in her harsh voice. She had one lit and puffing in a flash. 'My car done broke down today in front of Piggly Wiggly, and I had to call Melanie here to give me a ride.'

Normally I would have expected Sandy to pick up the conversational ball, but not tonight.

'What's wrong with the car?' I asked, after a beat.

'My boyfriend says it might be the alternator,' Carla said. 'I sure hope it's something cheaper. Tamsin not here yet?'

'Her car is over there,' Sandy said resentfully, pointing to Tamsin's modest Honda Civic. 'But she won't open the door!'

Melanie and Carla gave Sandy the same kind of careful sideways look I'd found myself delivering.

Firella came walking from the darkness at the other end of the small parking lot, pepper spray in one hand and keys in the other.

'Hey, y'all!' she called. 'We meeting out here in the parking lot tonight?' Carla laughed, and Melanie smiled. As Firella drew closer, she counted us and observed, 'One of us hasn't made it here yet.'

'Oh, Janet's car's here, too,' Sandy snapped. 'See?'

We all looked over to note that Janet's dark Camaro was half concealed by Tamsin's Honda.

'So where's Janet, and why won't the back door open? You think Tamsin and Janet are in there doin' it?' asked Carla. She didn't sound angry about the possibility – only ready for them to finish and unlock the back door, so she could get in the air conditioning.

Sandy was almost shocked out of her odd mood. 'Oh, my gosh,' she said, rattled to the core. 'I just never believed I could know anyone that . . . oh, my Lord.'

Though I was pretty sure Carla had just been blabbing – for the pleasure of hearing her own voice, and to shock Sandy – I didn't comment. I got a phone book from the front seat of my car, pulled my cell phone from the pocket of the drawstring sheeting pants I was wearing because they were cool, and dialed the health center number.

Inside the building, we could hear the phone ring, very faintly. That would be the one at the main reception desk, inside the front door.

A voice came on the line. 'You have reached the Hartsfield County Health Unit. Our office hours are nine to five, Monday through Friday. If you know the extension of the person you're calling, please press it now.' I did.

From inside the building, we heard another phone begin to ring, this time closer. We counted the rings. After four, the female voice came back on the line, to tell me that the party I wanted to contact was away from her desk and to ask me to call back during office hours. She also told me what to do in case of emergency.

'This seem like an emergency?' I asked, not sure I'd said it out loud until Firella said, 'It's getting to be.'

I stood back and looked at the door. Made of a heavy metal and painted brown, it was intended for staff use, so therapists wouldn't have to enter and exit through the reception area. It was kept locked every evening but Tuesday, as far as I knew, though there might be other kinds of therapy groups that met using the same arrangement. Tamsin always locked the door when the six of us were assembled inside, and something she'd said once had made me think she only unlocked it about ten minutes before group time.

The light wasn't crystal clear in the area around the door, but I could tell when I aimed my tiny key-ring flashlight at the crack that the deadbolt was not actually engaged.

So the door wasn't locked, after all. I tugged on it again, baffled. It didn't budge.

While the other women watched, I again punched the

'on' button of my tiny flashlight. My insurance agent would be glad to hear I'd found his giveaway so useful. This time, I shone the light all the way around the edges of the door, trying to spy something that would give me a clue as to why the door was being so stubborn. I was rewarded maybe the second or third time around, when I realized a chip of wood was protruding from the bottom.

'There,' I said, and squatted. I heard Melanie explaining to the others and many exclamations, but I ignored them. I tried to grip the sliver of wood in a pincer formed by my thumb and middle finger, but I didn't have much success. Tonight was the first time I'd ever wished I had long fingernails. I checked out the hands around me. 'Firella,' I said, 'your nails are the longest. See if you can grip this little piece of wood, here. That's what's got the door wedged shut.'

Sandy was suggesting in an increasingly nervous voice that we call the police right now, or at least her husband, but Carla put a hand on Sandy's arm and said, 'Hush, woman.' I noticed, while Firella crouched and tried to wriggle the strip of wood from its lodging, that Carla had put out her cigarette before it was smoked down to the filter. She was worried, too.

After a lot of shaking of her head and several little whispers of 'No, not quite . . . almost . . . damn thing!' Firella said, 'Got it!' and held up the thin strip of wood. About four inches long and two wide, it could have been no more than two millimeters thick, if that. It was just the right size to slip in the crack in the door, just thick enough to get wedged there when the first person tried to open the door to go to Tamsin's office.

I reached out to turn the knob, hesitated.

'What you waiting for?' Carla asked, her voice raspier than ever. 'Now we're late.'

I was waiting because I'd thought of fingerprints, but then I shrugged. By her own account, Sandy had already touched the door. 'Remember, she didn't answer the phone,' I said, my voice as quiet and calm as I could make it. I opened the door. The other women clustered around me.

The hall light was on, and Tamsin's office door was open, but not the door to the therapy room.

'Tamsin!' called Carla. 'You and Janet in there? You two stop messing around, you hear! The rest of us'll get jealous!'

Carla was trying to sound jaunty, but the atmosphere in the hall was too thick with anxiety for that.

Melanie said, 'I'm scared.' It was an admission, but it didn't signal that she was going to run away. She'd planted her feet and had that bulldog look on her face that meant she wouldn't back down.

'We're all scared,' Sandy said. Oddly, she'd gotten calmer. 'Do you think we had better just stay out here in the parking lot and call the police?'

'No,' I said.

They all turned to look at me.

'You can all stay outside,' I said, amending my words. In fact, I would've preferred they all stay out. 'But I have to see if they're . . . okay.'

Even slow Melanie read between the lines on that one. To my surprise she said, 'No. You go, we all go.'

'We all go,' Firella said, in a voice even more certain. Sandy didn't say anything, but she didn't walk away, either.

Oh, wonderful, I thought. The five musketeerettes.

We shuffled down the hall in a clump. I couldn't control my anxiety any longer and stepped out ahead of them, pivoted on my left foot and faced into Tamsin's office, my hands already floating up into the striking position. I was ready for something, but not for what I saw.

Behind Tamsin's desk, on the fuzzy wall where all the clippings had been stuck up with pins . . .

'Oh, dear God,' said Sandy, miserably.

'Shit, shit, shit!' Carla's blackbird voice, hushed with shock.

. . . was a body, and the whiteness of it was the first thing I noticed, the whiteness of the chest and arms and face. Then the blackness of her hair.

'Holy Mary, Mother of God,' Firella said, her voice more steady than I would have believed. 'Pray for us now, and at the hour of our death.'

But then there was the redness of it; that was startling, and considerable. The glistening redness mostly issued from the – stake? Was that really a metal stake? Yes, driven through the heart of . . .

'Who *is* that woman?' Carla said, more struck by this shock than by any of the others, apparently.

That naked woman, I amplified her statement.

'The naked and the dead,' I said, drawing from somewhere in the attic of my mind.

'So,' Firella said. Her voice was unsteady, and I heard her gulp back nausea. 'She's actually pinned to the wall?'

There was a groan practically under my feet, and I was shocked enough to lurch back, knocking everyone else into confusion.

Janet was lying on the floor in front of the desk. We'd been so transfixed by the dead woman that we hadn't even seen her. Janet rolled, with great effort, from her back to her front, and I saw a darkening bruise on her forehead. But her hand went to the back of her head, moving slowly and painfully.

In a moment, Firella was on her other side, and we tried to raise her. Though we believed we were the only ones in the building (at least I did) I wanted to get Janet out of there as fast as possible, as if the woman's deadness was contagious.

Janet began mumbling something, but I couldn't make it out. She moaned, though, as we tried to pull her to her feet. Without discussion, we lowered her back to the carpet.

'We gotta get out of here,' Carla said urgently, and I agreed. But we couldn't all go. I handed my cell phone to Melanie, who was silent and shocked.

'Go outside and call the police,' I said.

'Can't we just leave and call it in later?' Carla asked.

We all stared at her. She shrugged.

'I mean, take Janet to the hospital ourselves. Just so we won't be connected to the police side of this. I mean, someone offed this gal, someone really, really seriously sick. Right?'

Sandy said, 'That's true.'

'Look,' I said, and they did all look at me. I was feeling Janet's pulse, trying to decide if her pupils were even. I stopped and collected myself. 'We're listed on some schedule as coming here tonight, you know. All of us. Our names are written down somewhere, no matter how confidential Tamsin promised us this would be. I don't think we can opt out of this.'

'Do you think whoever killed this woman put her there for us to see?' Sandy asked in a quavering voice. 'Or for Tamsin?'

It was a funny question if you weren't there. If you were there, you could see the intention of display that had gone into arranging the body. To see the poor woman pinned up there, among the articles about rape and the empowerment of women, the accuracy of DNA testing and the heavier sentences being handed down to men who raped . . . we were meant to know we were powerless, after all.

We tried to look anywhere but at the body. 'White as a sheet' was a phrase that came to mind when I looked at my therapy group . . . except Firella, and she had turned an ashen color.

'So we can't dodge this,' Carla admitted. 'But . . . no, I guess, we just have to face the music.'

'After all, we didn't kill her,' Sandy said briskly – as if that cleared up the whole thing, and assured smooth sailing ahead.

When there was a long, thick pause, she said, 'Well, *I* didn't.'

'Enough of this, we have to get help for Janet.' I looked at Melanie. 'You and Carla and Sandy go out the door we came in,' I said. 'Call nine one one. Firella and I will stay here with Janet. Be sure to tell them we need an ambulance.'

'We haven't found Tamsin,' Sandy said.

The rest of us had forgotten all about Tamsin in the turmoil of finding the naked impaled woman and the unconscious Janet.

'She might be in here somewhere,' Sandy whispered. 'She might be the one who did this.' We stared at Sandy as though she'd sprouted another head.

'Or she might have been killed, too,' Carla reminded her.

'I don't think we better wander around here looking for her,' Firella said sensibly. 'I think we better call the cops, like Lily said. Janet needs an ambulance bad.'

Carla, Melanie, and Sandy turned to go, when Firella said, 'Just for the hell of it, any of you know this woman?'

'I do,' Melanie said. She started out, not looking back. 'That's my sister-in-law, who was married to the man who raped me.'

After a moment of stunned silence, Carla and Sandy hurried after her, down the hall and out into the parking lot. They stood holding open the door so we wouldn't be shut off from them, a piece of thoughtfulness I appreciated. I could hear Carla placing the phone call, having to repeat herself a few times. Firella and I stared at each other, side-swiped by the identification of the dead woman and uncertain how to react to it.

I turned my attention from what I couldn't understand to what I could, the fact that my friend had been attacked. But there didn't seem to be much I could do for her. Janet made little movements from time to time, but she didn't appear to be exactly conscious.

'She's not really stuck up there, is she? Like the newspaper clippings?' Firella said after a moment. Of course, the white-and-red display on the wall was what we were really thinking about.

'I don't see how the wall could be soft enough to drive the stake in far enough to actually hold her up.' Janet's color was awful, a sort of muddy green.

'I see what you're saying. I'm looking behind the desk.' Firella, proving she was tougher than I – I guess years of the school system will do it – stood and peered over the top of the desk.

She abruptly sat down on the floor again.

'I think she's kind of propped up,' she reported, 'with string around her arms in loops, attached to nails that have been driven into the wall. Her bottom half's kind of sitting on the back of Tamsin's rolling chair. There's a wadded-up doctor coat stuck under the wheels to keep the chair from moving.'

I couldn't think of anything to say to that.

'I wonder if one person could fix her that way. Seems like it would take two,' Firella said thoughtfully.

'I guess if one person had enough time it could be done,' I said, so she wouldn't think I was shucking her off. 'That's a lot of preparation. The wedge to keep us out until the scene was set, and the coat to keep the chair from moving.'

'I'm worried about Tamsin,' Firella said next.

'Me, too.' That was easy to agree with. I was wondering if Tamsin was in the therapy room. I was wondering if she was alive.

'Janet, help is coming,' I told her, not at all sure she could hear me or understand. 'You hang on one minute more.' It was true that I could hear sirens. I didn't think I'd ever been happier to know they were coming.

I hadn't talked to my friend Claude Friedrich in a while, and I'd just as soon not have talked to him that night. But since he's the chief of police, and since it was a murder scene in the city limits, there wasn't any way around it.

'Lily,' he greeted me. He was using his police voice; heavy, grim, a little threatening.

'Claude.' I probably sounded the same way.

'What's happened here tonight?' he rumbled.

'You'll have to tell us,' I said. 'We got here for our therapy group—'

'You're in therapy?' Claude's eyebrows almost met his graying hair.

'Yes,' I said shortly.

'Accepting help,' he said, amazement written all over him. 'This must be some doing of Jack's.'

'Yes.'

'And where is he, tonight?'

'On the road.'

'Ah. Okay, so you were here for your therapy group. You and these women?'

'Yes.'

'A group for . . . ?'

A very tall African American woman appeared at Claude's shoulder. Her hair was cut close to her scalp. She was truly almost black, and she was wearing a practical khaki pant-suit with a badge pinned to the lapel. A pale yellow tank top under the jacket shone radiantly against her skin. She had broad features and wore huge blue-framed glasses.

'Alicia, listen to the account of this witness. I know her, she's observant,' Claude said.

'Yes, sir.' The magnified eyes focused on me.

'Lily, this is Detective Stokes. She's just come to us from the Cleveland force.'

'Cleveland, *Ohio?*' Cleveland, Mississippi wouldn't have been surprising.

'Yep.'

Alicia Stokes would have to be classified as a mystery.

Focusing on the more pertinent problem, I explained to Claude and Detective Stokes that we were a group composed of rape survivors, that we met every Tuesday night at the health center, that we were led by a woman who was missing and might be somewhere in the building.

'Tamsin Lynd,' said Stokes unexpectedly.

I stared at her. 'Yes,' I said slowly. 'Tamsin Lynd.'

'I knew it,' the detective said to herself, so swiftly and in such a low voice that I wasn't sure I'd understood her correctly.

Stokes turned to a man in uniform and gave him some quick orders. He stared back at her, resentment all over his face and in his posture, but then he turned to obey. I shook my head. Stokes had her work cut out for her.

She caught the headshake and glared at me. I don't know how she interpreted my reaction, but she definitely didn't want sympathy.

Claude made a 'go-on' gesture, so I went on to explain how we hadn't been able to get in, had finally managed to do so, what we had found. I was glad to see the ambulance team taking Janet out, before I'd finished my account.

Stokes, who was at least four inches taller than my five foot six, said, 'Do you know the victim?'

'No.'

'Did any of you know her?'

'Ask them.'

Stokes clearly was about to come down on me like a ton of bricks when I caught sight of something that made me weak-kneed with relief. The officer Stokes had sent into the building was leading Tamsin Lynd out, his arm around her, and Tamsin appeared to be in good physical shape. She was walking on her own. She was crying and shaking, but she seemed to be unhurt. Not a drop of blood on her.

Following my gaze, Stokes and Claude saw her, too.

'She's your missing counselor?' Claude asked.

'Yes,' I said, relief making me almost giddy. I strode over to her and didn't even think about the other two, right on my heels.

'Lily, are all of you okay?' Tamsin called, pulling away from the officer to grip my arms.

'Except Janet,' I said. I told her Janet had gone in the ambulance.

'What on earth happened here?'

I became aware that the audience had grown quite large around us, listening to this exchange. One glare from Stokes sent them scattering, but she and Claude flanked me.

And at that moment, looking into Tamsin Lynd's eyes, I remembered the phone calls and the slit throat of the squirrel, and the fear she lived with. I had been very upset, deeply upset, but in that second I drew myself under control. 'There was a dead woman in your office,' I said, after a little pause to let the two cops stop me, if they would. 'Where were you?'

Only someone who'd witnessed at least part of Tamsin's problem would have understood her reaction.

'Oh, my God,' she moaned. 'Not again!'

'Again?' I repeated, because that hadn't been quite what I expected. Then, I said more harshly, '*Again?* You've found women killed in your office more than once?'

'No, no. I just mean . . . the whole cycle. You know, I called you about the squirrel being left hanging on my front porch,' she said tremulously, her shaking hand pointing to Claude.

'I know about your past problems,' Detective Stokes said curtly. Claude rumbled, 'I'd gotten a sort of outline picture.' Tamsin nodded. She made an effort to control her ragged breathing and tears.

After a moment, she went on. 'I was hiding in the therapy room,' she confessed. She looked at my face as if it were up to me to absolve her of this piece of self-preservation.

'Saralynn got there early so I could give her my little orientation speech. I said hi to her and then I remembered

I'd left some papers in the therapy room, so I went in there to fetch them, and while I was in there, I heard . . . I heard . . .'

'You heard the woman being killed?'

Tamsin nodded. 'And I shut the door,' she said, and shuddered and gasped. 'As quiet as I could, I shut the door and then I locked it.'

That was hard to swallow. We had ventured into a building we thought contained danger, to help Tamsin. But from her own account, Tamsin wouldn't open the door to try to save a woman's life. I made myself choke this knowledge down, shove it aside. Fear could make you do almost anything: I had known fear before, and I was willing to bet this wasn't Tamsin's first experience of it. 'Didn't you hear Janet come in?' My voice was as even as I could make it.

'That room's pretty soundproof,' she said, pushing her dark hair out of her eyes. 'I thought I heard someone calling down the hall, but for all I knew it was the same person who'd killed poor Saralynn, so I was too scared to answer. That was Janet, I guess. Then, later, I heard other sounds, other people.'

I'd have said we'd made enough noise to establish our identities, but it wasn't my business. Now that I knew the situation was more or less under control, I would be glad to leave, if Claude would give me a green light. I was finding that the idea of Tamsin cowering in a safe, locked room – while one woman was killed and another popped over the head – was not agreeing with me.

I had opened my mouth to ask Claude if I could go when another car pulled into the parking lot, toward the back where the police cars weren't as thick. Cliff Eggers sprang out as though he'd been ejected. He hurried to his wife.

'Tamsin!' he cried. 'Are you all right?'

'Cliff!' Our therapist hurled herself into the big man's arms and sobbed against his chest. 'I can't stand this again, Cliff!'

'What's happened?' he said gently, while Stokes, Claude, and I stood and listened.

'Somebody killed a woman and left her in my office!'

Cliff's dark eyes bored into Claude, another large white male.

'Is this true?' he asked, as though Tamsin often made up fantasies of this nature. Or as though he wished she had.

'I'm afraid so. I'm the police chief, Claude Friedrich. I don't believe I've had the pleasure?' Claude extended his hand, and Cliff disengaged from Tamsin to shake it.

'Cliff Eggers,' he responded. 'I'm Tamsin's husband.'

'What do you do, Mr Eggers?' Claude asked in a social way, though I could practically see Detective Stokes twitch.

'I'm a medical transcriptionist,' he said, making an obvious effort to relax. 'I believe your wife is one of my clients. Mostly I work out of our home, my wife's and mine.'

We must all have looked blank.

'Doctors record what they find when they examine a patient, and what they're going to do about it. I take the recordings and enter the information into a computerized record. That's paring my job down to the bare bones.'

I had no idea Carrie employed a medical whatever, and from his face Claude had either been ignorant of it, too, or had forgotten; he wasn't happy with himself. I was probably the only one present who knew him well enough to tell, though.

'You live here in Shakespeare?' Claude said.

'Right over on Compton.' Cliff Eggers's big hand smoothed Tamsin's hair in a cherishing gesture.

I was about to ask Tamsin if she'd heard anyone leave the building before our group had broken in, when I heard a voice calling, 'Lily! Lily!'

I peered around the parking lot, trying to find its source. Full dark had fallen now, and the lights of the parking lot were busy with insects. The people buzzed around below them, looking as patternless as the bugs. I was hoping all the police were more purposeful than they appeared. Claude was no fool, and he'd sent everyone in his department through as much training as he could afford. No wonder he was so quick to snap up a detective from a big force, one who was sure to have more experience than anyone he could hire locally. And though he'd never spoken to me of it, I was aware that Claude had quotas he had to meet, and his force was probably always trying to catch up on the minority percentage, especially since Shakespeare had had some racial troubles about eighteen months ago.

'Lily!'

And there he was; the most handsome young man in Shakespeare, prom king, and thorn in my side, Bobo Winthrop. My heart sank, while another part of me reacted in a far different way.

I turned a hose on myself mentally.

'Bobo,' I said formally.

He disregarded my tone and put his arm around me. Out of the corner of my eye I could see Claude's bushy eyebrows escalate toward his hairline.

'You okay?' Bobo asked tenderly.

'Yes, thank you,' I said, my voice as stiff as I could make it.

'Is this your friend, Lily?' Tamsin asked. She'd recovered enough to try to slip back into her therapist role, and the neutral word *friend* suddenly seemed to have many implications.

'This is Bobo Winthrop,' I told her. 'Bobo: Tamsin Lynd, Cliff Eggers.' I had done my duty.

'What happened here?' Bobo asked, giving Tamsin and Cliff a distracted nod. I was glad to see that Detective Stokes had drawn Claude away to huddle with him on real police business.

I wanted to be somewhere else. I started walking to my car, wondering if anyone would stop me. No one did. Bobo trailed after me, if a six-foot-tall blond can be said to trail.

'A woman got killed in there tonight,' I said to my large shadow when we reached my car. 'She was stabbed, or stuck through somehow.'

'Who was she?' Bobo loomed over me while I pulled my keys out of my pocket. I wondered where the rest of my therapy group had gone. The police station? Home? If Melanie didn't tell the police the identity of the corpse herself, they'd find it out pretty quick. She'd look bad.

'I didn't know her,' I said accurately, if not exactly honestly. Bobo touched my face, a stroke of his palm against my cheek.

'I'm going home,' I said.

'Jack there tonight?'

'No, he's on the road.'

'You need me to be there? I'll be glad—'

'No.' Clipped and final, it was as definite as it was possible to be. Dammit, when would Bobo find a girlfriend or stop coming home during the summer and the holidays? There must be a special word for someone you were fond of, someone who aroused a deep-rooted lust, someone you would never love. There was nothing as idiotic, as inexplicable, as the chemistry between two people who had almost nothing in common and had no business even being in the same room together. I loved Jack, loved him more than anything, and reacting to Bobo this way was a constant irritant.

'I'll see you around,' he said, abandoning his hope that I would prolong our encounter. He took a step back, watched me get into my car and turn the key. When I looked out my window again, he was gone.

Chapter Four

When Jack called that night, he sounded weary to the bone. He was following the trail of a sixteen-year-old runaway from Maumelle, a boy from the proverbial good home who'd become caught up in the subculture of drugs and then prostitution. His family hadn't seen him in a year, Jack told me, yet they kept getting hang-up phone calls from different cities and towns around the South. Convinced their son was on the other end of the phone, sure the boy wanted to come home but was ashamed to ask, this family was getting into seriously shaky financial shape in their search for him.

'How can you keep it up?' I asked Jack, as gently as I could.

'If I don't look, they'll hire someone else,' he said. Jack sounded older than thirty-five. 'People this driven always do. At least I'll really try my best to find the boy. Ever since we found Summer Dawn Macklesby, I'm the guy to see for missing kids.'

'Have you even had a glimpse of this kid?'

'Yes.' Jack didn't sound happy about it. 'I saw him last night, in the Mount Vernon area, on Read Street.' Jack was in Baltimore. 'He looks awful. Sick.'

'You didn't get to talk to him?'

'He went off with a man and didn't come back. I'll be out there again tonight. I might have to pay him for his time, but I'll have that talk.'

There was nothing to say.

'How is the surveillance going?' he asked, ready for some good news.

'She won't bend over. She's wearing a neck brace and walking with a cane, and any bending she does, she must be doing it where I can't see her. Maybe Beth Crider's really hurt. It would be nice to find an honest woman.'

'Not a chance. All the warning signs are there. She's a fraud. We gotta think of a way to catch this woman. Put your mind to it.'

'Okay,' I said. I said it very neutrally, because I am used to taking orders, but I am not used to taking them from Jack. However, I reminded myself in a flattening way, he was my boss now.

'Please,' Jack said suddenly.

'Okay,' I repeated, in a more agreeable tone. 'Now I have a thing or two to tell you.'

'Oh?' Jack sounded apprehensive.

'Therapy group was unexpectedly exciting tonight,' I told him.

'Oh, new woman?'

'Yes, in a way.'

'She'd gotten raped in some new way?'

'I don't know about the rape. She never got a chance to tell us. Someone killed her dead and left her in Tamsin's office.'

After Jack exclaimed for a minute or two, and made sure I hadn't been in personal danger, he became practical. 'That's all your group needed, right – a dead woman, on top of dealing with a pack of traumas. Who was she, did anyone know?' Jack was interested in my story, even more so when I told him about the dead woman, Tamsin's actions, and the new detective, Alicia Stokes.

'I can see why Claude would snap up a woman that qualified, but why in hell would a woman that qualified want to come to Shakespeare?'

'Exactly.'

'I don't know anyone on the Cleveland force, but maybe I know someone who does. I might make a few phone calls when I get back.' Jack's curiosity, which made him such a good detective, could also make him a little uncomfortable to be with from time to time. But in this case, I was just as curious about Stokes as he was.

I tossed and turned that night, seeing the wound in the woman's chest, the pale body and the red blood. I kept wondering why the body had been arranged in Tamsin's office. That was sending a message, all right: a woman murdered and displayed in the middle of all those articles about how women could overcome violence and keep themselves safe.

I thought time was overdue for Tamsin to give us a rundown on the stalker that was going to such lengths to terrorize her. After all, now the whole group was involved in Tamsin's problem, though we had come to her to get rid of our own.

Finally, I got out of bed and pulled on shorts and a T-shirt, socks and walking shoes. Jack wasn't home, and I couldn't sleep, so it was back to the old pattern. I slipped my cell phone and my keys into my pocket and left my house, making a beeline across the street to the arboretum that filled the whole block opposite mine. Estes Arboretum is one of the town's less popular bequests, since the land will only belong to Shakespeare as long as it remains in its leafy state. If the trees are cut down for another use, the city loses the land to the nearest living descendant of Harry Estes. Every now and then there's a flurry of resentment in the local paper about Estes. A group will protest that the city should either sell it or let it revert to the family because the trails through it are not being maintained and the trees are not properly labeled. Then there'll be a storm of cleaning up across the street, and dead branches and leaves will be carted off and new plaques affixed to the trees. The trails will be edged and new trashcans will be positioned discreetly. An elementary school class or two will visit the arboretum and collect leaves in the fall, and a few women from one of the garden clubs will come to plant some perennials in the spring. Then lovers and druggies will start visiting the park at night, trashcans will be vandalized, signs will disappear, and the whole cycle will begin again.

Right now the arboretum was in the upswing, and the petunias were being pinched back by the women of the Shakespeare Combined Church every week, Sandy McCorkindale among them, I was sure. The paths were free of downed branches and debris, and there weren't any used condoms decorating the bushes. I went over all the trails quickly and silently.

Suddenly and without warning, my right leg cramped. I hit the cement of the path a lot faster than I wanted to, and I made an awful noise doing it. The pain was intense. I knew if I could get up and stretch the leg I could recover. It was easier to imagine than to do, but I finally managed to push myself to a kneeling position, and from there I lurched to my feet. I almost screamed when I put my right foot to the ground, but within seconds the cramp had lost its hold on me.

I staggered home, my leg weak and aching. My face was covered with sweat and my hands were shaking. When I got into the house, I went to the kitchen and took an Advil. I didn't know if it would help, but a pain like that would surely leave soreness in its wake. Limping a little, I made my way into the bathroom and washed my face, patting a wet hand along the back of my neck as well.

I was grateful to be back in bed, and stretching the leg out felt so good that I was asleep within minutes of crawling between the sheets.

By the next morning I had almost forgotten about the incident. When I got out of bed to get ready to drive to my surveillance job, the muscle that had cramped was only a faint shadow of discomfort. I wondered if the cramp had anything to do with the approaching onset of my period, which was due any day, judging by my symptoms. I slipped a couple of plastic pouches in my purse to be on the safe side.

Beth Crider, the Worker's Comp. claimant, lived on a busy suburban street in Conway. The ranch-style homes, the small lots, the one-car garages all said 'lower middle class'. Crider had been the supervisor of a crew of men whose job consisted of shifting large boxes around a warehouse, more or less. The boxes left, the boxes arrived, but all the boxes were moved to correct areas on forklifts. Crider told the operators what to do, filled out paperwork on each and every transfer, and generally ran the place, except for the hierarchy she answered to. She'd been turned down for a promotion, and her raise hadn't amounted to what she felt she was due, according to her personnel file. So it had aroused her superior's suspicions when she'd had an 'accident' in the warehouse that had led to unverifiable back and neck injuries. A forklift driver had taken a turn too sharply and bumped Crider with the box he was shifting. She'd been knocked to the hard floor of the warehouse, and the frightened driver had called the ambulance when Crider didn't scramble right to her feet.

Crider now said she was too hurt to ever work again. She had a sore back, a stiff neck, and severe pain in one shoulder. All these conditions, she said, were chronic.

It would have been pleasant to believe her, but I didn't.

Even if I hadn't gotten the job trying to prove that very thing, I still wouldn't believe her. I had enough time, sitting there in my car, to reflect that this probably said something about me that most people might find unpleasant. So be it.

I'd alternated my car with Jack's, and now was back to mine. I'd pretended to visit the house for sale, which was on the opposite side of the street; I'd canvassed door-to-door for a nonexistent political candidate; and, I'm sorry to say, no one who was at home called me on that. They were all sufficiently uninformed to accept my assertion that there was a candidate they'd never heard of running for Congress in the district. I'd visited the convenience store, and I'd gotten gas. Beth Crider didn't go out much, and when she did, she stuck doggedly to the collar and cane. She didn't even go for walks. Hadn't the woman ever heard of exercise?

Of course, for all I knew, she had a home gym and was in her house now, minus all aids, bench-pressing up a storm.

I hated that idea, but when I thought of snooping closer, I was sure that any pictures I took through her window would not be admissible as court evidence. I would have to ask Jack about that.

After a couple of hours watching, I had expected to be antsy with pent-up energy. Instead, I found myself draggy and melancholy, inclined to think fruitless thoughts about situations beyond my control or affect. I wondered if the woman killed the night before had a big family. I wondered if Janet was all right, and if Tamsin could explain her behavior a little better than she had. I felt like I could take a nap.

Now, where the hell had that come from? Since when did I take a nap, or even think of doing so? I shook my head. I must be getting older. Well, of course I was. But lately I'd been thinking and feeling unlike myself. Was the difference my new living arrangement with Jack, or my new work, or the therapy?

I was doing a lot of new stuff at one time; that was for sure. Maybe all these new patterns and activities were having some kind of cumulative effect. Maybe I was being squeezed through a tube and would come out someone different.

The idea was deeply unsettling. I had perfected living the life I'd framed before I met Jack. Maybe that life had started to alter, to become more involved with the lives around it, even before he'd first come to Shakespeare on a job. But ever since I'd known him, change had become the norm.

I sat and brooded over this low-grade anxiety of mine, rousing myself every now and then to change the position of the car. I was beginning to worry about my mental state when I had a mild revelation. Of course, this was just a variation on PMS! Instead of my ordinary pattern of diminished patience, tender breasts, and backache, I was having all those plus cramps and mood swings.

But this deviation from my own body's norm was proof that my body was changing, that time was passing.

I finally convinced myself that the sanest response was, 'So what?'

Letting myself into my silent house in Shakespeare, I peeled off my sweaty clothes and headed for the shower. Fifteen minutes later, fluffing up my curls with my fingers, I checked my answering machine. My friend Carrie Thrush's voice said, 'When you come in today, give me a call, please. I know you're in the middle of learning a new job, but I have a cleaning crisis. Plus, I just want to talk to you.' I wrote her name on the notepad by the phone. The second message was from Melanie. 'Hey, I guess I got the right number, that sounded like your voice on the message. Listen, we all need to talk. Give me a call.' She read off her number, hesitated as if she was going to add something, then hung up.

For the first time, I looked at the message counter. Eight. I'd never had so many before.

A smoky voice began, 'Ms Bard, I hope you're over your shock today. This is Detective Stokes. I need you to come in to make a statement about last night.' Alicia Stokes bit out each word as though it would dissolve her mouth if it weren't perfectly enunciated.

The next call was from Tamsin, who wanted to reschedule our interrupted therapy session. I had to laugh out loud at that.

Firella had called. And Janet, sounding weak. And Carla. Everyone but Sandy. Her husband had called.

'Lily, this is Joel McCorkindale.' He had a rich, sincere voice that I would have recognized anywhere. 'I would like to speak with you about this therapy group you've been attending with my wife. I hope you don't think she broke whatever confidentiality you have to keep with the group; I just recognized you walking in last week when I dropped Sandy off. Please call me back at the church at your earliest convenience.'

I glanced at my watch. It was five-thirty. I looked up the church number and dialed.

He picked up the phone himself. His secretary must have

gone home. This must be an important conversation to the Reverend Mr McCorkindale.

'Lily' he said with elaborate pleasure, when I identified myself. 'I was hoping you could come down here and we could have a talk?'

I thought about it. I'd had my shower, and felt better, though still very tired.

'I guess,' I said reluctantly. 'I can be down there in a couple of minutes.'

I put on a little makeup to obscure the dark circles under my eyes, brushed my hair, and set out. Locking my front door behind me, I plodded down the front steps and over to the sidewalk, turning right. Watching my feet carefully because the sidewalk was cracked in many places, I went past the Shakespeare Garden Apartments and then around the corner (the big squared U that went around the arboretum road bearing three names was actually a cul-de-sac) to the parking lot and redbrick buildings of Shakespeare Combined Church. Joel McCorkindale's office was upstairs over the expanded Sunday school wing, and the daycare program it housed was closed for the day. The gym was busy, judging by the cars parked outside, but it was a separate facility on the other side of the church proper. So the big building was silent when I opened the glass door at the bottom of the stairs.

I plodded up, gripping the handrail, feeling more and more exhausted as I mounted. I didn't think I'd ever felt as washed-out in my life. I managed to get to the reverend's office and knock on the door without stopping to rest, but I had to push myself. And it was karate night, too, I groaned to myself. I'd just have to miss.

Joel came to the door to open it and usher me in. It was

one of those little courtesies that endeared him to so many of his congregation, especially women.

I sat down in the comfortable chair he indicated, and I was happy to do it. Joel sat in a matching chair a careful distance away – no desk between us for this conversation, another signal – and steepled his hands in front of him, his elbows resting on the arms of the chair.

'Lily, I don't know if you feel you're getting anything out of this therapy group, but I'm concerned about Sandy.'

'You should probably talk to the counselor about this.'

'I don't think she would be objective. She'll maintain Sandy needs her services, no matter what.'

'Now you've lost me,' I said, after a pause during which I tried to make sense of his words. I wondered if my mind were going through some sort of trough the way my body seemed to be.

'I have heard, not through idle gossip but through the concerns of members of my flock, that Tamsin Lynd has strong views about the relationships between men, women, and the church. Views that don't coincide with our interpretation of the Scriptures.'

I would have left then if I hadn't been too tired to get up.

'And this is my problem . . . how?'

'I come to you for your . . . advice.'

'I'm just not understanding you.'

'I understand that y'all know each other.'

I stared at Joel's smoothly shaved face, his carefully trimmed mustache, and his razor-cut hair. He wore a very good suit, not so expensive that the people of the church would whisper, but nice enough for sure.

'Joel.' He didn't like me using his first name. I'd always found him distasteful, but fair, and I didn't want to be as ugly as my first inclination led me to be.

'Joel,' I said again, trying to pick my words carefully. 'I don't think I've ever heard Tamsin say one word about any religion in our therapy group.' I took a deep breath. 'It seems to me you should be more concerned about your wife's mental health than about the possible theological opinions of her counselor.'

'Of course, Sandy's well-being is my primary concern,' Joel said. 'I'm just – why does she feel the need to go to this group at all?' he burst out, seeming genuinely puzzled. Suddenly, Joel looked like a real man, not like a little impervious god. 'We've prayed about it and asked for her healing and her forgiveness of the one who did such a terrible thing to her. Why does she need to talk about it?'

'Because your wife was raped,' I said, as if I was telling him this for the first time. 'She needs to talk to other women who've lived through the experience. She needs to be able to express her own true feelings about what happened to her, away from people who expect so many different things from her.'

He tilted back in his chair for a moment. At that second, he looked more vulnerable than I'd ever seen him. I didn't doubt that Joel McCorkindale loved his wife. I did doubt that he knew what a burden his public persona was on his wife's shoulders and what a struggle it was for her to preserve the image of the kind of wife she thought he deserved.

'My wife was accosted in college, over twenty years ago, from what little she's told me,' he said. 'Why would she need help now?'

Accosted? He made it sound as unthreatening as a panhandler asking you for spare change – though under some circumstances, that could be pretty damn scary. And I noticed that even Joel didn't seem to know exactly what had happened to his wife. 'Don't you ever counsel members of your congregation who've been raped?' I asked.

He shook his head. 'I'd be glad to help if someone came to me with that problem, but it hasn't happened.'

'Then you're not doing your job,' I said, 'in some sense. Because believe me, Reverend, your congregation contains rape victims.'

Joel looked unhappy at the idea, though what caused that unhappiness I couldn't guess. 'How many women are in your group?' he asked, staring at his fingers so evenly matched together in front of him.

'More than me and your wife, I can tell you that,' I said sadly. 'And we're just a fraction. How many women in yours?'

He blinked. Considered. 'Two hundred fifty, more or less.'

'Then you have about twenty-five victims,' I told him. 'Depending on whose estimates you use.'

He was shocked, no question.

'Now, Joel, I have to leave. I don't think I was any help to you. But I hope you can be to Sandy, because she definitely has some heavy problems.' I pushed myself to my feet, thinking this had been a waste of time and energy, and I left.

He was still sitting in the chair when I shut the door behind me, and unless I was completely wrong, Joel McCorkindale was deep in thought. Maybe he was praying.

I had more phone calls to return, so I ate a salad and some crackers to get supper out of the way. I was hungrier than I thought I'd be, and it was a little later than I'd planned by the time I called Carrie.

Claude answered the phone and bellowed Carrie's name.

I could hear her telling him she'd be there in a minute, then the sound of water being shut off.

'It's my night to do the dishes,' she explained. 'Listen, the reason I called you, the woman who's been coming in to clean every day – Kate Henderson – has taken a little sabbatical because her daughter had a baby. So I was wondering . . . I hate to mix friendship and business, but is there any way you can come in for a few minutes a day until Kate gets back from Ashdown?'

I'd cleaned Carrie's office until about eighteen months ago, when she'd found her increased patient load called for a daily cleaning, an obligation I couldn't schedule in at the time. 'I'm working in Little Rock this week,' I told her. 'But I can come Thursday and Saturday for sure. The other days, I'll have to see. I may finish up my job in Little Rock pretty soon.' That was probably optimistic thinking, but it was possible.

'I appreciate any time you can give me,' Carrie said. 'So, I'll see you tomorrow?'

'Sure. I'll get there first thing tomorrow morning before you start seeing patients, then I have to go to the Winthrops. But I can come back after you close.'

'So it'll be clean for Thursday morning and Friday morning, and you'll come in on Saturday so it'll be looking good on Monday. Great.' Relief was running high in Carrie's voice. I heard a rumbling in the background at her house.

'Claude wants to know if Alicia Stokes called you,' Carrie relayed.

'Tell him yes, and I'm just about to call her back.'

'She did,' Carrie called to Claude. 'Lily's returning her call after we hang up.'

'He says good.' Carrie listened to some more rumbling.

'He says to tell you Alicia Stokes might be almost as tough as you.'

I could hear from her voice she was smiling. 'Tell him, from me, that in that case I'll be extra careful,' I said.

Chapter Five

Alicia Stokes had her own little cubicle at the Shakespeare Police Department, which for the past three years had been 'temporarily' housed in an older home after the jail and the police station had been declared substandard and put on notice to meet the state requirements. The city had responded sluggishly, as Shakespeare always did when money was involved. After a couple of years, the new jail was completed. Prisoners could march extra yards and be incarcerated in a decent facility. To no one's surprise, the police station in front of it had run into work delays.

It was sort of nice to walk up onto a front porch to go in to see the police, but the old house really wasn't suited to the purpose, and it would be abandoned within the next two months. Alicia's cubicle was at the back of the former living room, and she'd already hung pictures of some of her heroes there. All her heroes were black and female. Alicia Stokes, obviously, had the courage to be different. And she was dedicated. She'd told me to come on in when I'd called, even though it was getting dark.

She stood to shake my hand, which I liked, and she gestured me into a chair that wasn't too uncomfortable. Unlike Joel McCorkindale, Stokes seated herself firmly on the power side of the desk. Then we both had to pretend that no one else could hear us, which wasn't easy, since the partitions were about as high as the detective's head.

'I'd like to review what happened last night,' the

detective said to open the interview. 'And then, we'll get a statement typed up for you to sign before you leave.'

So I'd be here a while. I nodded, resigned.

Detective Stokes had a legal pad in front of her. She opened it to a fresh page, wrote my name at the top of it, and asked, 'How long have you been attending this survivors' therapy group?'

'This would have been my third session. My third week.'

'And all the members of the group have been raped and are in the process of recovery?'

'That's the idea.' The air conditioning, probably as old as the house, could barely keep up with the heat.

'How were you contacted to join this group? Were you already a patient at the center?'

'No.' I told her about the flyer at the grocery store and described coming to the first meeting.

'Who was there?'

'The same people that were there last night.' I went through the list.

'Did Ms Lynd say anything about others who were supposed to come?'

'No, but that wouldn't be surprising.' I remembered my own reluctance. 'I'd expect someone to have second thoughts, or back out entirely.' I remembered Tamsin looking out into the hall that first night, as though she were waiting to hear someone knocking on the door at the end of the hall.

'I guess whoever killed that woman wore a lab coat,' I said. I hadn't been able to stop speculating about that lab coat, the one used to prop the rolling chair in place. 'Was it the nurse's?' There was a staff nurse who did drug testing.

She appeared not to hear me. 'Did you pass around any kind of sign-up sheet?' Her glasses magnified her dark eyes, which were large and almond shaped. Right now, they were fixed on me in a take-no-prisoners stare.

'No, we were supposed to have the illusion of confidentiality.'

'Illusion?'

'How could we remain secret from each other in this town?'

'True enough. Has Ms Lynd ever said anything to you about her own history?'

I shook my head. 'Well, not directly.' My inner thermostat seemed to have gone haywire. I took a tissue from the box on the desk and patted my face with it.

'What do you mean?'

'We saw the squirrel that was killed at her place. And I was there in the office when she got a phone call that seemed to upset her pretty badly.'

Of course I had to go over both incidents with the detective, but I'd expected that.

'So you had already formed the idea that Ms Lynd was being stalked?'

'Yes.'

'Did you report that to the police?'

'No.'

Detective Stokes looked at me almost archly, which was an unnerving sight. 'Why not? Wouldn't that have been the logical thing to do?'

'No.'

'Why not? You don't trust the police to help citizens?'

I was baffled by her manner. 'It would have been *logical* for Tamsin or her husband to call the police themselves. It was their business.' I shifted around in the chair, trying to get comfortable.

'Did you ever think that if you had called us, that woman might not be dead?'

I was in imminent danger of losing my temper. That would be very, very bad in this situation. 'If I had called here yesterday, and said that someone had killed a squirrel and hung it in a tree, what would you have done? Realistically?'

'I would have checked it out,' Alicia Stokes said, leaning forward to make sure I got her point. 'I would have warned Ms Lynd not to go anywhere by herself. I would have begun asking questions.'

I was figuring out things myself. 'You already knew, too,' I said, thinking it through as I went. 'You knew someone was stalking Tamsin Lynd. What did *you* do about it?'

For a long moment, I thought Stokes was going to lean across the desk and whop me. Then she collected herself and lied. 'How could we possibly know anything like that?' she asked.

'Huh,' I said, putting a lot of disgust into it. If Alicia Stokes was playing some kind of hide-and-seek, she could do it on her own damn time.

'She did look like Tamsin, didn't she?'

Detective Stokes laid her pen down on top of her yellow tablet. 'Just what do you mean, Miss Bard?'

'You know what I mean. The dead woman. She looked like Tamsin.'

'Who mentioned that to you?' Her interest was keen now.

'No one. I'm not blind. She was pale, she was plump, she was brunette. She looked like Tamsin.'

I had no idea what the detective was thinking as she regarded me.

'But as you know, I was told by . . . ,' she checked a note

on the tablet, 'Melanie Kleinhoff that the dead woman was her sister-in-law, that is, the wife of her husband's brother.'

'Melanie did say that,' I admitted. 'Saralynn, wasn't that her name?'

'And yet you told me last night you didn't know the name of the dead woman.'

'No, I told you I hadn't known her. You asked me if the others had recognized her, and I told you to ask them.' Splitting hairs, but I had technically told her the truth. 'I don't like repeating what other people tell me, when I don't know it for myself.'

Detective Stokes's face told me what she thought of that, and for once I wondered if I wasn't just being balky, like a stubborn mule.

'So where is Saralynn's husband, the one who raped Melanie?' I asked. 'I guess he raped Saralynn, too, since she was going to join our group?'

'Tom Kleinhoff's in jail,' Detective Stokes said, not confirming and not denying my assumption. 'He didn't make bail on the rape charge, because he already had other charges pending.'

It would have been good if he had been the guilty one. That would have been simple, direct, and over.

'Too bad it wasn't him, isn't it?' said Stokes, echoing my thoughts. I guess that wasn't too great a leap to take.

I nodded.

'So let me just ask you, Miss Bard. Since your boyfriend, I understand, is a private eye.' The distaste in her voice told me she knew all about the circumstances of Jack's becoming a private eye; he'd left the police force in Memphis under a black cloud. 'If you think the dead woman was killed in mistake for Tamsin Lynd . . . why? Was that supposed to send a message to Tamsin Lynd herself, that a woman resembling her was killed in her office? Was it a genuine mistake – the killer finds a dark-haired fat woman in the right place so he's sure he has the right victim? Or was the message for your group?'

I hadn't speculated that far, wasn't sure if that was a conclusion I'd have reached.

'Hadn't thought about that? Well, maybe you'd better.' Alicia Stokes's expression was definitely on the cold and hard side. 'Someone thinks they've killed the woman supposed to be helping five rape victims, you've got to ask yourself why.'

She was so far ahead of me all I could do was gape at her.

'How does your boyfriend feel about you being in this group?' she asked, pounding on down the track.

'He was the one who wanted me to go to it.'

'You sure he doesn't resent you giving such a big part of your time to a group of women? Maybe he doesn't like some of the advice Tamsin gave you? Maybe Tamsin told you to stand up to him? How long has he lived here?'

Scrabbling for the most recent question, I said, 'He's lived here in Shakespeare for only a few weeks. He lived in Little Rock for a few years.'

Angry with myself for babbling, I realized just how battered I felt.

Then I began feeling angry.

Even as I tried to remember all the other questions she'd asked so I could begin to respond, I thought, Why bother? I got up.

'You sit your butt back down in that chair,' Alicia Stokes told me.

I fixed my eyes on her face.

'Before I make you,' she added.

Rage hit me like fireball. 'You can't make me do shit,' I

said, slow and low. 'I came in to give a statement. I gave it. Unless you arrest me, I don't have to sit here and answer any questions.'

Stokes loomed over me, leaning across her desk, her knuckles resting on its surface. A patrolman I'd never met, a wiry freckled man, peered in the entrance to the cubicle, went wide-eyed, and backed away.

'This looks like the gunfight at the OK Corral,' Claude's voice said behind me.

I let out my breath in a long gust. I speculated on what could've happened if the new patrolman hadn't fetched him – would Stokes have launched herself across her desk at me? Would I have hit a police officer?

'I was just leaving,' I told Claude. I edged past him and strode out the front door, picking my way through the desks and chairs and a few assorted people with my eyes fixed on the floor. The freckled patrolman held open the front door for me. His nametag read 'G. McClanahan'. I made a mental note that I owed G. McClanahan a free house cleaning. Right now, getting in the car and driving away appeared to be my best move.

I wondered if Claude would have a talk with Stokes now, and what that talk would be like. I knew she would have no cause to like me any better afterward, that was for sure, and I didn't know if I'd care or not. What was more certain was the fact that as fast as I could think, the detective could think faster, and I added that to the list of her sins, as I was sure her fellow officers would. Stokes was northern, black, a woman, aggressive, very tall (and I'd bet strong), and smart as hell. She would have to perform like a one-woman band to be popular, or even tolerated.

How would she live in Shakespeare? Why had she taken the job?

To my mind, that was as much a puzzle as the woman pinned to the wall in the health center. Maybe the city paid better than I'd assumed, or maybe Stokes had a master plan that included some time in a small force – a very small force. Maybe Stokes had family in the area.

But it hadn't escaped my attention that a puzzling and bizarre murder had occurred in Shakespeare (where the norm was a Saturday night knifing) just when a puzzling and mysterious detective had turned up to solve it.

Some might think that suspicious, too.

I felt groggy when I woke up. I had to force myself to obey the clock. This was one of my days in Shakespeare, and I had to clean Carrie's office in addition to putting in a stint at the Winthrops' house. Forcing myself every step of the way, I got dressed and ate; though my head was aching and the rest of me felt exhausted already, as if I'd already put in a hard day. I wondered if I had dreamed a lot – dreams that were best forgotten – and had therefore slept restlessly. I caught no echoes of it as I cleaned my teeth and fluffed my hair. I expected my new sneakers to make me perk up; I don't often get new things, and these black high-tops had been on extreme sale.

But after they were laced and tied I stared down at them as if I'd never seen them before; or my feet, either, for that matter.

I saw a car already parked in the lot to the rear of Carrie's office, and I had a feeling I'd seen it before. I just couldn't place where and when. It was an hour earlier than any of the staff should appear. When I tried the back door, it was already unlocked.

'Hello?' I said cautiously, not wanting to scare anyone.

'Good morning!' called a horribly happy voice. Cliff

Eggers stuck his head out of one of the doors on the left. 'Carrie left a message you'd be coming in.'

I brought in my cleaning caddy and a few other things. I didn't know what Carrie's new cleaner kept here, so I'd piled my car with stuff. I had to do a great job for Carrie.

'And you're here so early to do medical transcriptions?' I said in a voice that would carry down the hall as I deposited my burdens.

'That's right.' Cliff appeared in the doorway again, beaming at me as though I'd said something very clever. 'It works out better for me this way. I can do the rest of my doctors at home.'

'And you like your job,' I prodded.

'It's fascinating. I learn something every day. Well, I'd better get back to it.' Cliff retreated to his desk, and I started with the waiting room. Dust, straighten, polish, vacuum, mop. In short order, the magazines were lined up on the square table in the middle of the room; the chairs were sitting in neat rows against the wall. The large mat in front of the door where most of the dirt from patients' shoes was supposed to fall had been shaken out the front door and replaced, exactly square with the door.

Cliff squeaked down the hall in rubber shoes, and I cleaned the glass barrier between the patient sitting room and the clerks' office. I saw with disapproval that Carrie's new maid had been slacking off there. And the counter in the reception clerk's area was just nasty.

'Want a cup of coffee?' he called to me after a few minutes had passed.

'No, thank you,' I said politely.

I was able to get on with the other rooms and the hall, and cleaned as fast as a dervish whirls until I reached the room in which Cliff was working.

The burly man was sitting at a desk, a headset on, and his fingers flying across the keys of a computer. His leg was moving slightly, and as I mopped behind him, I saw that he was operating a pedal. He wasn't listening to music on a CD player, as I'd at first believed. He was listening to Carrie's voice. I could barely hear it while I dusted. Carrie was saying, 'temperature of one hundred and one. Mr Danby said he'd had episodes of fever for the past two days, and his stomach had become very sore and tender to the touch. Upon examination, when the lower left quadrant of his abdomen was palpated . . .'

'You know anything about medicine?' Cliff said out loud, as I wiped the picture frames.

'No, not much,' I confessed.

'It's like listening to a soap opera every day,' he said, as if I'd asked.

'Ummm,' I said, lifting an open magazine to wipe underneath, ready to set it down exactly the same way.

'How's Tamsin doing?' I asked, just to stop him from asking me any more questions. I had seen his lips begin to form a phrase.

'She's doing well, considering what a shock she got,' Cliff said, his heavy face grim. He hesitated for a second, then said, 'And considering this has ruined our new life here.'

That seemed a strange way to put it. Here I was thinking it was Saralynn's life that had been ruined.

'It's awful about the woman who was killed,' Cliff went on, echoing my thoughts. 'But I'm Tamsin's husband, so I can't help worrying about her more than anyone. For someone whose joy is to help others, her life has been full of trouble this past couple of years.'

From what I'd seen, that was certainly true.

'You moved here from the Midwest?' I asked, trying to

confirm the accent. I realigned a stack of insurance forms and put a stapler in the drawer below.

'I'm originally from northern Kentucky,' he said. 'But we've moved a lot these past few years since we both got out of school. It's been hard to find a place where we both can have the jobs we like and a good lifestyle.'

Jack and I were facing the same sort of problem right now. 'So you've been here in Shakespeare for how long?'

'A little over a year, I guess. We really like it here, and Tamsin's finally making friends.'

I wondered how long Detective Stokes had lived here. Quite a Yankee invasion we were having, here in little Shakespeare. And there was the new freckled officer G. McClanahan at the police department. I had no idea where he'd come from.

As I cleaned around Cliff Eggers's bulk, as I bundled all my things back into the car, I deliberated over asking Tamsin about her allusions to problems in the past. Cliff seemed more than willing to talk, but I knew I'd feel uncomfortable discussing Tamsin's secrets without her permission or presence.

The silent Winthrop house was just what I needed after the unexpected and aggravating presence of Cliff Eggers at Carrie's office. Since school was out, I was a little surprised to find no one at home, and quite pleased. I was able to do things exactly in the order I wanted, up to the point when Amber Jean came in the back door escorted by about six of her friends.

Amber Jean was a whole different shooting match from her oldest brother, Bobo. She cast me a casual hello, as did two of her buddies, while the rest of them behaved as though I were invisible. Actually, I didn't mind that so much. I'd rather be ignored than the center of attention.

The three boys in the group were around fifteen or sixteen, and they were going through the goofy, pimply awkward phase where they could be adults one moment and silly children the next. I'd met Bobo when he'd been around that age.

The girls were more mysterious to me. Since I'd been one, and I had a sister, I should have understood these teenagers better. But with these particular girls, maybe it was the money their parents gave them, maybe it was the 'freedom' they had (which was really lack of supervision), maybe it was their mobility . . . they all had their own cars . . . Any or all of these factors made their lives different from any experience of mine.

I was relieved when the whole group trooped out to the pool. The boys pulled off their shirts and sandals and the girls took off various things. I supposed the shorts the boys were wearing could double as swimsuits, and the girls were already suited up under their clothing. They had small swimsuits on. Really, really small.

Amber Jean's two-piece was screaming pink with a pattern of green leaves. She looked very attractive in it. She stuck her head in the sliding glass door and called, 'Lily, could you bring us some lemonade and some snacks out to the pool?'

'No.'

She gaped at me. 'No?' she repeated, and the closest of the boys began sniggering.

'No. I clean. I don't serve.' I finished mopping the floor and squeezed out the mop.

Amber scrambled to catch hold of some superiority. 'Okay, no problem,' she said in a clipped, cold voice. 'Come on, guys!' she called over her shoulder. 'We got to get the food ourselves!'

I invented something for myself to do in the master bedroom to get out of their way, and when I heard the sliding glass door shut again, I ventured out. The floor had still been damp, and they'd tracked all over it. I'd have to mop again. Well, that was my payoff for not serving. Taking a deep breath, I took care of the floor for the second time. I thought it possible Amber Jean would invent a second reason to come in, and I waited for a few minutes just in case. When she and her friends stayed out, I scrubbed the sink and polished it in uninterrupted industry.

Just as I'd cleaned the counters, Howell Three came in. This second son was Howell Winthrop the Third, but he'd been called Howell Three since birth thanks to his mother, who thought the nickname was cute. Reedy, slender, plain, and an honor-roll student, Howell was the bridge between Bobo (beautiful and moderately book smart) to Amber Jean (fairly pretty and book dumb).

'Hi, Lily,' Howell Three said. 'Oops, sorry, the floor.' He took huge steps to get across the linoleum as quickly as possible.

'Quite all right,' I said. 'It's almost dry.' Now that he was on the carpet in the living room area, Howell Three heard the noise from the pool and looked out. A look of disgust crossed his face. 'Amber Jean,' he said angrily, as though she was right by him. 'She's sunning with her top off,' Howell Three told me, sounding about ten years younger than his age, which I realized with some surprise was seventeen. 'Lily, she shouldn't do that.'

'Will she listen to you?' I asked, after some hesitation. I felt a little responsible in a roundabout way. If I had brought her drinks and chips, Amber Jean would not be exposing her breasts now. That made no sense, but it was a fact.

'No. I'm gonna call Mom,' he said, reaching a resolution.

'I hate to rat on her, but this is embarrassing. She thinks she's being cool, that they won't talk about her, but that's not true. Those girls and those guys, they'll tell everyone.' He looked at me with some appeal in his face, but I had no authority to assume the role of Amber Jean's mother. I doubted if Amber Jean would listen to me, even if I did speak; she'd probably just strip off her bikini bottom, too, to spite me.

So while Howell Three called his mother (she was at one of the family businesses meeting with an accountant) and got her promise that she was on her way home instantly, I gathered up my stuff and got out of there. The last thing I wanted was to witness a Winthrop family blowup.

And to think, I'd been so happy a month or two before when Beanie had called me to come back to work for the family. I'd missed the income the Winthrops had given me, and in a weird way, I'd missed them. What had I been thinking? Was I falling victim to the Mammy syndrome?

Shaking my head at myself, I went home for lunch.

The afternoon was supposed to be free, but I had messages on my answering machine.

'Lily, hey, we're going to try to have our meeting tonight, since Tuesday didn't work out. I hate to lose our momentum,' Tamsin said. 'Oh, this is Tamsin Lynd calling. I hope I see you tonight, same time as usual.'

Tuesday didn't work out? That was one way to put it.

I trudged unwillingly into the building that night. It was still light, of course, but the day was lying on my shoulders like a heavy coat. I craved sleep, and the aching of my back and breasts reminded me that my cycle was coming full circle.

I saw Janet getting out of her car when I entered the parking lot.

'How are you?' I called.

'Lots better,' she said, trying to smile normally and failing. 'I still have a headache, but there wasn't any fracture and everything looks normal in the X rays.'

'What does the doctor think happened to you?' I fell into step beside her and tried to slow my steps to match hers.

Janet heaved a deep sigh. 'He thinks that someone hit me with something hard on the back of the head, that my head bounced forward and hit another hard surface, and that was all she wrote. I was completely out for maybe five minutes, total. I could kind of hear you and Firella when you were waiting with me. So I wasn't really out of it that long.'

'It felt like a long time to us,' I told her. 'We were pretty worried about you.'

'I'm glad you all came in. The detective told me what happened. I don't remember seeing the dead woman, so I guess I should thank the person who bopped me. That's not a memory I want.'

'So you don't remember seeing anyone in the building?'

'Nope. I just barely remember getting here Tuesday evening. It seems to me I sort of recall walking down the hall, but even that's not exactly clear.'

The rest of the group trickled into the therapy room in near silence. Janet and I were sitting on the left side of the table, Melanie and Carla on the other. Firella came in and pulled out a chair on my other side, and Sandy scooted in the room with her gaze cast on the floor. She worked her way down to the end of the table without meeting anyone's gaze. Tamsin came in last and sat at the end closest to the door.

'We needed to meet tonight to find out how everyone's handling what happened. As you all know by now, the woman you found dead was Melanie's sister-in-law,

Saralynn. She used to be married to the man who raped Melanie. They'd just gotten divorced.'

Firella shook her head. 'Sunday dinners must be hell in that family.'

Melanie nodded. Her plump, doughy face looked pinched and her eyes were definitely red. Her hair was frizzy as though she'd tried a home permanent that didn't work. But the same determination that had led her to prosecute her attacker when no one else in the world wanted to seemed to be getting her through this latest crisis.

'How are you getting along with your husband after all this?'

'We're fine,' Melanie said. 'He loves me and I love him, more than anything in the world, and he's not going to let me down. His brother is a no good piece of trash and Deke's always known it. Ain't Deke's fault his mom and dad turned out a bad 'un.'

'That's wonderful, Melanie,' Tamsin said. She didn't sound convinced, though. I leaned forward a little to get a good look at our counselor. 'Do you think your brother-in-law could be responsible for the death of his wife?'

'No, seeing as how he's in jail,' Melanie responded tartly.

I noticed that the ones who hadn't known this looked disappointed. Everyone, it seemed, would have been glad to have Tom Kleinhoff to blame for this murder.

'Why aren't you telling us how you feel about this?' Firella asked. She leaned forward so she could look right into Tamsin's face. 'Why aren't you telling us what happened in here Tuesday night?' This sudden aggression surprised almost everyone except me.

Tamsin flushed a deep plum color. 'I've admitted I was hiding in the therapy room when Saralynn Kleinhoff was killed,' she said in a low voice. I saw Sandy lean across the table to hear. 'I've admitted to being scared when I knew there was a killer in the building. I don't think that's too surprising.'

'But . . .' I began before I thought. I had leaned forward to focus on her myself. I stopped before I voiced my doubts.

'What, Lily?' Tamsin asked. But only because she had to; you could tell she was scared about what I was going to say. We were supposed to bare all to Tamsin; what about her being honest with us?

'Tell us exactly what happened,' I said, with careful emphasis. 'As far as we can tell, it could have been any one of us pinned to that wall in your office. How come Melanie's sister-in-law and Janet got attacked, and you didn't?'

'Are you blaming Tamsin for not getting hurt, Lily?' Firella asked. 'Are you blaming the victim for the crime, so to speak?'

'Yeah, where are you going with this, Lily?' Carla croaked.

Good question.

'I just want to know exactly what happened. We come here every week.' I simmered for a minute. 'We're supposed to feel safe here. How did this person who killed Saralynn get in? How'd he get out without us seeing him?'

Everyone around the table looked thoughtful after hearing my questions. I wasn't sure why I was maneuvering our therapist into telling us something that would surely upset her, but I was determined to do just that.

'As I told you the night of the incident, Lily,' Tamsin said with reluctance, 'Saralynn was supposed to come early so I could give her the little talk I give everyone before she joins the group. I'd asked her to come in at seven fifteen, a little earlier than I'd asked you to come. You were the last one to get the lecture the first night you all came, and I remembered I'd had to rush through.

'I was a little worried about Saralynn having such a close relationship with Melanie, how that would impact the group, and we talked about that a little bit.'

'You didn't hear anyone else in the building?' Firella asked.

'I may have. Now, I think I did. But it could have been someone staying late, or coming back in after something he'd left . . . anything.'

'The end door was locked?' Sandy wanted to be sure.

'No, the end door wasn't locked,' Tamsin flushed red. 'I knew you guys would be coming in. So I didn't lock it behind her.'

'Did you hear the door while you talked?'

'No. I don't think so.'

When I looked skeptical, she said, 'That's the most normal noise in the world, to me. I'm not sure I would have noticed!' She was getting angry.

'So there was a reason you had to leave Saralynn in your office?' Melanie said, to get Tamsin back on the track.

'Yes, I'd left the group list on the table in here, and I had to get it to enter Saralynn's name – just her first name – and phone number. You remember, I took that information from all of you in case we had to cancel sometime.'

'So while you were in the therapy room . . . ?' Melanie prompted.

'Okay, while I was in there I dropped everything. I spilled all my papers from my notebook and knocked my pop over.'

After a brief vision of Tamsin pushing down an old man with white hair, I realized she meant she'd spilled a soft drink. Maybe it was a northern or midwestern thing? We all waited, watching her. Janet's mouth was pulled tight against her teeth. Anger? Skepticism?

'I started picking everything up, and while I was doing that I heard someone going into my office.'

'Did you hear this person pass the door of the therapy room, or come from the direction of the end door?'

'I don't remember either way,' she admitted. 'I've tried and tried, but I don't remember.'

Sandy interrupted. 'What difference would that make, Lily?'

I shrugged. 'The difference between someone hiding in this building until he was able to catch a woman alone, and someone coming in from the parking lot – maybe after Saralynn – on purpose.'

An interesting difference, their faces said, and they turned to Tamsin again. She shook her head. 'No use, I just can't recall it. After I heard someone go into my office, I heard Saralynn say something, but I couldn't make it out. She sounded surprised but not scared. But after that, she said, "What?" and she made an awful sound. Then there was a lot of scuffling and grunting, and I knew what was happening. I was so scared. I know I should have gone to help her, but I was so scared. I crawled over to the door to the therapy room. It was shut, you know how it falls shut? So as quietly as I could, I locked it.'

She got a chorus of sympathy from everyone in the room except me. Her eyes traveled around the group of women, coming to stop at my face.

'Lily, I think we have to get this out in the open. Are you blaming me for not going to Saralynn's aid?'

'No,' I said. 'I think that was good sense.'

'Then are you angry I let Janet come in without warning her?'

'No. If you don't go help one, why go help another?' She winced, and I knew that had sounded as if I thought her callous. 'I mean, if you expected to be killed when he killed Saralynn, you would still have been killed if you'd tried to help Janet, I guess.'

'Then what issue do you have with me?'

I thought for a minute. 'You seem . . . already scared,' I said, picking my way slowly. 'Don't you think you should tell us the rest?' I could see the fear in her face, read it in the tightly drawn line of her mouth and the way her shoulders were set. I know a lot about fear.

'That don't make a lick of sense, Lily,' Carla said.

'Well, yeah, it does,' Janet said in her unnaturally husky voice. 'Like Tamsin's already been a victim and she's anticipating being a victim again.'

'The therapist isn't supposed to talk about her own problems,' Tamsin reminded us. 'I couldn't, even if I wanted to.'

'And why wouldn't you want to? We share our big problems with you,' Carla said illogically.

'This is where you come to get help,' Tamsin began.

'Oh, yeah, like the help we got Tuesday night?' Sandy's voice was bitter and shrill. The rest of us tried to look at her without actually turning our heads to stare, because Sandy was the least forthcoming of the group by far. We didn't want to startle her, or she'd run; it was like having a wounded deer in your backyard, a deer you felt obliged to examine. 'Seeing that dead woman in your office was the scariest thing that's happened to me in a long time, and if you know anything about it or if it happened because of you, I think we have a right to know that. Because what if it's connected to one of us?' I exchanged glances with Janet, not quite following Sandy.

'Sure,' said Carla, who evidently hadn't had the same problem. 'Think about it!' I was hopelessly confused.

'You're saying,' Firella clarified, 'that maybe if Saralynn's murder ties up with something in Tamsin's past, it hasn't got anything to do with us. Maybe we'd all been scared it did? Like maybe one of the bikers who raped Lily following Lily here and killing Saralynn as a lesson to Lily?'

'Right. Like that.' Carla sounded relieved that someone understood her.

'Or like whoever raped Sandy, not that Sandy has chosen to reveal that to the rest of her sisters in the group, which every one of the rest of us has,' said Melanie, and I thought through that sentence for a moment.

Sandy flushed a deep red. 'Well, then, missy, I'll just tell you that it couldn't be connected to me because the man who raped me was my grandfather, and I'll tell you what I did about it. I put rat poison in his coffee and that son of a bitch died.'

We all gazed at her with our mouths hanging open. In a million years, not one of us could have predicted what had come out of Sandy's mouth.

Firella said, 'Way to *go*, Sandy.'

So I had a sister under the skin. Another killer. I felt myself smile, and I was sure it was a very unpleasant smile to see. 'Good for you,' I told her.

Tamsin's face was a sight. A professional excitement that Sandy had spoken up was mingled with subdued dismay at Sandy's revelation, and concern over Tamsin's own situation.

'Didn't expect that, did you?' Carla jeered.

'No,' Tamsin admitted readily, 'I never suspected Sandy would share with us, especially to this extent. Sandy, do you feel good now that you've told us what happened to you?'

I observed that attention had turned away from Tamsin, which was undoubtedly what Tamsin had wanted.

Sandy looked as though she was rummaging around inside herself to discover what was there. Her gaze was inward, intensely blue, blind to all around her.

'Yes, I feel pretty good,' she said. Surprise was evident in her voice. 'I feel pretty *damn* good.' She looked happily shocked at herself. 'I hated that old man. I hated him. I was eighteen when it happened. You'd think an eighteen year old could fight off a grandfather, wouldn't you? But he was only fifty-eight himself, and he'd been doing manual labor all his life. He was strong and he was mean and he had a knife.'

'What happened afterward?' Tamsin asked. She kept her voice very even and low, so Sandy's flow would continue.

'I told my mother. She didn't believe me until she saw the blood on the bed and helped me clean up. He'd been living with us since my grandmother died. After my mom and dad talked, they took Grandpa to a hospital. They told him he had to stay in the mental hospital till he died, or else they'd tell what he'd done to me and he'd have to go to regular jail.'

'Did he believe them?'

'He must have, because he agreed. Oh, he tried to say no one would believe me. That was what I was afraid of, but then I turned up pregnant and of course,' and Sandy's face was too awful to look at, 'I would have had the baby to prove the paternity with.'

I felt nauseated. 'What happened with the baby?' I asked.

'I lost the baby, but only after Granddaddy was committed. And I thank God for that every day. Two days after I lost the baby, I visited Granddaddy in the hospital and I took him some coffee. It was spiked, so to speak. I was scared he'd talk his way out if he knew I wasn't pregnant anymore.'

Telling the bare and horrible truth takes its toll, and I could read that in the woman's face.

'You weren't prosecuted?' Firella, too, was keeping her voice very even and low.

'It's funny,' Sandy said, in an almost detached way. 'But though I wasn't trying to sneak in, no one saw me. Like I was invisible. If I'd sat and planned it a week, it couldn't've gone like that. No one at the front desk.' She shook her head, seeing the past more clearly than she could see the present. 'No one at the wing he was in. I pushed the button that opened the door myself. I went in. He was in his room alone. I handed him the cup. I had a plain one. We drank coffee. I told him I'd forgiven him.' She shook her head again. 'He believed that. And when the coffee was all gone – the tranquilizers had pretty much destroyed his sense of taste – I got up and left. I took the cups with me. And no one saw me, except one nurse. She never said a word. I just didn't register.' Sandy was lost in a dreamlike memory, a memory both horrible and gratifying.

'Have you ever told your husband?' Tamsin asked, and her more recent world came crashing back to Sandy McCorkindale.

'No,' she said. 'No, I have not.'

'I think it's time, don't you?' Tamsin's voice was gentle and insinuating.

'Maybe,' Sandy admitted. 'Maybe it is. But he may not want someone who's been through something so . . . sordid . . . my sons . . . the church . . .' And Sandy began crying, her back arching with huge, heaving sobs.

'He really loves you,' I said.

Her head snapped up and she gave me an angry look. 'How would you know about that, Lily Bard?'

'Because he called me into his office yesterday to ask me if I could tell him what was wrong with you. He doesn't know why you're in therapy, and he doesn't have the slightest idea how to help you.'

She stared at me, stunned. 'My husband is worried about how to help me? My husband wonders why I need therapy?'

I nodded.

Sandy looked intensely thoughtful.

Tamsin glanced down at her watch and said, 'This has already been a big night. And our time is up. Why don't we save the rest of this discussion until next Tuesday night?' She'd escaped from any further questioning, and her whole body relaxed as I watched.

With some grumbling, the rest of the group agreed. Sandy hardly seemed to be in the same room with us any more, her thoughts were so distant. As we left the building, I saw Sandy go to the end of the parking lot and slide into the car, where Joel sat in the front seat, waiting for her. I saw him lean over to give her a kiss on the cheek, and when he did, she gripped his arm and started talking.

Chapter Six

Some days everything just works out wonderfully. I didn't have many of those, and I enjoyed one when I got it.

I got two phone calls the next morning before I started for Little Rock and the stakeout. One was from Mel Brentwood, the owner of Marvel, who asked if I would work that day. I tried explaining to Mel that since the thief had been captured I had moved on to another job. Mel replied that he hadn't been able to find anyone to fill my position and if it was at all possible, he really wanted me to come in for my former shift. It would be worth the extra pay to not have to worry for one day.

'It might be a little awkward, Mr Brentwood, having me back now.'

'Oh, they don't know you were there as a private eye,' Mel reassured me. 'As far as they're concerned, you're a regular employee who had another job offer. I told Linda to put you on the substitute list.'

I wished Jack were there to advise me. I didn't want to alienate an important client of Jack's, but I didn't want to miss a day watching Beth Crider, either. Perhaps it might be good to lull her into security for a day? Maybe she'd been feeling watched; a day free from observation might make her careless. 'Okay, Mr Brentwood, I'll be there,' I said. I laid down the phone and it rang immediately.

'Yes?' I asked, a little apprehensive.

'Babe, it's me,' Jack said.

'How are you? Where are you?'

'Still at the hotel, but we're about to leave for the airport.'

'We?'

'He's agreed to come with me,' Jack said in a low voice. 'He's in the bathroom right now, so I can talk for a minute.'

'He just caved?' I asked, incredulous.

'He's sick and scared,' Jack said. 'And a trick beat the shit out of him two nights ago.'

If the boy had been fated to be beaten, this was the right time for it to happen, I thought, but I kept it to myself. I wasn't always sure if I believed in fate or not, but sometimes it was comforting to believe in something.

Jack went on to tell me he planned to drive the boy home after they landed. Then he'd come to Shakespeare. 'No matter how late it is,' he said.

So I was already feeling unusually chipper when I parked my car at Marvel, even though I was back to wearing the loathsome leopard-print unitard. As I slung my purse and lunch bag into my locker, Linda Doan, wearing a zebra-striped workout bra and puffy black shorts, asked me if I'd had a boob implant. Since she was pinning on her 'Manager' label at the time, I was tempted to ask her what she'd leak if she stuck her breast, but I abstained, which made me proud of myself.

'No, just me in here,' I said so cheerfully that I checked the mirror again to make sure I was myself.

Even Linda looked surprised.

'You musta gotten some last night,' she observed. 'You're mighty perky today.'

I sure was. Perky. Lily Bard, perky?

As long as I was being such a cheerful team member, I asked, 'Did you get any feedback from the calisthenics class?' That had been my idea. I got tired of the cute little classes taught in the aerobics room; they all pivoted around some gimmick. The set of calisthenics we did before karate class had seemed exotic to this bunch. And extremely painful.

Linda's face took on a reserved expression. Linda was brown from the tanning bed, streaked from the hairdresser, and hard bodied from exercise. She was a little cautious, too, when she perceived that her interest was at stake. 'A couple of the women said it was the hardest workout they'd ever had,' Linda said. 'And at least one of them wanted to try it again.'

'Great.'

'Byron was telling me you know Mel?' Linda was striving to keep her voice casual, but I could tell we'd come to the crux of the conversation.

I nodded.

'Did he send you here to keep an eye on me?' she asked, abandoning all pretense of having a normal conversation.

'No,' I said. My shoelace was loose, so I squatted down to retie it.

'You stop trying to dodge me,' Linda said in a furious whisper.

'I'm not. I'm just tying my shoe.'

'Well, I don't believe that you're just here to work this job.'

'Believe what you want,' I said. I picked up the bottle of spray cleaner and the paper towels and went over to the nearest mirror to begin my cleaning round. I glanced at Linda's reflection while I worked, and when I saw her expression I knew that she really hated me. I didn't particularly care, but it would have cleared the air if I'd been able to tell her why I'd really been hired. Mel Brentwood had been clear about that point, though. He wanted me to remain just an occasional employee to the staff at Marvel.

One of the regular clients, Jay Scarlatti, a tall, lean, bony man, had taken a shine to me. He came in every morning after his run to lift some weights; afterward, he'd shower and go to work in a suit his wife had brought in the afternoon before.

Jay was interested in me physically. He had no idea what my character was like. Today, as always, he saw the body in the unitard and not the person who was wearing it.

'Hello, you beautiful thing,' he said this morning, coming up behind me while I was spraying the upholstery of one of the weight benches. 'How are you today?'

I wasn't supposed to beat on the customers, so I replied mildly that I was fine, and I hoped he was well.

'And Mrs Scarlatti?' I asked.

'Katy's fine,' he said stiffly.

'That's good. She seems like such a nice lady, when she brings in your clothes in the afternoon. It's really too bad you never have time to do that yourself.'

Jay Scarlatti was scowling.

'Being a little emphatic, aren't you?' he asked, biting the words out.

'Seems like I need to. Are you going to try calisthenics today?'

He looked startled. 'Sure, I guess so.'

'Then let's get into line.'

I stowed away my cleaning things, blew my whistle, and collected a small crowd right away. Linda and Byron got in line, too, since I'd told Byron he might have to lead this exercise when I was off.

'You'll see,' said a young muscle-builder to his pal. 'This

is gonna make you sore in places you didn't even know you had muscles.' He looked excited at the prospect.

So we began, and the first time I asked them to touch the floor right in front of their toes, I heard a chorus of groans and cracking joints. But gradually they improved, and since I'd insisted on discipline from the beginning, I heard no complaints. Linda and Byron were red and panting, but they made it through the rest of the class.

Now that I wasn't watching for a thief, I actually enjoyed being in the gym all day. And I was so thankful not to be loitering in Beth Crider's neighborhood that I was extra-friendly all day.

Jack had thought he'd get home about ten, so I left some food out on a microwavable plate for him. I got ready for bed and read for a while, then heard the familiar snick of the key in the lock of the front door.

While Jack ate and brushed his teeth, I kept him company. He talked a little about the boy he'd found, about how halfway home the boy had decided he felt a little better and wanted to go back to the streets. He and Jack had had some conversation, and the boy had decided to stick to his original plan.

'What did you say to him to persuade him?' I asked.

'I just told him I'd carry him home, kicking and screaming if necessary. When he told me I wasn't capable of that, I pinched a nerve in his neck for a minute.'

'I bet that shut him up.'

'That, and me telling him I'd found and shipped plenty of runaways – just like him – home in coffins. And they never came back from *that*.'

'You've seen a lot of runaways.'

'Yeah. Starting back when I was a cop, I've seen way too

many. The ones like him, the ones that started selling their butts, didn't last three years. Sickness, or a client, or self-disgust, or drugs . . . mostly drugs.'

Every time Jack tracked a runaway, he went through a spell of depression; because the fact was, the kid often ran off again. Whatever grievance had led a child to leave home was seldom erased by life on the streets. Sometimes the grievance was legitimate; abuse, mental or physical. Sometimes it was based on teen angst; parents who 'just didn't understand'.

Catching a runaway often led to repeat business, but it wasn't business Jack relished. He'd rather detect a thieving employee or catch someone cheating on a disability claim any day.

'Did you get a chance to call anyone about the new detective here?' I asked, as Jack slid into bed.

'Not yet. Tomorrow,' he said, half asleep already. His lips moved against my cheek in a sketchy kiss. 'Everything tomorrow,' he promised, and before I switched off the lamp by the bed, he was out.

The next morning when I returned from cleaning Carrie's office, Jack was in the shower. He'd already worked out, I saw from the pile of clothes on the floor. Jack didn't believe in picking up as he went, a tenet that my mother had instilled in me when I was knee-high. I took a deep breath and left his clothes where he'd dropped them.

When he came out of the steamy little bathroom fifteen minutes later, vigorously toweling his hair, I was working on a grocery list at the kitchen table. He was well worth the wait. I sighed when Jack pulled on a pair of shorts and a T-shirt and began to brush through his long hair.

'When I got up, I called this woman I know on the force

in Memphis, and she knew someone on the job in Cleveland,' Jack said.

'And?' I said impatiently, as he paused to work through a tangle.

'According to this detective in Ohio, Alicia Stokes was a rising star in the office. Her clearance rate was spectacular, she handled community appearances well, and she was on the fast track for promotion. Then she got involved in a case she couldn't solve and it all kind of fell apart.' Jack frowned at the amount of hair that came off in his brush.

'What was the case?'

'One she wasn't even the primary on,' Jack muttered, still preoccupied by his hair loss. 'That is, she wasn't the detective in charge. She did some of the related interviews, that's all. No one knows what set her off the deep end about this case. Which,' he added, seeing the exasperation on my face, 'involved a woman who was being stalked.'

I felt a deep twinge of apprehension. 'Okay. What exactly happened?'

'I heard this secondhand, remember, and I don't know how well my friend's source actually knew Detective Stokes.'

I nodded, so he'd know I'd registered the disclaimer.

'In Cleveland, this woman was getting threatening letters. Stuff was being nailed to her door, her house got broken into, she got phone calls, her purse got stolen three times, her car was vandalized . . . everything happened to this poor gal. Some of it was just annoying, but some of it was more serious, and all of it was scary when you added it up.'

'What about the police?'

'They were onto it right away. But they couldn't catch anyone. This guy, who was like Stokes's mentor, was the primary, and he pulled her in to do some of the questioning of neighbors – had they seen someone they didn't know hanging around the neighborhood? Which of the neighbors had been home when the incidents happened? You know the kind of thing.'

'So she got wrapped up in it, I gather?'

'More so than was healthy. She began to spend her off time watching the house, trying like hell to catch the guy. She was so furious about what was happening to this woman . . .'

'I can understand why.' How would it feel to think that someone was watching your every move? Someone was waiting for you to be alone, your fear his only goal.

And that someone was able to get away with it. The police couldn't stop him; the officers who had sworn to protect you couldn't do their job. Despite everything, he would get you eventually.

Shaking my head, I leaned forward to rub my aching back. 'So she got as obsessed about finding the stalker as the stalker was about his victim?'

'Yes, that's about the size of it.'

'So, what happened?'

'She was warned off three times. The department gave her a lot of slack, because she was a good detective, she was a woman, and she was a minority. They didn't want to have to fire her. After a while, when she seemed to be watching the victim as much as the stalker was, they gave her a long leave of absence so she could get her head on straight.' Jack looked disapproving; no one had suggested he be extended the chance of a leave of absence when he'd misbehaved. They'd wanted him gone. If he hadn't resigned, he would've been fired.

'So, no matter what Alicia Stokes told Claude, she's really still an employee of the Cleveland Police Department.'

'Yes,' said Jack, looking surprised. 'I guess she is. Surely Claude called up there when she applied for a job here; that's one of the first steps, checking references. You call and get the official story. Then you use the network of cops you know to get the real story, like I did this morning. So Claude must know about her problems.'

But I wondered if Claude, chronically understaffed, had taken the extra time.

I shook my head free of problems that really didn't concern me and returned to work on my grocery list. It was taking me an awfully long time to finish my task. I couldn't seem to concentrate. Truthfully, I was feeling less than wonderful. When Jack showed signs of wanting to make up for his inattention the night before, I had to wave him off. It was the first time for that, and when he looked surprised I felt obliged to tell him I was about to have my monthly time, and that somehow it felt worse than usual. Jack was quite willing to leave our discussion at that; I think he feels it's unmanly to ask questions about my femaleness.

After thirty more minutes, my list was complete and I'd figured out the weekly menu. Also, I was in pain. Jack agreed to go to the store for us, and when I saw the worry on his face, I was embarrassed. I was seldom ill, and I hated it; hated going to the doctor, spending the money on prescriptions, not being my usual self.

After Jack left – after many admonitions and a lot of scolding – I thought I might lie down, as he'd suggested. I couldn't remember the last time I'd lain down during the day, but I was feeling very strange. I went back to our room and sat down very carefully on the edge of the bed. I swung my legs up and lay on my side. I couldn't get comfortable. I had a terrible backache. The weird thing was, it was rhythmical, I would feel a terrible tense clenching feeling, then it would back off. I'd have a few minutes of feeling better, then it would start again.

By the time I heard Jack unloading groceries in the kitchen, I was sweating and scared. I was lying with my back to the bedroom door, and I thought of turning over to face him, but it seemed like a lot of trouble to move. His footsteps stopped in the door.

'Lily, you're bleeding,' he said. 'Did you know?' There was lot of panic behind the calm words.

'No,' I said, in the grip of one of those pulses of pain. 'Gosh, and I put a pad on, just in case. I've never had this much trouble.' I was feeling too miserable to be embarrassed.

'Surely this isn't just your period?' he asked. He went around to the side of the bed I was facing and crouched down to look at me.

'I don't think so,' I said, bewildered. 'I'm so sorry. I'm just never sick.'

He glared at me. 'Don't apologize,' he said. 'You're white as a sheet. Listen, Lily, I know you're the woman and I'm the guy, but are these pains you're having . . . have you by any chance been timing them?'

'Why would I do that?' I asked, irritated.

'Your back hurts?' he asked, as though he were scared of the answer.

I nodded.

'Low down?'

I nodded again.

'Are you late?'

'I'm never very regular. Hand me the calendar.' Jack got my bank giveaway calendar from the nail in the kitchen and

I flipped back to the months before. I counted. 'Well, this one is late. I don't know why it's so painful, my last one was just nothing. A couple of spots.'

If I was as white as a sheet, we were a matching set. Jack lost all his color.

'What did you say?' he asked.

I repeated myself.

'Lily,' he said, as if he was bracing himself. 'Honey, I think you . . . I think we need to get you to the hospital.'

'You know I don't have insurance,' I said. 'I can't afford a hospital bill.'

'I can,' Jack said grimly. 'And you're going.'

I was as astonished as I could be. Jack had never spoken to me that way. He said, 'I'm going to call an ambulance.'

But I balked at that. It would take us only four minutes to get to the hospital in Shakespeare, and that's even if we caught the red light.

'Just put the bath mat down over your car seat,' I suggested, 'in case I leak any more.' Jack could see I wouldn't go unless he did as I'd said, so he grabbed the bath mat and took it out to his car.

Then he returned to help me up, and we went out to the car during a moment when I wasn't actively in pain. I got in and buckled up, and Jack hurried around to his side of the car and jammed the key into the ignition. We went backward at a tremendous rate, and Jack got out into the street as though there were never any traffic.

After a minute, I didn't care. I was really hurting.

Suddenly, deep inside me, I felt a kind of terrible wrench. 'Oh,' I said sharply, bending forward. I took a deep breath, let it out . . . and the pain stopped.

'Lily?' Jack asked, his voice frantic. 'Lily? What's happening?'

'It's over,' I said in relief. I looked sideways at Jack, but he didn't seem to think that was good news. Just when I was about to ask him if he'd heard me, I felt a gush of wet warmth, and I looked down to see blood. A lot of blood.

I felt very tired. I thought I would lean my head against the car window. It felt cool against my cheek. Jack glanced over and nearly hit the car ahead of us.

'What's happened to me?' I asked Jack from a far distance, as we pulled into the emergency room carport and he pushed open his door.

'Stay right there!' he yelled, and disappeared inside the building. The bath mat underneath me turned red. I congratulated myself on my foresight, trying not to admit to myself that I was terrified. In seconds, a nurse came out with a wheelchair. Jack helped me out of the car, and the minute I stood up my legs were drenched in a gush of fluid. I stared down at myself, embarrassed and frightened.

'What's happened to me?' I asked again.

'Hon, you're miscarrying,' the nurse said briskly, as if any fool should have known that.

And I guess she was right.

Chapter Seven

Carrie was there in five minutes, and she confirmed what the nurse had said. I was so shocked I didn't know which piece of knowledge was more stunning; the fact that I'd gotten pregnant without knowing it, or the fact that I'd lost a baby.

'Our baby,' I said to Jack, trying to absorb the loss, the impact of the facts. Tears rolled down my cheeks and I was too tired to blot them. I didn't know if I was exactly sad or just profoundly astonished.

He was just as amazed as I was at the whole incident. He left the cubicle in the emergency room abruptly, and I was left staring after him from the gurney.

Carrie re-entered. 'He's crying,' she whispered to me, and I could not imagine that. Then I remembered that when Jack's previous lover, Karen Kingsland, had been murdered, she had been pregnant. Carrie said, 'Did you really not know?'

'I never even thought of it,' I admitted. 'I never put everything together. I guess I'm just dumb.'

'Lily, I am so sorry. I don't know what to say.'

I shook my head. I didn't know what she could say, either.

'I thought I had too much scar tissue,' I told Carrie. 'I thought between the indications that I wouldn't be very fertile, and the fact that we used birth control every single time, I was safe as I could be.'

'Only abstinence is a hundred percent safe,' Carrie said automatically. Her round brown eyes fixed on me from behind her big glasses. 'Lily, I have to do a D and C.'

That meant operating room fees and an anesthesiologist and an overnight stay in the hospital. I began to protest.

'You don't have an option,' she told me firmly.

Jack said, 'You do what you have to do, Carrie. We're good for it.' He'd come back through the curtains behind her. His eyes were red. He took my hand.

'You know,' Carrie said very slowly, propping her bottom against the wall and hugging a clipboard to her chest, 'If this has happened once, this could happen again.' She rested her chin on the clipboard, and I could tell she was thinking of saying something she knew she ought not to say.

I looked over at Jack. His hair was hanging in tangles around his shoulders, and his scar almost gleamed in the harsh overhead light. He didn't seem to know what to think, and I couldn't even figure out how I felt about what had just happened to me, or at least how I fully felt. But the truth was, it was like being at the bottom of a deep pit of sorrow.

'A baby,' Jack said tentatively. 'A baby.'

'Lots of work,' I said, thinking of the Althaus home.

Carrie braced herself. 'Of course,' she interjected in a very low voice, looking anywhere but at us, 'I think it's always nice if a baby's parents are married.'

'Oh, no problem,' Jack said absently. Then he snapped to, and his eyes met mine. I shrugged.

Carrie perked up. Her glasses glistened as she raised her head. 'So, you guys are going to get married?'

'No,' I said. 'We already are.'

*

After all that 'parents should be married' preaching, Carrie gave us hell because we were married. I'd been her only bridesmaid, and I should've returned the compliment; Claude would've liked to have been at the ceremony; they would've welcomed the chance to give us a wedding present; etc.; etc. Blah, blah, blah.

'Listen, Carrie,' I told her. 'I am going to say this once because I am your friend. We don't want to talk about being married, we don't want to change the way we are, we don't want to put it in the papers. I haven't even told my parents, though Jack did tell his sister, since he can't seem to stop hinting.' I cast a look at Jack, who had the grace to look abashed. 'This isn't a good day for us anyway, right? Wait and hop on us when I feel better.'

'I'm sorry.' Carrie apologized thoroughly. 'Listen, Lily, I'm going to do your D and C in . . . ,' she looked at her watch. 'About an hour. The operating room'll be free then, Dr Howard's in there now.'

'What can I expect afterward?'

We went over that for a while, and I began to feel better. Carrie was sure I'd be feeling physically well very soon.

When she ducked out from the curtain, Jack took my hand. He hooked a chair with his foot, drew it closer, and settled in by the bed, resting his head against it. We were still and quiet together for a while, and it was wonderful after the hubbub of arriving at the hospital, the struggle to remove my jeans, the shock of the miscarriage. I felt drained, mentally and physically. I'd lost a lot of blood. After a while, I think I dozed a little, and Jack may have, too.

As I drifted in and out of uneasy napping, I was thinking that this was the first time I'd felt really married. It felt like a cord ran between Jack and me, an umbilical cord, pulsing with life and nutrients. Then I thought of the baby, the baby who'd been attached to me with a real umbilical cord, and I thought of Jack leaving this brilliant white cubicle to cry for our lost child. I stared at the wall, at the incomprehensible medical things attached to it, and I considered that if I had not allowed Jack into my life, none of this pain would have been mine or his. Dry eyed, I stared at the wall, from time to time stroking his dark hair, and I did not know if I was glad or miserable that I'd ever seen him.

That evening Tamsin and Cliff came to my room. It was a double, but there wasn't another patient in there, which was a relief I was sure I owed to Carrie. Jack had left to spend a little time at the house cleaning up the disorder we'd left behind us that morning and to shower and change. I'd been dozing again, this time from the anesthesia, and I was startled to open my eyes and see the couple standing in the doorway.

'Tamsin,' I said. 'Cliff.'

'I was visiting a client on my lunch hour and I saw your name on the admissions list,' Tamsin explained. She had a little arrangement of daisies and baby's breath in her hand. 'Are you feeling all right, Lily?'

'Yes, much better,' I said, being careful not to move. 'Thanks for coming by.'

Tamsin placed the flowers on the broad windowsill, and Cliff came to the side of the bed and peered down at me. 'We've had a miscarriage, too,' he said. 'Tamsin lost our baby about three years ago.'

Tamsin looked away, as if the mention of the loss was a reproach.

'How are you doing?' I asked her.

'You mean, about the death of Saralynn?'

I nodded.

'I'm adjusting,' she said. 'Her mother came to see me. That was bad.'

'I can well imagine,' I lied.

'I brought you some magazines.' Tamsin fumbled with a bag. 'Here, maybe one of them will distract you for a while.' She arranged a stack on my rolling table. She'd been smart enough to avoid *House Beautiful* and *Vogue*.

'Thank you,' I said.

'Then, I guess, we'll see you later. I hope you feel better.'

'Thank you.'

After they'd left the room, I was ashamed of my eagerness to have them gone. I didn't want to see anyone, not a soul, but normally I would have expended some effort to be more polite.

Between the slit left between the curtains, I could see the late summer sun setting on one of the longest days of my life. I was seeing only a slice of the brilliant ball of glory, the briefest flare of red and orange. I looked for a long time. Then I pressed my call button.

The nurse eventually arrived to help me to the bathroom. She was a burly middle-aged woman who had no sympathy for me at all . . . kind of a relief after the emotional fire-walking I'd had that day.

As I shuffled back to my bed across the bright linoleum, I realized that Tamsin herself must be going through much the same difficulty. Her life was churned and risky, and she and Cliff most probably could not see any end to that risk.

In my self-protective way, I wanted to hold my counselor at arm's length because I had too much trouble of my own to help her out of hers.

Whatever Tamsin was doing, or whatever was being

done to her, I wanted no part of it. I had worked myself into a state of revulsion for my increasing entanglement in the lives of others, even Jack. This was where it led, to this hard white bed in this hard white place, where pieces of me bled out of my body.

I caught my breath, revolted by my own self-involvement.

When Jack returned, he tried to hold my hand, but I pulled my fingers away and turned my eyes to the wall.

'I'll feel better before long,' I promised the wall. I forced myself to go on. If there was anything I hated, it was explaining myself. 'I'll just brood for a while and get it over with.'

I just couldn't, shouldn't, treat Jack this way. I was ashamed. I did my second least favorite thing, and began crying. My tears felt hot against my face. I bit my lips to keep from making a sound, but it didn't work.

'I'm sorry,' I said, 'I'm sorry I couldn't hold on to our baby.'

'Move over.'

I scooted as much as I could in the narrow bed. I heard Jack's shoes hit the floor and then the mattress took the weight of his body. He wrapped himself around me. There was not anything to say, but at least we were together.

Chapter Eight

The next morning, right after Carrie checked me over, I went home. Jack was silent for the short drive, and so was I. When we got to the house, he came around the car and opened my door. Slowly, I swung my legs out and got up, glad he'd brought me clothes to replace my ruined jeans. Trying to be modest in a hospital gown would've been just too much. I was a little shaky, but he let me make my own way into the house.

When I looked around the living room, I was stunned.

'Who?' I asked. Jack was focused on my face, his own dark and serious. 'What . . . ?'

A vase of pink carnations was on the table by the double recliner. Three white roses graced the top of the television. A small dried bouquet was arranged in a country basket on my small bookshelf.

'Go lie down, Lily,' he said.

I shuffled into our bedroom, saw two more little flower arrangements and two cards. I sat gingerly on the edge of the bed and eased back. I swung my legs up.

'Where'd these come from?' I was realizing that my initial idea, that Jack had gotten them all, was just plain crazy.

'Carrie and Claude. Janet, the dried arrangement, and she brought some chicken. Helen Drinkwater left a card in the door. Marshall brought you a movie to watch; a Jackie Chan. Birdie Rossiter sent flowers and included a card from her dog Durwood.' Jack's voice was very dry. 'The Winthrops sent flowers, Carlton from next door dropped by and left a card, the McCorkindales brought flowers.' Jack picked up a notepad he'd dropped on the night table. 'Let's see. Someone named Carla brought you a sweet-potato pie. Someone else named Firella called, said to tell you she'd be bringing by a ham tonight.'

People here in Shakespeare had been kind to me before, helped me out when I needed it, but this was a little overwhelming. The Drinkwaters, for example. Since when had they cared about my well-being? The McCorkindales? I'd been beaten black and blue before and they hadn't noticed. Something about my losing a baby had struck a chord.

'How did they find out so fast?'

'You were brought up in a small town and you haven't figured that out?' Jack tried to sound teasing, but couldn't quite manage it.

I shook my head, not feeling smart enough to figure out how to untie my shoes.

'McCorkindale, the minister, visits at the hospital every evening. Beanie Winthrop is a volunteer Pink Lady. Raphael Roundtree's oldest daughter is an admissions clerk, so Raphael carried the news to Body Time. I had to call your clients and tell them you couldn't come in this week, so they knew. I arranged with the sister of the woman who does Carrie's office for the Winthrops and the Althauses to be covered this week, and she's best friends with Carla's little sister.'

'You did?' I was so startled by all this that I was caught off balance. 'I won't go to work this week? But Carrie said I would be okay tomorrow,' I said. I could feel the blood rush into my face. 'I could—'

'No,' Jack said flatly.

There was a long silence.

'What?' My fingers began to roll into fists.

'No.' Jack's face was quite expressionless. 'You are not. And before you get that look on your face, listen to me. What Carrie actually said was, you would be feeling fine tomorrow if you took it easy. That means no work. That means you really do stay home and take it easy. Now,' and he held up a warning hand, 'I know you're going to get into the "I have to earn my living" speech, and I know you're going to get mad.'

He was quite right about that.

'But, I am telling you, you are finally going to take the time you need to recover from something, and I am going to make sure you do it.'

'Who are you to tell me anything?' I was starting off low, but I could feel the pressure building.

'Lily, I am . . . your . . . husband.' With the emphatic spacing of someone who wants to be clearly understood.

And all at once, like the tidal wave that precedes a hurricane, understanding washed over me. As though it would hold me in the room, my fingers clenched the bedspread as I stared without focus, the stunning facts washed off my anger. I had lost *our baby*. This man was *my husband*. I gasped air in desperately, fearing I would choke.

Jack stepped closer to the bed, obviously worried.

I felt tears run down my cheeks. I couldn't seem to let go of the bedspread to get a Kleenex.

'Lily?'

Wave after wave of complete comprehension swept over me, and it felt as though no sooner did I rise to my feet in the surf than another surge swamped me. I was weeping for the second time in two days. I hated it. Jack handed me tissue after tissue, and when the worst had passed, he stayed there, not moving, clasping me against his warmth.

'I'm sorry,' I said, trying hard not to care that I sounded quavery and weak. 'Jack, I'm sorry.' I felt guilty that I hadn't been able to carry his child, guilty I hadn't managed better than Karen Kingsland, though there was no comparison between us. 'This is so stupid,' I managed to say, and was grateful when he didn't agree.

I didn't know I'd gone to sleep until I woke up. Jack had had a bad night, too, and I could tell from his breathing that he was dozing behind me. I thought over what he'd said to me. I made myself admit that he'd made sense. I made myself admit that before, when I'd gone back to work early after an injury, I'd done myself harm.

Even though I'd known I loved Jack for months, I was shocked by the power he had in my life. I hadn't thought this through; I guess you can't, you love someone without counting the change. I began to wonder what influence I exerted over Jack. He didn't smoke or drink; though he'd formerly done both to great excess. He'd hardly had time to think about another woman, and I knew ahead of time how I would handle that: it would be very bad.

I couldn't think of anything that I wanted Jack to do, or not do, differently. So . . . Jack was perfect? No, that wasn't really how I felt. I knew Jack was imperfect. He was impatient, which meant he didn't always take time to plan things out. He relied too much on intuition. He had a hard time handling his pride.

I rolled over to face him. I looked at his eyelids, at the relaxed face with its thin nose and slightly puckered scar. Jack had been divorced twice, and he'd had the disastrous affair with Karen Kingsland, a cop's wife. Karen had been in her grave for five years now. For the first time, I wondered what the other wives had looked like, where they were now. For the first time, I was admitting to myself that I was one of those wives. One result of keeping our marriage secret was that I hadn't had to consider myself really Jack's wife, hadn't had to acknowledge the whole load of baggage and implication that was carried in the word *wife*.

Well, we could make of it what we would.

Sooner or later, I had to tell my parents.

I could picture them doing cartwheels in the streets, but I could also imagine them sobering up when they thought of the fact that Jack had been married twice before. And they'd have to consider Jack's notorious affair with Karen, whose husband had ended up shooting Karen dead in front of half the Memphis Police Department – and on television.

Well, all those women – including Karen, who'd been using Jack to make her husband pay attention – were idiots. Anyone who let Jack go was, by definition, a fool.

I didn't often think of cosmic systems, but in this instance I had to conclude that these other women had only parted with Jack so I could have him.

The doorbell rang, and when Jack didn't twitch, I eased off the bed and padded barefoot down the hall through the little living room, to answer the front door.

Carol and Heather Althaus were wearing matching short sets, pink-and-purple plaid cotton camp shirts tucked into pink shorts. Carol was holding Heather's hand, and in her other hand she had a Hallmark gift bag. Carol looked far uneasier than her daughter.

'Oh, I'm afraid we woke you up!' she said, eyeing my rumpled hair.

'I was awake. Come in.' I stood to one side, and Heather was across the threshold in a flash, tugging at Carol to follow. Once the two were seated, Heather said socially, 'This is such a nice little house, Miss Lily.'

'Thank you.' I wasn't often called upon to show company manners. 'Can I get either of you a glass of ice water or some cranberry juice?'

'Thanks, no, we can only stay a minute. We don't want to wear you out.'

'Are you feeling better?' I asked Carol.

'Oh, yes! You know how it is. Once the morning is past, I'm fine.' Then she realized I certainly did not know how it was, and she closed her eyes in mortification. She made a little waving motion with her hand, as if she were erasing what she'd said. Heather was looking at her mother like she'd grown horns.

'If I'm not up to par by next Monday, I believe Jack called you to say he'd arranged for someone else to help you out?' Social talk was definitely uphill work for me.

'You're gonna come back, though, aren't you, Miss Lily?' Heather's narrow face was tense as she leaned toward me.

'I plan on it.'

Her shoulders collapsed with the weight of her relief. 'We brought you a present,' she said, and slid off the loveseat to carry the bag over to me. She gave it to me ceremoniously, her face serious.

Jack came from the hall to sit on the arm of my chair. He introduced himself while Carol eyed him much as she would have a pet tiger. Heather seemed less anxious and more interested.

There was a card in the bag, one with a teddy bear on the front. The bear's arms were spread wide and the legend inside read, 'Big Hug'. Okay.

The gift had been picked out by Heather, I knew as soon as I extricated it from the nest of yellow tissue. It was a figurine of a harassed-looking blonde with a dustcloth in one hand and a broom in the other.

'That's you,' Heather explained. 'Do you like it?' She edged very close while she waited for me to speak.

'That's just the way you stand at the end of the day,' Jack said, over my shoulder. I could tell he was smiling from the sound of his voice. I re-examined the slumped posture of the figurine and suppressed a snort. 'I like it very much,' I told Heather. I glanced at Carol to include her in my thanks. 'I'm going to put it on these shelves over here, so my company can see it.'

Jack was off the chair arm and carrying the figurine very carefully over to my small bookcase. He positioned it dead center on top, looked to me for my approval.

'Thanks,' I said. 'Heather, does that look okay?'

'I want a hug,' Heather said.

I tried to shove my surprise aside quickly. I scooted forward in the chair and opened my arms. It was like holding a bird. A sharp grief lanced through me, and I had to restrain myself from holding the child tightly to me. I sighed as silently as I could, patted Heather on the shoulder, and gently let her go.

Jack drove in to Little Rock on Monday morning, leaving me with a long list of restrictions: only a light amount of exercise, only a little driving, no cleaning.

After I ate a slow breakfast, I realized I felt much better – physically, anyway. It was still only seven fifteen, and I was already at loose ends. So I went to Body Time and got on the treadmill for a while, and did a little upper body work. Marshall Sedaka, the owner of the gym, came out of his office to talk to me, looking more muscled up than ever. I thanked him for giving me the Jackie Chan movie. After he'd commiserated with me awkwardly over the miscarriage, he told me about the woman he was dating now. I nodded and said, 'Oh, really?' at the right intervals, wondering if he'd ever look at Janet Shook, who'd been doing her best to attract him for years.

Tamsin and Cliff were being shown the ropes by one of the young men who seemed to stream through Body Time on a regular basis. They liked working out, Marshall had told me one day when he was feeling discouraged, so they thought they'd like working at Body Time. The fact was, as I'd found myself from my recent experience at the gym in Little Rock, that working for low pay in a gym is just the same as working for low pay at any other job. This particular young man was one I vaguely recognized as being a friend of Amber Jean Winthrop. In fact, I was almost certain he was one of the crowd by the Winthrops' pool, the day Howell Three had gotten so upset.

Tamsin was looking lumpy and lost in her Wal-Mart workout ensemble of cotton shorts and black sports bra, topped with a huge T-shirt that must have been borrowed from her husband. Cliff was not faring any better, projecting discomfort and uncertainty though he was wearing an old pair of sweatpants that he must have saved from college and an equally ancient T that was full of holes.

'What a role reversal,' Tamsin said, with a wan smile. 'Here we are in your place of power, instead of mine.'

She hadn't taken the words right out of my mouth, since I never would have said that out loud, but she'd taken the thoughts right out of my head. And it was interesting that she thought of the health center as her 'place of power'. The assault that had taken place in her own office must have shaken her to her mental and emotional foundations. Considering that, she'd made a great recovery.

'You're gonna start coming in every morning?'

'Well, we're going to try. Cliff and I both have been eating too much; we've just been so nervous. That's what I do when I'm nervous, I head for the doughnuts. Jeez, do you have any body fat at all?'

'Sure,' I said, feeling awkward.

'I'm glad you feel well enough to come in this morning,' Tamsin said, her dark eyes uncomfortably sympathetic.

'Thanks for your visit while I was in the hospital,' I said dutifully. 'I enjoyed the flowers.'

'When I lost my baby . . . ,' she began, to my discomfort. But just at that moment, Cliff gestured to her to rejoin him, since the young man was explaining yet another piece of equipment.

I left before Tamsin could speak to me again, on purpose. At the moment, I didn't want to assume anyone else's problems, since my own were bearing down on me.

But later that day, I would've been glad to have listened to Tamsin talk her heart out. Correction. Maybe not glad, but I would have tolerated it with a much better grace. Hanging around doing nothing was not a state of affairs I was used to. I cleaned my kitchen cabinets, slowly and carefully, only slightly violating Jack's dictum. I was in a silent house, since Jack had assumed my stakeout on Beth Crider. He called home once on his cell phone to find out how I was feeling and to tell me he was having no more luck catching her out than I'd had.

That night, when he was drying the dishes while I washed, Jack expressed disgust that we hadn't closed the books on Beth Crider.

'Maybe she's really hurt,' I said, without conviction.

'Huh.' Jack didn't seem troubled by doubt about that. 'In the years I've been a private detective, I've investigated one case where the guy was really hurt as badly as he claimed. One. And every now and then, I still drive by his house to check, because I can't quite believe it.'

'The level of cynicism here is pretty deep.'

'Absolutely. Did you have any time to check Beth's credit rating today?'

'Sure did,' I said. Jack had a computer program that seemed able to call up anything about an individual's financial history. To me, it seemed frightening that he didn't have to produce any kind of ID, or explain his purpose, in buying this program. Joe Doe could buy one as easily as law enforcement personnel. 'If I did everything right, nothing seems to have changed on her credit history.'

'Then she's smarter than most of them, but we'll nail her,' he said, confidence running strong in his voice. 'Next week, you can take over surveillance, if you feel well enough. I should spend some time in the office, returning phone calls.'

I managed to keep my face still, but I had to acknowledge to myself that I was feeling gloomy. Jack would be spending some nights in Little Rock next week. He had rented a room in his friend Roy Costimiglia's house, the room vacated by Roy's son when he'd gotten married the year before. Jack could come and go as he pleased and not bother with renting an apartment, so the arrangement suited him perfectly. I'd known when Jack moved in with me that he would have to stay in Little Rock some of the time. I just hadn't counted on missing him.

'Sure,' I said. 'Listen, did you find out anything else about Saralynn's murder?' Jack and Claude had shared a beer the night before while Carrie and I talked. Claude had kind of taken to Jack, since there were few people in town he could talk to freely. Jack, an outsider experienced in law enforcement and married to a woman who didn't gossip, was heaven-sent to Claude.

'I don't think they're making any progress on the case,' Jack said, 'though maybe I'm reading in between the lines. And the new detective – well, everyone except the new guy, McClanahan, has come to Claude to complain about her. Too Yankee, too black, too tough.'

'You'd think they'd want a fellow officer to be tough.'

'Not if she's a woman, apparently. She ought to be able to back them up on the street, but then she ought to let them take the lead in everything else. And she ought not to want to be promoted as much as they do, because they deserve it more, having a wife and children to support.'

'Oh,' I said, enlightened.

'Right.'

'You think she's crippled as a police officer, down here?'

Jack mulled this over, as he brushed back his hair and secured it at the nape of his neck.

'No, but she'll have to try like seven times as hard as a guy, and probably twice as hard as a Southern white woman,' Jack said. 'I'm glad I'm not in her shoes.'

That very day, who should drop by to see me but Detective Alicia Stokes. I opened the door, hoping I didn't look as surprised as I felt. Instead of her career clothes, Stokes was looking good in walking shorts and a sleeveless T-shirt, serious walking shoes instead of sandals at the end of her long legs.

'You feeling better?' Stokes asked, but not as if she actually cared.

'I'm fine,' I said with equal enthusiasm.

'I need to talk to you.'

'Okay.' I stood back and let her into the (by now) spotless little house. 'Would you like a Coke?' Letting Jack do the grocery buying had had its consequences. He had gotten a bag of Cheetos, too.

'Sure.'

'What kind?'

She stared at me.

'You said Coke. That's what I want.'

I didn't bother explaining that I called all soft drinks 'Coke', like most Southerners. I just got her some. I didn't often drink carbonated drinks, but I joined her in a glass. Once I'd gotten her settled in a chair, and had satisfied the dictates of hospitality, I asked Alicia Stokes what I could do for her.

'You can tell me what you think about Tamsin Lynd.'

'Why do you care what I think?'

'Because everyone in the damn town says you are the one to ask.'

I found that inexplicable. But it seemed to me that it would look like I was being falsely modest if I asked for her to tell me more about that, so I shrugged and told her I hardly knew Tamsin well.

'And she's your counselor?'

'Yep.'

'Because you were raped.'

'Yes.'

'All right. What kind of job do you think she's doing?'

'A pretty good one.'

'How do you figure that?'

I said carefully, 'Those of us who weren't talking at the beginning are talking now. I don't know how she did it, and maybe she didn't have a lot to do with it at all, but it's a fact that we're all dealing with what happened to us, in some way or another.' There, hadn't I put that well?

'You think I'd fit in the group?'

'No.'

'Why not? Cause I'm Yankee? Cause I'm black?'

'Tamsin's a Yankee. Firella is black.'

'Then why?'

'Because you haven't been raped.'

'How do you know that?'

I shook my head. 'You wouldn't have to worry about fitting in with the counseling group if you had been raped.' And that mark just wasn't on her, though I wasn't about to say that. She'd ask me how I knew, and I just couldn't tell her. The mark was not on her.

'So, in your opinion, how can I get close to this woman?'

'Why do you want to?'

'I need to watch her.'

I was getting a growing feeling of doom.

'It's her,' I said.

'What?'

'It's her. You took a leave of absence from the Cleveland force to watch her.'

'How did you know that?'

I shrugged.

'You better tell me now.'

'Jack made a few phone calls.' I didn't want her to think I'd had a look at her personnel records or learned something out of school from Claude.

She sat back in her chair, tall and black and tense and angry.

'I know about you, too.'

'Most people do.'

She didn't like that. I didn't like her. I felt a certain grudging admiration for someone who would pursue a case with such relentless determination. At the same time, it seemed kind of nuts. Like the man who'd pursued Jean

Valjean . . . what was his name? Inspector . . . Javert, that was it.

'What about this has you so hooked?' I asked, in honest puzzlement.

'I think she's doing it herself,' Alicia Stokes said. She sat forward, her long hands capping her knees, her Coke forgotten on the table beside her. 'I think she's fooling everyone, and I can't let her get away with it. The man hours we wasted in Cleveland . . . enough to work four extra cases, cases where people really needed us. As opposed to trying to protect one neurotic woman who's actually persecuting herself. She had everyone else fooled. Everyone.'

I gave Stokes a long hard look. 'You're wrong,' I said.

'On what basis?'

'She's done good. She can't be that crazy. We would know.'

'Oh yeah? You a licensed shrink? You know there have been cases like this before. They're almost all women. All the men, they feel sorry for the poor persecuted woman. They feel frustrated because they can't protect her from the evil demon who's doing this to her. Then it turns out she's doing it all herself!'

Alicia Stokes certainly believed what she was saying. I looked down at my hands, considering. I was trying to reconfigure my world, trying to see Tamsin as Stokes saw her. Tamsin, with her medical transcriptionist husband and her little old house. Tamsin, with her nice conservative clothes and her plump belly, her good mind, her compassionate nature. Nothing I got from Tamsin added up to the kind of emotional horror that could plan and execute such clever schemes against herself.

But I could be wrong. As the detective had pointed out, I was no therapist.

What if Stokes was right? The consequences – to me, to the whole group – would be devastating. We had all placed our trust in each other and begun to build on that; but the basis of this trust was the foundation laid by Tamsin Lynd.

I looked up to find the detective leaning forward, waiting patiently for me to finish my thoughts.

'Could be, couldn't it?'

'I guess,' I said, my voice reluctant and unhappy. 'I guess you realize that your own behavior is pretty damn fishy.'

Stokes was startled, and almost lost her temper. For a long, tense moment, I could see the war in her face. Then she pinched her lips together, breathed in and out, and collected herself. 'I know that,' she said.

'It's not my business,' I said slowly, surprising myself by telling her what I was thinking, 'but what are you going to do when this is over? Sooner or later we will know the truth. The Cleveland Police Department may not take you back. Claude will be very angry when he finds he hired you under false pretenses. How did you get past his checking your references?'

'My superior owed me the biggest favor in the world,' Alicia Stokes said. She put the palms of her big hands together, bumped her chin with the tips of her fingers. I'd seen her make the gesture before, and it seemed to indicate that she was feeling expansive. 'So I knew when Claude called him, he'd get a good recommendation from Terry. I passed the physical and psychological tests, no problem.' She smirked. 'The others were glad I was going. They wouldn't say anything – or I might stay.'

I tried not to let my surprise show on my face. Quite a change of heart, here: Stokes was sharing more than I wanted her to. But then I thought, Whom else could she talk to? And she must want to talk, want it desperately.

Detective Stokes needed a good therapy group.

Something twittered in the room. I looked around, startled.

'It's my phone,' Stokes said. She pulled it from a small pouch clipped to her belt. 'Yes?' she said into the unfolded phone, which looked very small in her hand.

Her face became hard as she listened, and the fire burned hotter in her eyes. 'I'll be there,' she said abruptly. The phone went back into the depths of her purse. 'Take me to Tamsin Lynd's house,' she said.

So she'd walked to my place. As I grabbed my keys, I looked back at the detective. Oddly, Stokes looked almost happy – or at least, less angry.

'Is Tamsin all right?' I asked, venturing onto shaky ground.

'Oh, yes, little Miss Counselor is just fine. It's her husband, Cliff, who's hurting.' Stokes was positively grinning.

I could find out what had happened without leaving my car, as it turned out. Cliff was on the lawn bleeding, and the ambulance attendants were bent over him, when we arrived within three minutes of the call.

'Stay here,' Alicia ordered, so I sat in the car and watched. I think her goal had been to keep me out of the crime scene, or the situation, whatever it was. If she'd been thinking straight, instead of being so intent on the scene, she would've sent me home. What did she need me for, now that I'd provided transportation?

It wasn't too hard to read the evidence. Cliff's leg was gashed and bleeding, as they say, profusely. In fact, the medics had cut away his pants leg. I could see that one of the steps going up to the side door of the house, the door nearest the garage, was missing its top. Splintered wood painted the same color as the other step was lying on the ground.

Well, this could have been an accident. Hefty man meets weak board. Cliff's leg could have gone through the step, scraping his shin in the process. However, that wouldn't really fit the facts. The leg was gashed, not scraped; I could see that much, more clearly than I really wanted to. And surely, for that kind of ordinary accident, one wouldn't call an ambulance.

Someone tapped on my window, making me almost jump out of my skin. It was the new policeman, Officer . . . there was his nametag, McClanahan. I lowered the window and waited.

'Ma'am? You need to move on,' he said apologetically. He laid his hand on the door. He was wearing a heavy gold ring, and he tapped it against the car door as he stared off at the paramedics' activities.

I looked at him, really looked at him, for the first time. He wasn't tall, or fat, or pumped, or handsome. In fact, he was a plain pale man with freckles and red hair, a narrow mouth, and light green eyes that were much the color of a Coke bottle. But there was intelligence there, and assurance, too, and then there was the odd coincidence of his always being at hand whenever I was with Detective Stokes.

'Then you will have to tell Detective Stokes that you told me to go home, since she told me to stay right here,' I said.

We took each other's measure.

'Oh, really,' he said.

'Really.'

'Lily Bard, isn't it?'

'You know who I am?' People never looked at me in the

same way once they knew. There was always some added element there: pity, or horror, or a kind of prurient wonder – sometimes even disgust. Curiosity, too. McClanahan was one of the curious ones.

'Yes. Why did the detective ask you to wait here?'

'I have no idea.' I suspected she'd just plain forgotten she didn't need me any more, but I held the knowledge to myself.

He turned away.

'Where are you from?'

It was his turn to jump. 'I haven't lived here long,' he said noncommittally. His bottle green eyes were steady and calm.

'You're not . . .' But I had to stop. To say, 'You're not an ordinary cop,' would be unbearably patronizing, but it was true that Officer McClanahan was out of the general run of small town cop. He wasn't from around here; he wasn't from below the Mason-Dixon Line at all, or I'd lost my ear completely. Granted, the accents I heard every day were far more watered down than the ones I'd heard in my youth; a mobile population and television were taking care of that.

'Yes, ma'am?' He waited, looking faintly amused.

'I'll leave,' I said, and started the car, I had lost my taste for sparring with this man. 'If Detective Stokes needs me to come back, I'll be at home.'

'Not working today?'

'No.'

'No cleaning jobs?'

'No.'

'Been ill?' He seemed curious, mildly amused.

'I lost a baby,' I said. I knew I was trying to erase 'Lily Bard, the victim' from his mental pigeonhole, but replacing that version of me with 'Lily Bard, grieving Madonna' was not much better. If I'd been fully back to myself, I would've kept my mouth shut.

'I'm very sorry,' he said. His words were stiff, but his tone was sincere enough to appease me.

'Good-bye,' I said, and I pulled away. I went to Shakespeare's Cinema Video Rental Palace, picked out three old movies, and drove home to watch them all.

Maybe I would take up crocheting.

Chapter Nine

Bobo Winthrop stopped by that night. He knew the whole story about Cliff Eggers.

'There was a stake hidden under the steps,' he told me, the relish of the young in his voice. We were sitting on my front steps, which are small and very public. I wanted the public part. There were good reasons I should not be alone in a private place with Bobo. I had my arms around my knees, trying to ignore the ache in the pit of my stomach and the unpredictable flares of misery.

'Stake a-k-e, not steak e-a-k?'

He laughed. 'A-k-e. Sharpened and planted in the dirt under the steps, so when the step gave way, his leg would go down into the area and be stuck by the stake.' He pushed his blond hair out of his face. He'd come from karate class, and he was now in his *gi* pants and a white tank top.

'I guess that would've happened to anyone's leg,' I suggested.

'Oh. Well, yeah, I guess so. If his wife had come home before he did, she would've gotten hurt instead of him.'

I hadn't thought of that, and I winced as I pictured Tamsin going through the step and being impaled on the stake. 'Did he have to stay at the hospital?' I figured if Bobo knew all this, maybe he knew even more.

'Nope, they sent him home. It was really an ugly wound, Mary Frances's aunt told me – she's an emergency room nurse, Mrs Powell is – and she said it looked worse than it really was. But it's going to be really sore.' Mary Frances was one of Bobo's former girlfriends. He had a talent for remaining on their good side.

Janet Shook came jogging down the street then, her small square face set in its determined mode, and her swinging brown hair darkened with sweat around her ears and temples.

'Stop and visit for a minute,' I called, and she glanced at a watch on her left wrist and then cast herself down on the grass. 'Want a lawn chair?'

'No, no,' she panted. 'The grass feels good. I needed to stop anyway. I'm still not a hundred percent after that knock on the head. And I had karate class, tonight. You should have been there, Lily. Bobo and I got to teach two ladies in their sixties how to stand in *shiko dachi*. But I missed running. I've signed up for a ten K race in Springdale next month.'

Janet and Bobo began a conversation about running – wearing the right shoes, mapping your route, maximizing your running time.

I laid my cheek on my knee and closed my eyes, letting the two familiar voices wash over me. At the end of a day in which I'd done mighty little, I managed to feel quite tired. I was considering Cliff's leg going through the step – what a shock that must have been! – and the hostile visit of Detective Stokes. I mulled over green-eyed Officer McClanahan. I wondered if he'd seen the body of poor Saralynn Kleinhoff, if he'd looked at her with the same cool curiosity with which he'd eyed me.

Surely his face was familiar to me, too? Surely I had seen him before? I had, I was sure, after a moment's further thought. I began to rummage around in my memory. He hadn't been in a police uniform. Something about a dog, surely? A dog, a small dog . . .

'Lily?' Janet was saying.

'What?'

'You were really daydreaming,' she said, sounding more than a little worried. 'You feeling okay?'

'Oh, yes, fine. I was just trying to remember something, one of those little things that nags at the edges of your mind.'

'What Marshall doesn't realize,' Bobo said to Janet, evidently resuming a conversation that my abstraction had interrupted, 'is that Shakespeare needs a different kind of sporting goods store.'

I could feel my eyebrows crawl up my forehead. This, from a young man whose father owned a sporting goods store so large there was a plan to start producing a catalog.

'Oh, I agree!' Janet's hands flew up in the air to measure her agreement. 'Why should I have to drive over to Montrose to get my workout pants? Why shouldn't the kids taking jazz at Syndi Swayze's be able to get their kneepads here? I mean, there are some things *you just can't get* at Wal-Mart!'

I'd never seen Janet so animated. And she sounded younger. How old could she be? With some astonishment, I realized Janet was at least seven years younger than I was.

'So, are you totally satisfied with your job?' Bobo asked, out of the blue.

'Well.' Janet scrunched up her face. 'You know how it is. I've run Safe After School for four years now, and I feel like I've got it down. I'm restless. But I don't want to teach school, which is the only thing I'm trained for.'

'My family, we're all merchants,' Bobo said.

It was true, I realized, though I'd never have thought to put it that way. Bobo's family had made their money selling things; the sporting goods store that leaned heavily toward hunting and fishing equipment, the lumber and home supplies store, and the oil company that had supplied the money to build the Winthrop empire.

'So,' he resumed, 'I guess it's in my blood. See, what I've been thinking lately – now you tell me if you think this is a good idea, Janet, and of course you, too, Lily – I think that the sporting goods store isn't really the kind of place most women and kids want to come into. What they want, I think, is a smaller store where they can come in without going through a lot of crossbows and fishing rods and rifles, a smaller store where they can find their running shorts and athletic bras and those kneepads you mentioned – the ones you need to wear when you take jazz dancing.'

'Tap shoes,' said Janet, longing in her voice. 'Ballet slippers.'

'I think we really have an idea here.'

'It would be great,' she said, philosophically. 'But ideas aren't money to underwrite a store start-up.'

'Funny you should mention that,' Bobo said. He was grinning. He looked about eighteen, but I knew he was at least twenty-one now. 'Because my grandfather's will just got probated, and I happen to have a substantial amount of money.'

Janet gaped at him. 'We're talking serious? You weren't just dreaming? You really think there's a possibility of doing this?'

'We need to do a lot of figuring.'

'We?' Janet asked, her voice weak.

'Yeah. You're the one who knows what we need. You're the idea woman.'

'Well.' Janet sounded out of breath. 'You actually mean it?'

'Sure I do. Hey Lily, would you mind if we finished Janet's run and went over to her place to talk? What do you think about this idea?'

I felt rueful and old. 'I think it's a great idea for both of you.'

Janet's face lit up like a torch. Bobo's was hardly less excited. In a second, they were stretching before they began running. I noticed Bobo's eyes running over Janet's ass when she bent over. He gave a little nod, all to himself. Yep, it was a nice ass.

As they set off down the street, I had to smile to myself. All those hours I'd worried about Bobo's inappropriate affection for me, all the times I'd tried to repulse him, hate him, fight my own shameful physical attraction to him . . . and all it took was Janet Shook's brain, ass, and a dash of mercantile blood.

I went inside, and when I'd locked the door behind me, I laughed out loud.

The next morning – the next boring, boring, morning – I went to the library. I needed to swap my books, and I thought I might do some research on runaways. Jack had discussed printing a small pamphlet on the search for runaways, since so much of his business came from such searches. It would be good to feel I'd accomplished something.

The modest Shakespeare library was in the oldest county building, which was about the rank at which most Shakespeareans placed reading. In the summer, it was hot, and in the winter, the pipes clanked and moaned and the air was warm and close. The ceilings were very high. In fact, I believed the building had been a bank at one point in time. There was a lot of marble.

To humanize the building, the librarians had added curtains and area rugs and posters, and on pretty days the attempt worked. But today was not such a day; it was going to rain, and the uniform sullen gray of the sky was echoed in the marble. I stepped from the damp heat of the morning into the chilly marble interior and shivered. Through the high windows, with the happy yellow curtains pulled back to show the sky, I could see a silver maple tossing in a strong wind. The rain would come soon.

I consulted one of the computers, and began scribbling down a list of books and magazine articles. One article was very recent. In fact, it should still be in the current magazine area, a sort of nook made comfortable by deep chairs and an area rug.

After I'd read the article and made some notes, I picked up a copy of *People* and flipped through it, amazed all over again that the reading public would be interested in the outsider's view of the life of someone they would never know. Why would a hairdresser in Shakespeare care that Julia Roberts had worn that designer's slacks to the premier of a new movie? Would a bartender in Little Rock ever be the richer by the knowledge that Russell Crowe had turned down a part in that film?

Of course, here I was, reading the same article I was deriding. I held the magazine a little closer to peer at a ring some singer had paid a third-world budget to purchase. A ring . . . a celebrity magazine. Suddenly, some synapsis fired in my head.

The picture I remembered wasn't in this magazine in particular, but I associated the picture with a magazine very like it.

How had I happened to see the picture? These things weren't on my normal reading agenda. I pulled and prodded at my faint memory until I'd teased a thread loose. I'd seen the picture when I'd been at Carrie's office, when I'd been dusting. The magazine had been left open in one of the rooms – which one? I could almost see the cover after I'd automatically flipped the magazine shut and returned it to a pile. The cover had been primarily ivory, with the picture of an actress – maybe Julia Roberts again – dressed in jeans and boots and a handkerchief, looking brilliant against the neutral color. Carrie's office!

Trying to keep hold of the image in my memory, I drove to Carrie's. Of course, her office was open and full of patients, and I explained to the receptionist that I wasn't there to see the doctor, that I was trying to find something I'd lost the last time I'd cleaned. Gennette Jenks, the nurse, gave me a suspicious look, but then Gennette was always suspicious of me. A hard-faced woman in her fifties, Gennette was chemically brunette and naturally efficient, which was the only reason Carrie kept her on. I looked around the small front office, which was crammed with a fax machine, a copier, a huge bank of files, and mounds of paper everywhere. No magazines.

And no magazines in Carrie's office besides a tattered old *Reader's Digest* left there on the little table by the chair in front of the desk. That was the bad-news chair; because most often when Carrie invited patients into her office and sat behind her desk, that meant she was about to deliver bad news. I twitched the chair to a more hospitable angle.

The magazine I'd been seeking was in the big pile on the table by the waiting area, a few chairs at the end of the hall where caregivers could wait while their charges were being examined. I shuffled through the stack and extracted the cover I'd been searching for. I stepped sideways into the little room where the part-time clerk, a milkmaidish blonde with a lust for Twinkies, worked on insurance claims. This was the same room where Cliff Eggers had been working the morning I'd cleaned, and this was where I'd picked up the magazine and returned it to the pile. That explained why I'd remembered the magazine. I'd stood in there for such a long time while he talked to me, I'd had time to memorize the cover.

After nodding to the clerk, who gave me an uncertain smile in return, I began paging through the magazine. Once, twice . . . I was beginning to doubt myself when I noticed the jagged edge. Someone had removed a page from the magazine. Maybe it had had a great recipe for chicken salad on the other side – but on the whole, I doubted that. Someone besides me had found the picture interesting.

Now that I knew what issue of what magazine I needed, I returned to the library, dashing through the first blast of rain to push through the heavy glass doors. Lightning was making patterns in the sky and the wind had increased in pace, so the view through the high windows was ominous. Mary Lou Pettit, the librarian working the circulation desk, was clearly unhappy about the violence of the weather. As I crossed the large open area in front of the desk to reach the periodicals area, she caught my eye and gave an exaggerated wince, inviting me to share her anxiety. I raised my hand to acknowledge her, and shrugged,

To tell you the truth, I've always liked a good storm.

I'd checked the date on the magazine at Carrie's office. Now I found that the one I wanted had been put away. I filled out a slip, handed it in, and waited ten long minutes while an aide looked in the periodicals storage room. I passed the time by watching the rain lash the windows in irregular gusts.

Refusing to peek until I was by myself, I sought out a half-concealed table in a corner behind the stacks. I turned to the page that had been clipped from the copy I'd checked. 'Author protects privacy' was the uninspired headline, and I checked the other side to see if there was anything more interesting there. But it turned out to be an ad for a diet supplement, one I'd seen in many, many other periodicals, so I flipped back.

The author in question was a man of medium height and build, swathed in a track suit and baseball cap, further shielded with sunglasses. He was holding leashes with two little dachshunds trotting at the ends.

Okay. So this wouldn't be an instant answer. I scooted my chair closer to the table and began to read. There was only one other person in sight, a bony and lashless young man who worked as a bagger at one of the grocery stores. He was reading a computer magazine. He seemed completely engrossed.

So I began scanning. Author of true-crime bestsellers *Baby Doll Dead* and *Mother and Child*, reclusive Gibson Banks . . . blah, blah, blah . . . real name kept completely secret by his publisher . . . only picture his publisher is allowed to release . . . 'He probably rented the dogs for the picture,' said Gary Kinneally, the photographer. 'He didn't seem to care for them at all.'

I examined the picture again. I whipped out the little magnifying glass that attached to my key chain, a stocking stuffer last Christmas from my sister. I'd never had occasion to use it before, but now I was glad I had it. It took a moment's practice to learn how to use it effectively, but finally I had it on the man's face. I looked at his skin very carefully. The picture was not in color, but I could tell the hair was not dark. No mustache. I analyzed his body.

He was probably five foot ten, maybe one fifty-five or one sixty. I moved the magnifying glass over his hand, the one extended holding the leashes.

I looked at his hand real close. And then I looked again.

And then I got mad.

He wasn't at the police station. It was his day off, the dispatcher told me. I was lucky not to encounter Claude on my way out.

How'd I know where his house was? I'd seen him coming out of it as I took one of my night walks. At the time, I hadn't realized who he was, or at least what his cover identity was. At the right modest house on Mimosa Street, I pulled up in front, not caring that I was halfway onto his lawn. I was across the sodden grass and onto his front porch before you could say, 'Traitor.' I was too angry to raise my hand to knock. I turned sideways, raised my leg, and kicked.

Officer McClanahan looked up from his computer in understandable surprise.

Chapter Ten

'Miss Bard,' he said, getting up very, very slowly. 'Are you all right?'

'I think not,' I said, softly. The rainwater was trickling down my face. I shivered in the air conditioning because my clothes were soaking wet.

'I have no intention of attacking you,' he pointed out, and I realized I had dropped into fighting stance, my body aligned sideways to him, my knees bent, my hands fisted; the left one in chamber, the right one poised in front of me.

'I might attack you, though,' I said. I circled to the right a little. He was stuck behind his computer desk, and it was hard to see what he could do about it. I was interested to find out. 'I know who you are,' I told him.

'Damn. I ripped the picture out of the magazine at the doctor's office when I was there for my allergy shot. I knew there were lots more copies around town, but so many people could see that one.'

I sensed movement and glanced toward the door that led into the back of the house. Two little dogs stood there, the dachshunds from the picture. They didn't bark, but stared at me with round brown eyes and wagged their tails in a slow and tentative way.

I looked back quickly to 'Officer McClanahan'. He hadn't budged.

'Was it them that gave me away?' he asked. His voice

was calm, or he was working mighty hard to make it seem so.

'The ring.'

He looked down at his finger. 'I never even thought of it,' he said, his voice heavy with chagrin. 'The dogs, yes. But I never thought of the damn ring.' It was heavy and gold, with a crest of some kind with one dark blue part and one white, as background; I hadn't been able to tell the colors from the picture, of course, but I could tell dark and light. 'My college ring,' he told me.

'The dogs weren't just props,' I said.

'No, and I laughed like hell when I read that story,' Gibson Banks said. He pointed at the dogs. 'This is Sadie, and this is Sam.' His face relaxed into a smile, but mine didn't. If he thought cute names for his dogs would charm me, he had the wrong woman. 'I can tell you're very angry with me,' he continued, the smile fading.

'No shit,' I said. I moved a little closer and the dogs came in to sniff me. I didn't react to their cold noses pressing my ankles, and I didn't take my eyes off him.

'Well, what are you going to do? Are you going to hit me, or what?'

'I haven't made up my mind,' I said. I was at ease with standing and thinking about what to do, but he was getting jumpy. My breathing was even and good, the discomfort in my pelvis now only a slight ache, and I was fine with kicking him. I wondered if Jack would come back to Shakespeare to bail me out of jail, and I wondered if the trial would take very long.

'You betrayed me, and my friend Claude,' I said.

'I misled you.'

'You came to write about my life, without telling me.'

'No, not your life.' He actually looked indignant.

I found myself feeling strangely embarrassed, guilty of some form of hubris. 'Jack's?'

'Not even Jack's, as fascinating as it is to any aficionado of true crime that you two are a couple.'

'Who, then?'

'Tamsin Lynd,' Gibson Banks said.

'Does Claude know who you are?' All the fire left me, abruptly and without warning. I eased into a chair close to the desk.

'He knows I'm Gerry McClanahan, a police officer who wanted to live in a small town.'

'That's who you really are? Your real name?'

'Yes. I spent fifteen years on the St. Louis force before I found out I liked writing just as much as I liked being a cop. Since then, I've lived all over America, moving from case to case. Europe, too.'

I held up my hand to stop his digression. 'But Claude doesn't know you're also Gibson Banks.'

Gerry glanced down, and I hoped he really was feeling a little ashamed. 'No. I've never taken a real job to be closer to a story before. I figured it was the only way to stay hidden in a town this small.'

I ran a hand over my face. Claude had one cop who was a writer in disguise, another who was obsessed with proving her own version of a current case. 'I'm going to tell him,' I said.

'I wish I could persuade you not to, but I hear Chief Friedrich and his wife are your friends.'

'Yes.' Gerry McClanahan, aka Gibson Banks, didn't sound upset enough to suit me.

'What about Tamsin Lynd?'

'She's my counselor.'

'What do you think about what's happening to her?'

'I'm not giving you a quote. If you think you're going to put me in your book, you deserve anything you get.' I felt like someone was boring through me with a giant awl. My poor life, so painfully reconstructed, and it was all about to be destroyed. 'Don't write about me,' I said, trying not to sound as though I were begging. 'Don't write about Jack. Don't do it.' If he could not hear the despair, he was a stupid man.

If he had smiled I might have killed him.

But – almost as bad – he looked cool and detached. 'I'm just here in Shakespeare following the Tamsin Lynd story,' he said after a long pause, during which the sound of the rain dripping from the roof became preternaturally loud. 'A middle-class woman of her level of education, in her line of work, being stalked by a madman as she moves around America? That's a great story. You know Tamsin and Cliff have moved twice to escape this guy? But somehow he always finds out where she is and begins leaving her tokens of his – what? His hatred of her? His love of her? And she's this perfectly ordinary woman. Bad haircut, needs to loose some pounds. It's amazing. It could happen to anyone.' Gerry McClanahan was speaking with such gusto that I could tell he was delighted to have someone to talk to.

'But it's happening to her. She's living this. You're not watching a movie,' I said, slowly and emphatically. Talking to this man was like talking to glass. Everything I said bounced off without penetrating.

'This case has even more twists than even you can imagine. Look at finding you, such a name in true crime books already, and Jack Leeds, whose television clip is a true piece of Americana.'

He was referring to that awful footage of Karen's brains

flying all over Jack's chest when her husband shot her. I had a moment of dizziness. But McClanahan hadn't finished yet.

'And you're just sidebars! I mean, think. One of the counselees getting killed in the counselor's office? That's amazing. This case has turned upside down. When it's over, and I wrap up my book, think of how much women in America will know about being stalked! Think of all the resources they'll have, if it ever happens to them.'

'You don't give a tinker's damn about the resources available to the women of America,' I said. 'You care about making money off of someone else's misery.'

'No,' he said, and for the first time I could tell he was getting angry. 'That's not it. This is a great story. Tamsin is an ordinary woman in an extraordinary situation. The truth about this needs to be told.'

'You don't know the truth. You don't know what is really happening.'

He put his hands on the yellow legal pad on his desk and leaned on it as if he were guarding its contents. He focused on me. 'But I'm very close. I'm right here; working on the investigation into the murder that took place in Tamsin's office! The death of a woman who was killed just to make some weird point to Tamsin! How much closer can you get?' He was flushed with excitement, the bottle-green eyes alight with elation.

I thought of many things to say, but not one of them, or even all of them, would have made any impression on this man. He was going to ruin my life. I once again thought of killing him.

'I'll bet that's how you looked before you pulled the trigger,' he said, his eyes eating me up. For an interminable moment I felt exposed before this man.

'Listen,' he said. 'Keep quiet, let me see this through, and I'll leave you out.'

I stared at him. Bargaining?

'I'm doing as good a job as any other policeman on this force. I'm really working, not just playing at it. If you let me follow this story to the end . . . you're home free.'

'And since you're so honest, I should believe you?'

He pretended to wince. 'Ouch. The truth is, I've done more watching out for Tamsin than any cop could ever do. In case you hadn't realized it, I bought this house because it backs catty-cornered to Tamsin and Cliff's. I watch. Every moment she's home and I'm not at work, I watch.'

'Let me get this straight,' I said slowly. 'You're stalking her, too?'

His face flushed deeply. He'd never put it that way to himself, I was willing to bet. 'I'm observing her,' he said.

'No, you're waiting for someone to get her.'

I got up and left his house.

'Remember!' he called after me. 'If I get to keep my job, you get to keep out of the book!'

I went right to Claude. I was in that period of grace, the time between the moment the bullet hits and the moment you begin to feel the pain; in that period of grace, you actually felt numb, but you knew something dreadful was coming. (At least, that was what some gunshot victims had told me.) If I waited, I would consider Gerry McClanahan's offer. I couldn't let myself hesitate.

The old house, temporary home of the chief of police's office, looked especially forlorn in the renewed rain. I was so wet that getting out again hadn't posed a hardship, and I walked into the station with my hair dripping in streams to the floor, much to the amusement of the desk clerk. She went into Claude's office after I asked for him and ushered me in after a brief consultation. She also handed me a towel.

It was hard to know what to dry first, but after I rubbed my face and hair, I began to work my way down. Then I folded the towel, put it in the uncomfortable chair that faced Claude's desk, and sat on it.

Claude was wearing his work face, serious and hard, and I was wearing mine, blank and equally hard. We were just two tough people, there in that little office, and I was about to tell my friend Claude some tough things. Before I opened my mouth to speak, I found myself wishing I were rich enough to hire someone else to come in here and tell Claude all this unpleasant news. And I was still undecided about whether or not to talk about Alicia Stokes.

In the end, I only broke the news about Gerry McClanahan. If Claude had researched a little more he would've found out about Stokes's obsession. Or maybe he did know. Maybe he needed her more than he cared about her quirks.

At least I told myself that was my reasoning; but actually, I suspect I just didn't want to give Claude so much bad news at one time.

'So,' Claude rumbled, when I'd finished, 'My newest officer is a famous writer?'

I nodded.

'He's a qualified police officer, right? I mean, his references checked out.' These words were mild, giving no hint that Claude was truly and massively angry.

'Yes, he is a qualified police officer.'

'He told me he had taken a few years off to travel on some money he'd inherited.' Claude swiveled his chair to look out at a dripping world. 'He didn't have a record.' Claude kept staring out the damn window for a good while.

'And he intends to write about the murder of Saralynn Kleinhoff?'

'He's writing a book about the stalking of Tamsin Lynd.'

Another shock for Claude, who ran a hand over his seamed face. 'So, though she never told us squat and I wouldn't know about it to this day if Detective Stokes hadn't remembered it from her former job, Tamsin Lynd has been stalked for a while. Persistently enough to make it a notable case.'

'According to McClanahan, yes. He says she's moved twice.'

'And whoever this is, just keeps following her.'

'Alicia Stokes has a theory about that.'

'Yeah, Alicia said she thinks Lynd is doing all these things herself. She played me a tape about a similar case that occurred a few years ago, the woman was doing it all herself. Smearing manure on her own door, setting off smoke bombs on her porch, sending herself threatening hate mail.'

I couldn't help but realize that Tamsin's stay in the conference room while Saralynn was killed and Janet attacked was much more explainable if it had been Tamsin doing the attacking. I tried to imagine Tamsin pinning the body of Saralynn up on the bulletin board, and I just couldn't. But I knew better than anyone did what could be inside someone, unsuspected. However . . . I shook my head. I just couldn't see it. I didn't want to see it.

'Lily, what did he threaten you with?'

'What?'

'You told McClanahan you were coming over here?'

'Yes.'

'He didn't try to stop you?'

I didn't answer.

'I know he did, Lily. Don't you lie to me. There's been enough of that.'

The numbness had worn off by then, and Claude's question drew my attention to the wound. The pain hit me broadside. I realized, fully, that my new life was gone. Possibly Jack's, as well. We would go through the whole thing again, both of us, and I didn't know if we were strong enough to withstand it.

'Lily?'

Looking down at my hands folded in my lap, I told him.

After a moment of silence, Claude said, 'Damn him to hell.'

'Amen to that,' I said.

We sat in silence for a moment.

'What about telling Tamsin?' I asked.

Claude rubbed a finger over the surface of his badge. 'Lily, you go home and rest up,' he said finally. 'That isn't your responsibility. I'm sorry it's mine, but I guess it is. It's someone I employed who's watching her.'

'But not illegally,' I said, having thought it over. 'He stays on his property. He doesn't trespass. He's just . . . observing Tamsin's life. From a safe distance.'

'He doesn't communicate with her or try to scare her?' Claude asked, thinking it through.

'No. He just watches and waits for something else to happen to her.' I couldn't help it; I shuddered.

'Maybe I should just tell her husband, that Cliff.'

'Cliff Eggers, martial medical transcriptionist? I don't think that'd do a lot of good.'

'Me, either.' Claude reflected for a moment. 'Well, Lily, I'm sure Jack will track me down and beat me up if you don't go home to rest.'

For whatever reasons, he wanted me to go. There was

nothing else I could say or do. I just had to wait, and watch the consequences coming at me. Nothing I could do would stop what was going to happen. I had sworn to myself that I would never again feel helpless in this life; to that end, I had trained myself and remained vigilant. But now, all over again, I was a victim.

I felt very tired. I returned the towel to the receptionist on my way out, and when I got home I was happy to get in a shower, get even wetter, and then put on some dry clothes. I sat in my reclining love seat, began rescreening one of the movies I'd rented, and without a premonitory blink I fell asleep.

Someone had hold of me, and I wrenched my arm away.

'What? Stop!' I mumbled, heavy with sleep.

'Lily! Lily! Wake up!'

'Jack? What are you doing here?' I focused on him with a little difficulty. I wasn't used to napping, and I found it disagreed with me.

'I got a phone call,' he said, his voice clipped and hard. 'Telling me I better get back fast, that you were in trouble.'

'Who would have said that?'

'Someone who didn't want to leave a name.'

'I'm okay,' I said, a little muddled about all this, but still pretty sure I was basically all right. 'I just fell asleep when I left Claude's office. You won't . . . you're going to be really mad when I tell you what's happened.'

'It must have been something, to make you sleep through karate class,' Jack said. I peered past him at the clock. It was seven thirty. I'd been asleep about two hours, I realized with a great deal of astonishment. I could count the naps I'd taken as an adult on the fingers of one hand. 'How are you feeling?'

'Pretty good,' I said. 'Let me go clean up a little. My mouth is gummy. I can't believe I fell asleep.'

When I came back from the bathroom I was sure I was awake, and I knew I felt much better. I'd washed my face, brushed my teeth, and combed my hair. Jack looked calmer, but he was angry now, the false phone call having upset him badly.

'Did you try calling me before you rushed back from Little Rock?' That would have left the puzzle of who had called him, but relieved his anxiety.

Jack looked guilty, 'Once.'

'No answer.'

'No.'

'Did you try my cell phone?'

'Yes.'

I took it from the table and looked at it. I'd never turned it on that day. 'Okay, let me tell you where I was.' I could hardly upbraid Jack because he had rushed back to Shakespeare under the impression I was in deep trouble, either physically or emotionally. 'I was at the police station.'

Jack's dark brows arched up. 'Really?' He was determined not to overreact, now.

'Yes. I was there because of the new patrolman.'

'The red-haired guy?' There wasn't much Jack didn't notice.

'The very one. It turns out he's Gerry McClanahan, all right, but he's also the true-crime writer Gibson Banks.'

'Oh, no.' Jack had been standing by the window looking out at the darkness of the cloudy night. Now he came and sat beside me on the love seat. He closed his eyes for a second as he assessed the damage this would do us. When he opened them, he looked like he was facing a firing squad. 'God, Lily. This is going to be so bad. All over again.'

'He's not after us. We're only an interesting sidelight to him, something he just happened on. Serendipity.' I could not stop my voice from being bitter or my face from being grim.

Jack looked at me as though I better not draw this out. So I told him quickly and succinctly what Gerry McClanahan, aka Gibson Banks, had proposed to me. And what I had done.

'I could kill him,' Jack said. I looked at Jack's face, and believed him. 'I can't believe the son-of-a-bitch made you that offer.' When Jack got mad, he got mad all over; there was no mistaking it. He was furious. 'I'm going to go over and talk to him right now.'

'No, please, Jack.' I took his hands. 'You can't go over there mad. Besides, he might be on patrol.' I had a flash of an idea, something about Jack and his temper and impulsive nature, but in the urgency of the moment it went by me too fast for me to register it.

'Then I'll find him in his car.' Jack shook my hands off. I could see that something about my becoming pregnant had smothered Jack's sure knowledge that I was a woman who could definitely take care of herself. Or maybe it was because our brief life together was being threatened; that was what had shaken me so badly.

'You can come with me if you're afraid I'll kill the bastard,' Jack said, reading me correctly. 'But I'm going to talk to him tonight.' Again, I felt as if I ought to be drawing a conclusion, as if somewhere in my brain a chime was ringing, but I couldn't make the necessary connections.

I didn't feel as though I had enough energy left to walk to the car, much less trail after Jack over to the writer's house. But I had to. 'Okay. Let's go,' I said, getting to my feet. I pulled my cheap rain slicker from the little closet in the living room, and Jack got his. I grabbed my cell phone. 'We need to take the car,' I said, trying not to sound as shaky as I felt. 'I don't want to walk in the dark.'

That didn't fool Jack. I could see he knew I was weak. He shot me a sharp look as he fished his car keys from his pocket, and I saw that even concern for my well-being was not about to divert him from his goal of confronting the writer. Jack waited, barely holding his impatience in check, until I climbed in the passenger's seat, and then we were off. Jack even *drove* mad.

There were lights on in the small house. Oh, hell, McClanahan was home. No matter how he'd upset me that day, I'd found myself wishing he'd be at the police station, or out on patrol, anything but home alone. I got out of the passenger seat to follow Jack up the sidewalk to the front door. He banged on it like the cop he'd formerly been.

No answer.

The author could have looked out to see who was visiting, and decided to remain silent. But Gerry had struck me as a man who would relish such a confrontation, just so he could write about it afterward.

Jack knocked again.

'Help!' shouted a man's voice, from behind the house. 'Help me!'

I vaulted over the railing around the porch and landed with both feet on the ground, giving my innards a jolt that sent them reeling. Oh, God, it hurt. I doubled over gasping while Jack passed me by. He paused for a second, and I waved my hand onward, urging him to go to the help of whoever was yelling.

I was sure I needed to go home to wash myself and

change my pad. I felt I was leaking blood at the seams. But the pain abated, and I walked to the voices I was hearing at the back of the house.

I could barely make out Jack and – was that Cliff Eggers? – bent over something huddled in the darkness by the corner of the hedge that separated the rear of this house from the house behind it. I could see the back of Tamsin's house to my right, and its rear light was shining benignly over the back door. There was a bag of garbage abandoned on the ground beside Cliff, who was covered with dark splotches. I'd only seen him dressed for work, but I could make out that Cliff was wearing only a formerly white T-shirt and ancient cutoff shorts.

'Don't come closer, Lily,' Jack called. 'This is a crime scene.'

So I squatted in the high grass next to the house, while I eased the cell phone out of my pocket. I tossed it to Jack, who punched in the numbers.

'This is Jack Leeds. I'm at 1404 Mimosa,' he said. 'The man living here, Gerry McClanahan, a police officer, has been killed.'

I could hear the squawk of the dispatcher over the phone. I pushed myself up and leaned over the steps at the back porch, which was covered by a roof. There was a light switch. I flipped it up, and the backyard was flooded with a generous amount of light.

Gerry was on his stomach, and underneath his head was a thick pool of blood.

'Yes, I'm sure he's dead,' Jack said, circling his thumb and forefinger to thank me for turning on the light. 'No, I won't move him.'

Jack pressed 'end' on the phone and tossed it back to me.

Cliff, big burly Cliff, was crying. He rubbed his eyes with the back of his hand, staring down at the body on the ground beside him, his face contorted with strong emotions. I couldn't figure out which feeling would get the prize for dominant, but I figured shock was right up there. There was a hole in the hedge to allow passage between the yards, and in that hole lay another white garbage bag cinched at the top.

'I came out to put the garbage in the can,' he said, his voice thick with tears. 'I heard a sound back here and I came to look.'

'What's happened to him?' I felt I should know.

'There's a knife in him,' Jack answered.

'Oh my God,' Cliff said, his voice no more than a whisper, and the night around us, the pool of light at the back of Cliff's house, became alien in the blink of an eye, as we all thought about a knife and the person who'd wielded it. I have a particular fear of knives. I found myself crossing my arms across my breasts, huddling to protect my abdomen. I was feeling more vulnerable, more frightened, than I had in years. I thought it was because my hormones were bouncing up and down, perhaps, unbalanced by my lost *pregnancy*, a word that still gave me a jolt when I thought of it.

I made myself straighten up and walk into the dark front yard. Looking up into the sky, where there was a hole in the clouds through which I could see an array of stars, I realized that I wanted to go home, lock the door, and never come out again. It was a feeling I'd had before. At least now, I wanted Jack locked in with me. That was, I guess, progress. I could hear the sirens growing closer. I slipped back to my previous post.

'Where's Tamsin?' I heard Jack ask Cliff.

'She's inside taking a shower,' Cliff said. 'Oh God. This is just going to kill her.'

I was horribly tempted to laugh. Tamsin wasn't the one who was dead, her biographer had died in her place. Instead of writing the last chapter in Tamsin's story, Gerry McClanahan had become a few paragraphs in it himself! Was that poetic justice? Was that irony? Was that the cosmic balance of the universe or the terrible punishment of a god?

I had no idea.

But I did know taking a shower would be a good idea if, say, you had bloodstains on your hands.

I was glad that I hadn't exposed Alicia Stokes to Claude, because he certainly needed her that night. One of his other detectives was on vacation and the third was in the hospital with a broken leg, suffered that very afternoon at the home of a man arrested for having a meth lab on his farm. The lab had been set up in an old barn, one with rotten places in the floorboards, as it turned out.

Alicia's dark face was even harder to read in the dramatic light provided by the dead man's back porch fixture. I wondered if she would automatically assign guilt to Tamsin Lynd. Her suspicions had well and truly infected me.

When Jack and Cliff had been ordered away from the heap on the ground, I had seen more than I wanted to see of what was left of Gerry McClanahan. Dressed in shorts and a T-shirt, he lay in a heap, a terrible wound in his throat. From it protruded the wooden handle of a knife. He had no wounds on his out-flung hands, or at least none that I could see. There were no weapons in his grip. As we stood there in the tiny backyard, the rain blew in again. The sky was a solid dark mass of clouds. They let go their burden, and soon our hair was again wet and plastered down. So was the red hair of the corpse. It was too bad about the crime scene; though plastic tents were put up as quickly as possible, I was sure if there were any small clues in the hedge and the yard, they were lost. A portable generator powered lights that exposed every blade of grass to a brilliant glare, and people up and down the street began coming out of their back doors to watch, despite the rain.

It was very lucky I'd told Jack I'd come with him, since Jack would have made a dandy murder suspect, given the mood he'd been in after he'd learned Gerry McClanahan's other identity. Claude had thought of that, too. I could tell from the way his eyes kept returning to Jack. The two men liked each other, and they were well on their way to being as good friends as Carrie and I were – but I'd always known Claude recognized the wild streak that more than once had led to Jack's downfall.

I said, 'I was with Jack every second until we heard Cliff yelling.'

'I believe you, Lily,' Claude said, his voice deceptively mild. 'But I know why you were coming over here in the first place. This man could've caused you no end of trouble.'

'That's why Jack got the call,' I said, feeling as if I'd just seen a piece of machinery crank up smoothly.

'What?'

I told Claude – and Alicia Stokes, too, since she drifted up at that moment – about the anonymous call Jack had gotten at his office in Little Rock. It was hard to tell if Detective Stokes believed me or not, but I made myself assume that Claude did. It was a pretty stupid story to tell if it wasn't true, since Jack's phone records could be checked.

Stokes seemed more interested in questioning Cliff Eggers. Someone who was spying on Tamsin would naturally be in Cliff's bad graces, but Cliff gave no sign of realizing that the policeman had been leading a double life. It was a piece of information Claude seemed to be keeping under his hat, at least for the moment. It would have to come out soon. Most often, writers aren't celebrities the way movie stars are, but Gibson Banks had very nearly attained that status.

Cliff was telling Alicia (for the third time) he'd just come out to put two bags of garbage in the can when he'd heard a moan, or anyway some kind of sound, in the backyard catty-cornered to his. That noise, of course, had prompted him to investigate. If I had been the object of as many vicious attacks as Cliff and Tamsin had, I am not sure I would have been so quick to find out what was making the noise.

Just as Cliff wound up his explanation, Tamsin emerged from the house wrapped in a bathrobe with wet hair. The bathrobe and hair made her look faintly absurd when she crossed the backyard under an umbrella. Predictably, she crumbled when she learned why we were all out in the rain. Stokes showed her the knife, encased in a plastic bag. 'I never saw it before,' she said.

'Did you know Officer McClanahan?' Stokes asked, her voice cold and hard. Did Stokes know, yet, about Officer McClanahan's secret identity? I thought not.

'Yes, we'd talked over the hedge. It made me feel so much safer to have a policeman living so close!' Tamsin said, which struck me as the height of irony. I could feel my lips twitch, and I had to turn my back to the group clustered in the yard, a group at that moment consisting of Alicia, Claude, Cliff, Tamsin, and a deputy I didn't know.

Stokes sent Tamsin over to stand by me to clear the way for the hearse. Tamsin was shivering. 'This is so close to home, Lily. First Saralynn gets killed at my office, and now this Officer McClanahan gets killed right behind my house. I have got to start carrying something to protect myself. But I can't carry a gun. I hate them.'

'You can get some pepper spray at Sneaky Pete's up by Little Rock,' I said. 'It's on Fontella Road.' I told her how to get there.

After all the recent rain, the heat of the night made the atmosphere almost intolerable. The longer we stood in the steamy night, the less inclined we were to talk. I could feel the sweat pouring down my face, trickling down the channel between my hips. I longed for air conditioning, for a shower. These small concerns began to outweigh the far more important fact that a man had died a few feet away, a man I'd known. I closed my eyes and leaned against the house, but the aluminum siding still felt hot from the day and I straightened back up. Tamsin seemed to have control of herself and she pulled a comb out of her pocket and began trying to work it through her hair.

She spoke once again before Jack and I were allowed to leave. She said, 'I don't know how much longer I can live like this. This . . . terrorism . . . has got to end.'

I nodded, since I could see the strain would be intolerable, but I had no idea what to reply. You couldn't stop it if you didn't know the source.

Jack came over to me and held out his hand. Though it was almost too hot for even that contact, I took it, and with a nod to Tamsin, went back to his car with him. We were glad to get home, take a blissful shower, put on clean things, and stretch out in the cool bed, to lie there close to each other with sufficient air conditioning to make that pleasant. I don't know what Jack was thinking about, but I was acknowledging to myself how glad I was that Gerry

McClanahan wouldn't be writing his book now. Jack and I could lead our lives again, and we would not be exposed. Tamsin, at least for a while, would be spared some scrutiny, though if it were ever discovered who was stalking her, there was sure to be some newspaper articles about her persecution. As of now, she and Cliff had come out of it well, too. Only Gibson Banks and his publisher were permanently inconvenienced.

I could live with that.

Chapter Eleven

I went to Little Rock with Jack the next morning. I couldn't stand another day in the small house doing nothing.

I had to promise Jack I wouldn't do anything too vigorous. I was absolutely all right, and I was chafing a little more each day under the weight of his protectiveness. Since I was just going back to surveillance on Beth Crider, it was easy to swear I'd limit my exertions.

I was beginning to hate Beth Crider.

Jack dug in at his office to begin clearing up backlogged paperwork and returning calls. I organized my campaign and drove to Crider's neighborhood yet again. Maybe we should just buy a house close to her. Maybe when Jack was pushing my wheelchair down the street she might slip up and discard her walker.

Today I'd come prepared. I'd brought a hand vacuum, a load of cleaning materials, and a bucket, plus some Sneaky Pete paraphernalia. I parked in front of a house with a For Sale sign in the yard, about three doors west of Beth Crider's, and I got out.

After I got everything set up, I began to work. In no time at all, sweat was trickling down my face and I was fighting an urge to pull off my socks and shoes. Jack's car had never been cleaned more slowly and thoroughly. When I needed water, I got it at the outside faucet. I was lucky they hadn't had the water turned off, since I had to go back and forth several times refilling the bucket.

I received my reward when Crider came out of her front door, with envelopes in her hand. It didn't take a genius to figure out she was going to put some outgoing letters in her mailbox. In this neighborhood, they were on posts by the ends of the driveways. With my back to her, I watched her progress in the passenger-side rearview mirror, while I polished it with a rag and glass cleaner. I reached inside the car to turn on the movie camera I had set up, loaded and ready. It came inside a stuffed panda. I had the panda propped and positioned to cover just that area, since Beth normally mailed her letters at about this time.

She slid her letters into the box, shut it, and raised her red flag. Then she hesitated, and I could see she was looking at the ground.

'Come on, bitch,' I whispered, polishing the rearview mirror yet again. 'Fall for it.'

She looked back and forth, up and down the street. I was the only person out, and I had my back to her.

Down she squatted, supple as you please, to pick up the ten-dollar bill I'd torn and stuck to a tattered Arkla bill next to the curb. I'd tossed this out the window on my way down the street. I'd hoped it would seem as though the stiff morning breeze had picked up some of the trash from the car, and lodged it in front of her home on the ground.

Beth Crider straightened and walked back to her house, only remembering to resume her halting gait when she was about five feet from the steps. I knew the camera would catch the transition from robust to rehabilitative. Inside, I laughed my ass off.

And Jack's car was clean, too.

He looked up when I came in the office, having his own little transition from businessman and detective to my lover. I had the panda tucked under my arm.

'I did it,' I said, knowing I sounded proud but unable to keep it out of my voice.

'Yes!' He was up like a shot and hugged me. 'Let's see!'

Together we watched the film of the temptation of Beth Crider.

'So what will happen now?' I asked.

'Now, United Warehouse will approach Beth and ask her to drop her suit. She'll probably accept. United will give her some cash, she'll sign some papers, and that'll be it.'

'She won't be prosecuted?'

'Staying out of court saves money and time and publicity.'

'But she cheated.'

'Saving time and money is more important than vindication, in business. Except in very special circumstances, when public punishment will ward off more troublemakers.'

I wasn't as happy any more. 'That's not right,' I said, not caring if I sounded sullen.

'Don't pout, Lily. You did a good job.'

'Pout?'

'Your bottom lip is stuck out and your eyes are squinted. Your hands are in fists and you're swinging your legs. You look like I'd just told you about Santa Claus. That's what I call pouting.'

'So, United Warehouse will pay you lots of money?' I said, reforming my mouth and unclenching my fists. I opened my eyes wide.

'They'll pay. You'll get a percentage, like any trainee.'

I felt deep relief. Now, I could feel better about having quit my cleaning jobs.

'Let's go eat lunch,' Jack said. He turned off his computer after saving what he'd been working on. 'We're meeting Roy and Aunt Betty.'

I tried to be pleased about having lunch with Jack's friends, but I just didn't know the two older detectives well enough to take a personal pleasure in their company. I'd met them both before, and talked to them on the telephone several times.

As we were led to their table in the Cracker Barrel (a favorite of Roy's) I spied Aunt Betty first. With her fading brown hair, nice business suit, and sensible shoes, Elizabeth Fry certainly did look like everyone's favorite aunt. She had the kind of slightly wrinkled, well-bred, kindly face that inspires universal trust. Betty was one of the best private detectives in the Southeast, Jack had told me.

At the moment, Betty was telling Roy some story that had him smiling. Roy doesn't smile a lot, especially since his heart attack. Though he has a sense of humor, it leans toward the macabre.

When I sat across from him, I could look Roy right in the eyes. He's not tall.

'Hey,' I said.

Betty leaned over to pat my hand, and Roy looked stricken. 'Hey, baby, you feelin' okay?' He reached over with one of his stubby hands and patted the same place Betty had. 'Thelma and me, we're sorry.' Thelma was Roy's wife, to whom he was devoted.

Of course, Jack had told them about the miscarriage. I should have expected that.

'I'm feeling much better,' I said, trying very hard not to sound cold and stiff. I failed, I could see, by the glances Roy and Aunt Betty exchanged. Personal exchanges with near strangers in public places are just not my thing, even though I knew I was being a pill. I made a tremendous effort. 'I'm sorry, it's hard to talk about.' That was truer than I'd realized, because I could feel tears welling up in my eyes. I grabbed up a menu and began trying to focus on it. It persisted in being blurry.

'Lily caught Beth Crider this morning,' Jack said. I knew he was diverting them, and from their hasty exclamations I could tell they were glad to be diverted. I recovered, after a minute or two, and was able to look pleasant, if nothing else.

I had my back to the entry, so I couldn't see what made Roy stiffen and look angry a moment or two after we'd ordered. 'Crap,' he said under his breath, and his eyes flicked to my face, then back over to Jack. 'Trouble coming,' he said, a little more audibly.

'Who is it?' Jack asked, sounding as though he were afraid he already knew the answer.

'Her,' Aunt Betty said, her voice loaded down with significance.

'Why, it's the private detective table, isn't it?' said a voice behind me, a youngish woman's voice with a Southern accent so heavy you could have used it to butter rolls. 'My goodness me, and I wasn't invited along. But who have we here, in my old place?' A navy-and-beige pantsuit, well packed, twitched by me, and I looked up to see a pretty woman, maybe a couple of years my senior, standing by the table. She was looking down at me with false delight. The perfect makeup and honey-colored shoulder-length tousled hair were designed to distract attention from a nose that was a little too long and a mouth that was a little too small.

'You are just too precious,' said this sleek newcomer. I don't believe anyone had called me 'precious' in my life, even my parents. 'Let me introduce myself, since Jack seems to have lost his tongue. His *wonderful* tongue.' She gave me a roguish wink.

Well, well, well. I didn't dare to look at Jack. I wavered between amusement and anger.

Roy said, 'Lindsey, this is Lily. Lily, Lindsey Wilkerson.'

I nodded, not extending my hand. If I shook with her, some of my fingers might come up missing. You don't often meet people who will lay an unattractive emotion out on the table like that. Showing your hand so clearly is a big mistake.

'Dear old Betty, how you been doing?' Lindsey asked.

'Fine, thank you,' said "dear old Betty", her voice as weathered as old paint. 'And I hear you're flourishing on your own.'

'I'm paying the rent,' Lindsey said casually. She was carrying a leather handbag that had cost more than two of my outfits, which mostly come from Wal-Mart. Her beautiful shoes had two-inch heels, and I wondered how she walked in them. 'Lily, how do you like working under Jack?'

I shrugged. She was about as subtle as a rattlesnake.

'You watch out, Lily, Jack's got himself a reputation for fooling around with his co-workers,' Lindsey warned me with mock concern. 'Then he just leaves 'em high and dry.'

'Thanks for the advice,' I said, my voice mild. I could feel Jack relax prematurely.

'Where'd he find you?' she said. Her southern Arkansas accent was beginning to grate on my nerves. 'You' comes out 'yew', and 'where'd' was awful close to 'whar'd'.

Not under the same rock he found you, was my first, discarded answer. I exercised my option of not speaking at all. I looked into her eyes, instead. She began to shift from pump to pump, and her nasty smile faded.

But she rallied, as I'd been willing to bet she would.

'Jack,' she said, leaning over the table right in front of me,

'I need to come by your place and pick up some clothes I left there.'

Her throat was exposed, right in front of me. I felt my fingers stiffen into Knife Hand. At the same time, the part of my brain that hadn't lost its temper was telling me that it's not right to hurt someone just because she's a bitch.

'I don't believe I have anything of yours,' Jack said. From the corner of my eyes I could see his hands clenching the edge of the table. 'And I don't live in that apartment any more.'

She hadn't known that. 'Where'd you move to?'

'Are you a detective, too?' I asked.

'Why, yes, honey, I sure am.' She straightened up, now that she knew I'd had a good time to look at her impressive cup size.

'Then you can find out.' She would also find out we were married.

'Listen, bitch . . .' she leaned back down toward me, extending a pointing finger. People around us were beginning to stop eating in order to listen.

My hand darted up, quick as an arrow, and I seized her hand and dug my thumb into the pit between her thumb and first finger. She gasped in pain. 'Let go of me!' she hissed. After a second's more pressure, I did. Tears had come into her eyes and she stood there nursing her hand until she understood that she had become ridiculous, and then she did what she had to do – she walked away.

Aunt Betty and Roy began talking about something else right away, and the other diners went back to their own concerns, leaving Jack and me in a sort of cocoon. I picked up a long-handled spoon and stirred my iced tea. It was too weak. I like tea that's something more than colored water.

'Uh, Lily,' Jack began, 'listen, I . . .'

I made a chopping motion with my hand. 'Over and done.'

'But she never meant—'

'Over and done.'

Later, when Aunt Betty and I were discussing a recent court verdict, I heard Roy ask Jack if I'd really meant it when I'd said we'd never talk about Lindsey again.

'Absolutely,' Jack's voice somewhere between amused and grim.

'That's a woman in a million,' Roy said, 'not wanting to hash over every little thing.'

'You said it.' Jack didn't sound totally delighted.

Later, when we'd eaten, paid, and gone back to Jack's car, we found a long scratch down the paint. I looked at Jack and raised my eyebrows.

'Yeah, I figure it was her,' he said. 'Vindictive is her middle name. Lindsey Vindictive Wilkerson.'

'Will this be the end of it?'

'No.' He finally looked me in the eyes. 'If Betty and Roy hadn't been there, maybe. But she got beat, and in front of witnesses she cares about.'

'If she keeps this up,' I told him, 'she'll be sorry.'

Jack gave me a look. But at length, his troubled face gave way to a smile. 'I have no doubt of that,' he said, and we went back to the office for the afternoon. He filed, and I cleaned. He gave me another lesson on the computer, and a lecture on billing procedures. As a kind of treat for Jack, on our way back to Shakespeare we stopped at Sneaky Pete's, one of Jack's favorite businesses. Jack wanted to report to Pete on the success of the panda-bear camera.

As was often the case, Pete's was empty of customers but crammed with goods. Most of the store's income came from a stock of high-end cameras and home security systems, but Pete Blanchard had founded the shop with the idea that you could buy any sort of expensive electronic surveillance device there.

Pete Blanchard hadn't made up his mind about me yet, and I wasn't sure what to think of him, so our conversations tended to be tentative and oblique. Mostly, I was content to watch Jack prowl around and have fun, but Pete seemed to feel it was his duty to entertain me while Jack shopped. The fact that Jack seldom bought anything didn't seem to bother Pete. He'd known Jack for several years, and he liked him.

Every time I'd seen him, Pete had been wearing the same sort of clothing. He wore a golf shirt and khakis and Adidas. He seemed to have several versions of this outfit, but he liked it and that was what he wore. I could respect that. A former cop, Pete had probably had trouble fitting into a patrol car; he had to be six foot four or five. His mustache and hair were graying, but his toffee-colored skin had few wrinkles, and I couldn't begin to guess his age.

This particular afternoon, Pete's son was working in the store. A college student who picked up some money wherever he could, Washington Blanchard considered himself much smarter than his father and vastly more sophisticated. Jack had told me he just hoped Wash, as the young man was called, would learn better before too long. Otherwise, in Jack's opinion, someone was likely to sock Wash in the mouth. Jack had had a gleam in his eye that had said the sight wouldn't be unwelcome.

Though I hadn't noted it on my calendar that morning, today had apparently been designated as Pick a Fight with Lily Day. Most men are put off by me. I just don't seem, I don't know, womanly or something. Especially if they know what happened to me. A small sampling of men, the ones that are sick, are turned on by that very same thing. Wash Blanchard was a member of that small group.

While Pete showed Jack a pair of glasses that took pictures, Wash asked me questions about the woman who'd been murdered in Tamsin Lynd's office. That death had made the Little Rock paper mostly due to its bizarre circumstances. Little Rock as a whole seems to try to forget there's anything south of it in the state.

I hadn't checked this morning to see if Gerry McClanahan's death had made the paper, but I figured it hadn't, since it had occurred so late. At any rate, Wash didn't bring it up, so neither did I.

Wash wanted to know if I'd known the health center murder victim.

'No.'

'There can't be that many women in Shakespeare, Lily.'

'I didn't know her.'

'What was she doing in that building, I wonder. The paper didn't make that clear.'

'She was coming to attend an evening self-help group.'

Wash was astonished. He said, 'How do you know that?'

I shrugged, sorry I'd said anything at all.

'Did you see her?' he said. Wash had the usual prurient desire to hear secondhand about blood and death. If he'd ever happen to see it close up, he'd lose that in a jiffy.

'Yes.'

'What did she look like? Was she really impaled?'

I looked longingly at the door.

'Don't talk to me any more,' I said. I began to look at a rack of cameras, the kind that did everything but snap their own buttons. That was my kind of camera. I liked photographs, as aids to memory and as art, but I was not interested in taking them myself.

'Because I'm black? Huh?' And there he was, right in front of me again, determined to bother me. It's like people don't understand English, sometimes.

'It doesn't have a thing to do with your skin. It has to do with your obnoxious character,' I said, my voice still under control but inevitably rising.

Big Pete interposed. I felt the presence of Jack behind me.

'Something wrong, here?' Pete was trying to sound calm.

'She's treating me like trash, ignoring me and calling me names,' Wash said, though his voice was not as full of righteous wrath as it might have been.

'I can't imagine Lily doing that,' Pete said.

Explaining. People always want you to explain. I yearned to walk out speechlessly, but this was one of Jack's favorite places.

'I don't care to discuss crime scenes and how this woman died. The woman who was killed in Shakespeare.'

Pete stared at his son. 'Wash, you want to talk about dead bodies, remind me to show you some pictures of things I saw in Viet Nam.'

'You got pictures, Dad?' Wash sounded stunned and happy.

''Scuse us, Jack, Lily. Wash and I got some talking to do.'

Jack and I left in a hurry.

I tried to figure out if I needed to apologize to Jack, but no matter how I looked at it, this little run-in was not my fault. However, Jack wasn't talking, and I wondered if he was angry.

'It's really weird, isn't it,' he said suddenly. 'You'd think nice people like Pete and Marietta, his wife, would have such great genes their kids couldn't turn out bad. And then, look at Wash. He has to learn every lesson over and over, lessons he shouldn't even have to be taught. Things he should know by . . . instinct.'

Where had that come from? I followed the trail of that thought for a moment. Genetics. Kids turning out differently from their parents. Okay.

'Do you want a baby, Jack?' We'd been dodging this conversation ever since I'd lost the baby.

'For the life of me, Lily, I don't know.' It was clear he'd only been waiting for me to open the subject. 'If you had kept the baby, if everything had gone okay, I would have been proud to have a baby with you. When the baby . . .' He hesitated.

'Miscarried,' I supplied.

'When the baby miscarried, I guess you could tell how sad I was. But the next day, I maybe felt a little relief, too. What changes that would have made in our lives, huh?'

I nodded when he glanced over to check my reaction.

'Can you tell me how you feel?' he said.

'Like you.'

'No elaboration on that?'

'It surprised me when you cried. It made me love you more.' If we were going to say things, we might as well say everything.

'I hated to see you bleeding and weak. It scared me to death. And I would have loved to have been the father of our baby.'

'Didn't ever want to be the dad of Lindsey Wilkerson's baby?' I asked, keeping my face poker-straight. I was able to dodge Jack's hand when it slapped in my direction, because I was waiting for it.

'The world's best argument for birth control,' he said.

I didn't laugh out loud, but I smiled. His sideways glance caught it, and he grinned at me, that wicked look I loved.

Tamsin and Cliff came over that night. They called first, and I said it was all right, but I shouldn't have. I really didn't want to see them, didn't want to hear about Tamsin's multiple problems. But she had helped me, so I was obliged to her, a yoke I found nearly intolerable. I reminded myself not to ask for help again.

I should have been ashamed of my grudging attitude. And maybe I was, a little. But being close to Tamsin now seemed a risky thing.

'How are you feeling?' Tamsin's question seemed on the perfunctory side, especially since she didn't meet my eyes to hear my answer.

'I'm all right. You and Cliff?' I motioned them to chairs and offered them drinks, as I was obligated to do. Jack got Cliff a Coke, but Tamsin waved the query off.

'You can imagine how strange it is to find out that this policeman was really a famous writer,' Tamsin told me.

I nodded. I could imagine that.

'And then I finally recognized that woman last night. Detective Stokes.'

Jack reached over my shoulder to hand Cliff his drink.

'And, Lily, what I want to know is, why me?'

I couldn't believe I'd heard her correctly. Tamsin Lynd, of all people, was asking the unanswerable. Was this something some victims were just bound to go through, no matter how smart or clearly victimized they were?

That couldn't be true. And why had she decided to talk to me about it? Because I was Supervictim?

I thought for a minute, but I decided there was no way to get around this but to talk to Tamsin about it.

'Why are you different?' I asked her.

'What do you mean?'

'Would you let us ask that question in counseling group?'

She flushed red. 'I see what you mean.'

'Do you think you're better than us, because you're being stalked instead of being raped?'

Cliff looked horrified and upset, and his hand moved as if he were going to get my attention to signal to me, but I gave him a quelling look. Tamsin had dragged him along, and Jack was in the room, but this conversation was between me and her.

'Oh, Lily, I hate to see that in myself!' Tamsin was really upset, now. But upset in a more intelligent way.

'Why not you, Tamsin? What makes you superior or invulnerable?'

'I've got it, now,' she breathed. 'I see that. But I guess what I was thinking, was not that I should be spared because I was superior, but because I'm not. I'm an overweight, nearly middle-aged woman in a crowded and poorly paid profession. There's nothing remarkable about me. How did I attract the attention of someone so determined?'

'There is plenty special about you, honey,' Cliff said, his voice desperately earnest. 'You are the most sweetnatured, kindest—'

'Oh, Cliff.' Tamsin's face was radiant with pleasure, but deprecating. 'You're the only one who believes that,' she added with a little laugh.

I wasn't going to sit here and bathe Tamsin in compliments. She was quite right. I liked her – a little – and I appreciated her, but there was nothing exceptional about Tamsin Lynd in my eyes . . . except her victimization.

'You just got picked by the Claw.' That was as good an explanation as I could come up with.

'The Claw?'

'You know that game they have out in the Wal-Mart

entryway? The one where you put in some quarters and the metal claw swings down over a bin of stuffed animals and swoops down at random, and maybe picks one up, maybe not? That's the Claw.'

'Lily!' Tamsin looked at me with the oddest quizzical, expression. 'That's the most depressing philosophy I've ever heard.'

I shrugged. I wasn't in the Pollyanna business. 'The Claw picked you up, Tamsin. So you have a stalker, and Janet doesn't. I got raped, you didn't. Saralynn was murdered, Carla wasn't. The claw passed her over.'

'So you don't believe a divine plan runs the universe?'

I just laughed. Some plan.

'Don't you believe that most people are innately good?'

'No.' In fact, I found the fact that some people did believe that to be absolutely incomprehensible.

Tamsin looked really horrified. 'You don't believe that we're only given the burdens we can handle?'

'Obviously not.'

She tried again. 'Do you believe in the eventual punishment of evildoers?'

I shrugged.

'Then how do you go on living?' Tamsin was tearful, but not as personally tearful, as she had been before.

'How do I go on living? A day at a time, like everyone else. A few years ago, it was an hour at a time. For a while, it was minute by minute.'

'What for?'

Cliff looked like he wished he was anywhere but here. But Jack, I saw, was leaning forward to hear what I was saying.

'At first, I just wanted to beat the . . . ones that attacked me.' I picked my words carefully. I was being as honest as I knew how. 'Then, I couldn't add to my parents' miseries any more by dying. Though I did think about suicide, often. No more fear, no more scars, no more remembering.

'But after a while, I began to get more involved in trying to make living work. Trying to find a way to make my days, if not my nights, productive and make a pattern to stick to.' I took a drink from my glass of water.

'Is that what you think I should do?'

'I don't know what you should do,' I said, amazed anyone would ask advice of me. 'That's for you to figure out. You're a professional at helping people figure out what they should do. I guess that doesn't really help you right now.'

'No,' she said, her voice soft and weary. 'It's not helping, right now.'

I gave her the only piece of advice, the only philosophy, that I cherished. 'You have to live well to defeat whoever's doing this to you,' I said. 'You can't let them win.'

'Is that the point of living, to not let him win? What about me? When I do I get to live for myself?'

'That is entirely up to you,' I told her. I stood up, so she'd go.

'I thought you, of all people, would have the answers, would have more sympathy.'

'The point is, that doesn't make any difference.' I looked Tamsin straight in the eyes. 'No matter how much sympathy I have for you, it won't heal you faster or slower. You're not a victim of cosmic proportions. There are millions of us. That doesn't make your personal struggle less. That just increases your knowledge of pain in this world.'

'I think,' said Tamsin, as she and Cliff went through the door, 'that I should have stayed at home.'

'That depends on what you wanted.' I shut the door

behind them. I could see Jack's face. 'What?' I asked, sharp and quick.

'Lily, don't you think you could have been a little more . . .'

'Touchy-feely? Warm?'

'Well, yeah.'

'I told her exactly how it is, Jack. I've had years to think about this. I don't know why everyone feels like they're supposed to be safe all the time.'

Jack raised an eyebrow in a questioning way.

'Think about it,' I said. 'No one expected to be safe until this century, if you read a little history. Think of the thousands of years before – years with no law, when the sword ruled. No widespread system of justice; no immunizations against disease. The local lord free to kill the husbands, husbands free to rape and kill their wives. Childbirth often fatal. No antibiotics. It's only here and now that women are raised believing they'll be safe. And it serves us false. It's not true. It dulls our sense of fear, which is what saves our lives.'

Jack looked stunned. 'Why have you never told me you feel this way?'

'We've just never gotten around to talking about it.'

'How can you even share a bed with me, if you hate men that much?'

'I don't hate men, Jack.' *Just some of them. I despise the rest.* 'I just don't believe – no, let me turn that around. I do believe that women should be more self-sufficient and cautious.' That was probably the mildest way I could put it.

Jack opened his mouth to say something else, and I held up my hand. 'I know this isn't fair, but I've talked as much as I can for one evening. I feel like I pulled my guts out for inspection. Can we be quiet from now on? We can talk more tomorrow if you want to.'

'Yes, that would be okay,' Jack said. He looked a little dazed. 'You sure you want me sharing the bed tonight?'

'I want you in the bed every night,' I said, forcing myself to reveal one more bit of truth.

And for the first time since the miscarriage, that night I gave him proof of that truth. After a long, sweet time, we slept that night back to back, me feeling the comfort of his warm skin through the thin material of my nightgown. I never felt he was turning away from me when our backs touched; we were just attached in a different way.

I lay awake, thinking, longer than I liked. Since I was on a roll with the truth, I had to think of what I hadn't told Tamsin, what I couldn't tell anyone else in the world. My healing had accelerated when I began to love Jack. Love weakens, too, makes you vulnerable; but the strength, the power of it . . . it still amazed me when I considered it. I would die for him, be hurt for him, give anything I owned for his happiness; but there were parts of me that could not change for him. There were traits and attitudes I required for my hard-won survival. Knowing this left me with an uneasy feeling that some day I would have to face this fully and in more detail, an idea that I detested.

Jack gave a little gasp in his sleep, much like the one he often gave when I surprised him in lovemaking. It was a sound I found infinitely comforting, and hearing it, I fell asleep.

Chapter Twelve

I woke the next morning feeling very clearheaded and relaxed. After Jack had left for a meeting with a client in Benton, I decided stretching and mild calisthenics would do me a world of good. When that was done, and I felt much better overall, I changed the sheets, taking pleasure in the order of clean smooth percale.

The phone rang just when I was wondering what to do next.

'This is Dani Weingarten,' announced the caller. There was a silence.

'Yes?' I said finally.

'Dani Weingarten, the mystery writer,' said the voice, less firmly.

'Yes?' I read very little fiction, so her identity was not an exciting fact, which the caller soon seemed to realize.

'I'm the fiancée of Gerry McClanahan,' she said, by way of redefinition.

'Okay.' Sooner or later, she'd get to the point.

'I'm flying in from Florida tomorrow to take charge of the arrangements for having Gerry's body flown back to Corinth, Ohio . . . his hometown.' So far, Dani Weingarten had not given me one bit of information that interested me. There was a long pause. 'Did you hear me?' she asked, in a testy way.

'I didn't realize that required a response.'

Another long pause. 'Okay,' she said, 'Let's try this. I

have talked to the police department there in Shakespeare, and the chief of police there recommended you as the best housecleaner in town. Whatever that means. So, if you have time, I'd like you go to over to Gerry's little rental house and start packing up his things. I'll ship them to my house to go through them.'

I almost turned her down. I'd spent enough time sorting through the detritus of the dead. But I thought of the hospital bills coming soon, and of my improved health, and I said I would do it. 'Key?' I asked.

'You can pick one up at the police station,' Dani Weingarten told me. Her voice sounded softer now, as if she'd used up all her forcefulness. 'I told them it was okay. Did you know Gerry?'

'Yes,' I said. 'I knew him a little.'

'He told me Shakespeare was a fascinating little town.' She sounded on the verge of tears.

'He talk about his work much?' I asked cautiously.

'Never,' Dani Weingarten told me. 'He only discussed it when his first draft was ready.'

So she didn't know I was one of the fascinating things in Shakespeare. Good. 'Will you be staying at the house?' I couldn't pack up all the bed linens, if so.

'No, I couldn't stand it.' Her voice was getting heavier and heavier with unshed tears. 'I'll check into a motel. If you have motels in Shakespeare.'

'We have one. It's a Best Western. Do you want me to make a reservation for you?'

'That would be great.' She sounded surprised, and I didn't blame her. 'I'm going to rent a car at the airport. I should get there about three thirty.'

'I'll tell them.'

'You know,' she said suddenly, 'I don't believe any of this.' And she thunked the receiver down.

She would believe it by tomorrow. I called the motel, and went over to the police department yet again. Claude had left the key with the dispatcher, along with a verbal message that the police department would finish its search of the house by eleven. I could have the house to myself once they were out.

I felt energized at the idea of money coming in, and I had time to kill, so I drove to the Winthrops' house. Bobo's car was there, but no one else's. I let myself in, calling for him, but got no answer. The pool was empty. Maybe he'd gone somewhere with a friend.

After glancing around at the mess in sheer disbelief, I got to work. There was so much to do I hardly knew where to start. Just in case Bobo was asleep upstairs, I decided to concentrate on the ground level.

Living room, kitchen, game room, wash room, pantry. Master bedroom and master closets, master bath, smaller hall bath. In due time, they were gleaming and dustless. A couple of times, I thought I heard a voice; maybe Beanie had left the radio on? But I checked, and found nothing.

As I closed Beanie's walk-in closet door (with its newly polished mirror) I was beginning to feel a little tired. Well, pretty tired. But it went against my grain to stop without finishing. I wondered if I could just do a little straightening upstairs? Just as I started up, I heard a sound above me, and I looked up to see a very startled Janet, followed by an equally surprised Bobo, coming down the carpeted steps.

Since Janet was buttoning her blouse, it was impossible for her to pretend they'd been up there planning their sporting goods store. They had certainly been engaged in another joint venture.

I raised my eyebrows.

'Hey, Lily,' Janet said, squeezing the words out as though they were toothpaste. She looked anywhere but my face, which I was struggling to keep neutral.

'Lily,' Bobo said. 'Ah, we didn't hear you come in.' His face was scarlet from the awkwardness of it; if he'd been observed by anyone in the world but me, this would be easier for him. Janet, not knowing that Bobo had harbored feelings for me once, was free of worry. She was suppressing laughter; her eyes swung over to mine and she made a little face.

'No, I guess you didn't.' I was really glad I hadn't decided to do the upstairs first. I nodded gently, trying very hard not to smile, and began to make my way up the stairs. Bobo seemed to wake up from his shock, then followed Janet across the living room. They made it to the kitchen in silence, then I heard Janet begin to giggle, and Bobo join in.

I laughed myself, once I was safely up the stairs. It would be tacky of me, I decided, to go in Bobo's room and make the bed or change the sheets. So I cleaned the upstairs bathroom, leaving all three bedrooms as they were. Beanie would be glad I'd come at all. I didn't think she'd be overly upset about the kids' bedrooms. A little order is better than none at all.

A little later, after lunch and some rest, I let myself into Gerry McClanahan's house on Mimosa. It is never a pleasure to deal with the belongings of the dead. But the dealing would be nominal in this case: as I'd noticed on my previous visit, the furniture was very sparse. I wondered if it was rented like the house. The dispatcher at the police department had told me the dachshunds had gone home with Officer Stuckey, who had two small boys, so I knew they were okay; but somehow their abandoned toys seemed more desolate than Gerry McClanahan's abandoned computer.

I walked through the quiet house. All the rooms were empty except for the front room, with its big desk and couch and television, and the larger bedroom, which had the usual furnishings. In a kitchen drawer was the rental agreement for the furniture, so I left that out for Dani Weingarten to see. A quick examination told me there'd be precious little to pack. I called the older couple who'd rented the house to Gerry McClanahan. They hadn't turned on their radio that morning, so they hadn't heard the news. I had to hear lots of exclamations and lamentations before I was able to ask the pertinent questions about to whom the linens and pots and pans belonged. Those items, I found, were Gerry's. I wondered a little about the cage I found just inside the back door; it didn't seem large enough for one of the dogs, though it had definitely been used. I might ask Dani Weingarten if she recognized it. Now that I had an idea about the scope of the job, I went to the garage that was the local outlet for a big moving company and bought some boxes, keeping the receipt so Ms Weingarten could reimburse me.

I turned on a radio at the rental house, just so I could have some company while I packed up the dead man's clothes. Normally, I don't like distractions. But this house was sad. Though it had been years since I had a pet, I almost wished the little dogs were there.

Folding McClanahan's clothes didn't take long. I packed his uniform carefully, wondering if he'd be buried in it. What had this man been, in his core: a policeman or a writer? He had certainly been a researcher. There were at least three shelves of nonfiction books, like Gavin de Becker's *Gift of Fear*, and David Simon's *Homicide: A Year on the Killing Streets*. I looked at de Becker's book, repressing a snort. McClanahan hadn't read that carefully enough: he hadn't known to be scared, when he should've been. The only thing I was sure of about his death was that he had seen it coming and not recognized it.

A trio of books actually piled on the desk were more disquieting. They were thinner and had a scholarly look, like books you wouldn't get in a regular store unless you ordered them. The one on top was titled, *The Psychology of Two; the Selection of a Mate* by Lauren Munger, and the thinner black and blue one underneath it was by Steve Coben and called *Pathological Pairs: Duos with Bad History*.

I felt a flash of rage so intense I had to sit down. Despite everything he'd said, it was evident that Gerry McClanahan had planned to write about Jack and me. He had been studying us. Maybe his interest had begun as a sidelight to the stalking drama of Tamsin Lynd, but that interest had evolved. I took some deep breaths, told myself over and over that nothing could be done about it now, and packed those books along with the rest.

I found a biography sheet, I guess one that his publicist was preparing; Gerry had made little corrections here and there. He'd won prizes and awards, and his books had been translated into twenty different languages. I'd had other things on my mind when I'd scanned the *People* story. Reading the biography sheet, I understood for the first time what a furor there would be when it was discovered that Patrolman Gerry McClanahan was also Gibson Banks. I wondered how much time we had before that connection was made; not much, I was sure. There was an accordion file, full of notes for other projects. Gerry was tentatively planning a book on a serial killer in Minnesota. That would have been a change of climate, for sure.

The house had been gone over by the police, and I knew I wouldn't find anything remarkable they hadn't already seen. Plus, they would've taken anything interesting with them. But as I picked up a pen that had rolled onto the floor, I saw the edge of a sheet of yellow paper torn from a legal pad, protruding very slightly from under the desk. I remembered that Gerry had had a legal pad in front of him while we talked. A legal pad and a computer; that had seemed like overkill to me at the time. Why both?

Now, I pinned the paper to the floor with the point of the pen, and raked it out. It was a sheet covered with tiny black handwriting.

I peered at it and switched on the desk lamp to see it better. It was a log of the comings and goings at Tamsin's house. Nothing much, it seemed, had happened at Tamsin's that particular day. The Lynd-Egger couple had gone to work, come back home. Various lights had gone off and on. Tamsin had swept the back porch, and Cliff had spent five minutes in the little tool closet by the back porch some time after that. The date was the night before Jack and I had heard Tamsin yell on her front porch.

I was sure the rest of this log, which was a terrible document in and of itself, had been taken by the police. Perhaps Gerry had ripped this day's observations out to discard because nothing much had happened, and I hoped that the other notes he'd made proved of more value. The person stalking the counselor – it was hard not to think of this person as some kind of evil entity, since he was so invisible – hadn't liked anyone else stalking them, I was willing to bet. Gerry's obsession with the stalker's obsession had led to his own death.

As I locked the door behind me, my job completed, I suddenly realized that Gerry must have found out, there at the end, who the stalker was. I hoped, after all he'd sacrificed for the knowledge, he'd had a moment's satisfaction. Had he been dreadfully surprised . . . or had the killer's face been well known to him?

I was glad to lie down when I got home, but it was a good, tired feeling; not exhaustion. I watched a few shows on television: a biography of an actor I'd only heard of in passing, a documentary on the CIA. It was embarrassing to realize that the phone ringing actually woke me up.

'Yes?'

'Lily.' Jack.

'Hi.'

'I won't be home tonight. I'm going to start this job right away. If the CEO likes the job I do, there'll be more business from this firm.'

'What does he want you to do?'

'She.' I felt embarrassed. 'She wants me to do very thorough background checks on the applicants for this very sensitive job.' He was telling me the essence without the particulars, but that was all right with me. 'Have you been taking it easy?' Jack asked, suspicion evident in his voice.

'Well, I did do a little work today.'

'You know what Carrie said, Lily!'

'I just couldn't stand it any more. I had to do something or die of boredom.'

'Lily, you have to mind the doctor.'

'Yes,' I said, keeping my voice gentle.

'I love you.'

'I know. I love you, too. I got to go, Jack. Someone's at the door.'

'Answer it while I'm on the phone.'

I went to the door and looked through the peephole Jack had installed for me. 'It's Bobo, looks like.'

'Oh, okay,' Jack said, relieved. I cocked my head as I opened the door. Jack, who was sometimes jealous, had never gotten the fact that there was actually something to be jealous of with Bobo. I was grateful for his lack of acuity where this particular Winthrop was concerned. I sometimes felt very guilty when I caught an unexpected glimpse of Bobo and experienced a definite physical reaction to the sight of him.

'Bye, Jack,' I said, and he told me he would see me the next day.

I waved Bobo inside, feeling unusually curious about what he would have to say. This time, sure I was safe from – well, safe – I let him in and shut the door behind him.

'Are you okay with . . . ?' he tried just waving his hands a little, not wanting to come right out and say it.

'With you having sex with a friend of mine?'

'Yeah, that.'

'Of course, Bobo. You're over eighteen and so is Janet.' Not for anything in the world would I have explained my more complicated feelings. I would hardly admit them to myself.

But, as he often did, Bobo surprised me. And this was why I never quite lost a link to this unusual golden boy, this was why despite the difference in our ages and our lives there was a relationship between us. 'It's not just that, and you know it,' he said, his anger evident in the way he was standing, the tension in his arms.

I held up my hands in front of me, palms outward. I meant him to stop; we were not going to get serious, here. I'd had enough of that the night before. My long talk with Tamsin Lynd still griped me.

'You have to tell me if it's true.'

Suddenly, everything grew clear. 'You heard I was married.'

'Yes. Is it true?'

'Tell me you didn't take Janet to bed out of spite.'

'Is it true?'

'Yes, it's true.'

'How long?'

'A month.'

'Why were you keeping it a secret?'

'It isn't anyone's business,' I said, not caring if I sounded harsh.

'But it is,' he said. 'It is. You should have told me.'

I lost my temper. 'Why? Were you going to marry me?'

'No! But a married woman, you shouldn't even think about her!'

'So, if I'm married, I'm sacred to you, you can't lust after me.'

'That's right! That's exactly right!'

'Then end this, right here and now. I am married.'

'Can you give up thinking of me? Has being married made any difference to you? Because I know you. I know you think of me.'

'Bobo, this is too weird. Neither of us has any business thinking of the other. This is all wrong.'

'And now you're married.'

'Yes.'

'You love him?'

'Of course. More than anything.'

'But—'

'But nothing. This – we have to seal this off. This is over.'

'We've said this before. Or you have.'

'Are you saying I'm encouraging you in this idea you have, that we should go to bed together?'

'No, I'm not saying that. What I'm saying is, I can tell in your eyes that you know that if we did it would be great, that you want to fuck me as much as I want to fuck you.'

'But we can't do that, because there are trails leading up to and away from any act of sex.'

He took a deep breath. 'That's right.'

'So we won't talk about this again.'

'No,' he agreed, more slowly, with less conviction.

'I don't want to answer this door when my hair has gone gray, to find you still talking about it.'

He laughed a little. 'No,' he said. 'I have to get on with my life.'

'And Jack and I have to get on with ours.'

'Lily,' he said. He reached out and brushed his knuckle down my cheek. 'Do you love me just a little?'

'Yes,' I said. I owed him that. 'Just a little.'

I closed the door.

My unremembered dreams must have caused me to toss and turn in the night, because I woke up tired the next day. I took a cup of coffee out onto the tiny back porch and sat listening to the birds. My rosebush, growing up a cheap plastic trellis to one side of the porch, was in bloom. The rose had been chosen for smell, not appearance, and I closed my eyes to enjoy it to the fullest. My neighbor, Carlton Cockroft, waved at me from his back porch, and I raised my hand. We knew it was too early to talk to each other. The slope up to the railroad tracks was covered with flowering weeds that were full of bugs of all sizes and dispositions. I didn't know much about bugs, but I could appreciate their industry and appearance when they weren't in the house. I watched a butterfly, and a small bee, as each made the rounds of the flowers. When I'd had enough of that, I unrolled the small local paper that I'd gotten from the end of the sidewalk.

Man Stabbed by Stranger read the lead headline. I began to read what I assumed was going to be an account of Gerry McClanahan's murder, which had occurred too late to be featured in yesterday's paper. Stabbing is rare in Shakespeare, and stabbing by a stranger almost unheard of. Most killings in Shakespeare are male-on-male violence, of the Saturday-night-drinking-binge variety. I was actually shaking my head, anticipating the national news stories about Gerry's double life, when my eyes caught the name in the story.

> CLIFF EGGERS of 1410 Compton was taken to the hospital late yesterday evening after he said he was stabbed by a stranger, local police stated. Eggers, who has been a resident of Shakespeare for about a year, said he was walking out to his car after dark when an assailant rushed from the hedge to the side of his property. The assailant struck Eggers in the back and ran away. Hampered by a bandaged leg, Eggers did not pursue. At first, Eggers said, he didn't realize he'd been stabbed.
>
> 'It just felt like he hit me,' Eggers said. 'I called my wife, and she called the police.'
>
> A city policeman, Gerry B. McClanahan, was stabbed to death almost to the rear of Eggers's house two nights before. (See related article, page 2)
>
> 'We may have a deranged person in the neighborhood, or we may have someone who's targeted the Eggers household,' said Claude Friedrich, chief of police. 'We have every available officer assigned to the case.'
>
> Asked if he had any leads in the case, Friedrich responded, 'New information is coming in constantly.'

Eggers was treated and discharged from Shakespeare Regional Hospital.

I assumed Claude's comment meant that he didn't have a clue. Carrie had called me the night before to thank me for cleaning her office. 'I knew it was you,' she'd said, 'because you always make the magazine stacks so neat.' She'd confessed her regular cleaner had gotten held up, and she was up a creek. But she hadn't said anything about Cliff Eggers.

Of course, she couldn't. I could see that now. She couldn't blab any more about her husband's business than I could about Jack's. I was glad, just the same, to see Carrie's old car parked behind her office. She often came in on Saturday mornings to catch up on paperwork.

'No one in the hospital?' I called as I went in the back door.

'Not a soul, can you believe it?' She came out of her office with a mug in her hand. She was wearing her weekend outfit of cutoffs and T-shirt.

'Not even Cliff Eggers,' I said.

'No, he bled like a stuck pig, but it wasn't that deep.'

'Where was he cut?' I asked, since Carrie seemed to be in a chatty mood.

'In the back, oddly enough,' Carrie said. 'It was a funny kind of wound. Started here,' and she touched a point just above my waist slightly left of my spine, 'and ended here,' which turned out to be a spot about midway down my right hip. 'It was deeper toward the end.'

'Kind of low for a blow from another man,' I said, after I'd considered it.

'Yes, isn't it. I don't think I've ever seen a knife wound quite like that.'

'Maybe . . .' I thought for a minute. 'Okay, what if Cliff

was walking away, and the knifer was swooshing down.' I raised my arm with an imaginary knife in it, and brought the arm down in an arc. 'So if Cliff stepped away just then, the end of the knife would slice through the hip, rather than penetrating him higher up by the spine, as it was intended to.'

'Could be. Could be,' Carrie said, looking at my back doubtfully. 'Of course, Cliff's at least six inches taller than you. But still, I would say his assailant had to be shorter than Cliff. Or kneeling, but I can't quite visualize that.'

I couldn't either, but it was an interesting idea. 'What was Tamsin doing while all this was going on?' I asked, trying to sound casual. I assumed that since Tamsin and Carrie were both in some sense medical professionals, they would know each other, and I was right.

'In the kitchen cooking, she told me,' Carrie said, still staring at my back as if it would tell her the answer.

'I guess she came to the hospital with Cliff.'

'Oh, yeah, as upset as she could possibly be. I don't know how much longer she's going to be able to do her job, if things like this keep happening around her. She said something about moving again.'

I looked at Carrie. 'What was she wearing?'

'Oh, I don't know. Ah, a pair of old jeans and an Arkansas Razorbacks T-shirt, seems like.'

'No apron?'

'No. Either she's one of these women who cooks without, or she pulled it off before she came. Why?' Carrie seemed to realize that this was an odd question.

'Just wondered.' I was relieved when the phone rang, because Carrie once more immersed herself in work. I didn't want to have to explain to Carrie what I didn't even want to admit to myself, that I'd been infected with Alicia

Stokes's suspicions. I was wondering if it was my mental health counselor who had stabbed her husband in the back.

As I polished the sink in the women's bathroom, I longed for Jack. It was always easy to talk things over with him. He seemed to enjoy the process, too. Jack understood people a little better than I did. I was repulsed by people who were messy with their emotions; just look at the tangled mess of Bobo and me. It felt good to have encapsulated and pushed away our mutual attraction.

I had a sudden and unprecedented flight of fantasy. I pictured myself telling Beanie Winthrop that Bobo and I were going to be married, and the expression I could just imagine on her face tickled me all morning. Though Beanie had some admirable characteristics, we had never liked each other. It almost seemed worth telling her the lie just to see her face. I wondered if her only daughter, Amber Jean, would turn out to be a good woman. Her teen years were obviously shaky ground. Amber Jean had her picture in the paper this morning, helping with the canned goods drive for the soup kitchen maintained by Shakespeare Combined Church, Calvary Baptist, and First Presbyterian. She'd looked glossy and preppy in the picture; not the kind of girl who would take off her shirt in front of a group of boys, not the kind of girl who would try to subordinate a woman older than herself. 'A picture is worth a thousand words' did not apply in Amber Jean's case.

What about my mental picture of Tamsin? Tamsin looked like the average young professional, the kind who didn't care terribly about money, the kind who really, really wanted to help. But she'd been stalked, or so it seemed, through three jobs and two states. Small animals around her died, unpleasant things happened to her everywhere, and people around her were beginning to drop like flies. She was in the center of a circle of destruction; she was the eye of a storm.

I drove to the gym thinking hard about Tamsin and her situation. She was the first person I saw when I stepped into Body Time. She was talking to Marshall, and she was looking haggard and unkempt. Her sweats looked dirty, and her hair was disheveled. Marshall gave her a dismissive pat on the back and glided over to me. Marshall is so fit that you could bounce a dime off his abs, so dangerous as a martial artist that he's made me cry from pain. I was glad to have him for a friend.

I could tell he wanted to ask me if it was true that Jack and I were married, but he couldn't quite bring himself to do it. He knew I hated personal questions, so he was determined to avoid that most personal one.

'Since Jack's not here, why don't we work out together?' he suggested. I agreed, since it's always nice to have a spotter, and the workout always goes better with a partner to challenge you. It was triceps day for me, though I was so far behind my normal schedule I could start just about anywhere. Triceps were fine with Marshall, so we went over to the heavy weights rack to begin. Assuming the pushup position, my hands on the pair of seventies on the top rack, I began my first set, concentrating on my breathing. Marshall was propped on the hundreds farther down the rack, and his body moved as though he had springs embedded in his arms.

'Tamsin was telling me about Cliff,' Marshall said, as we rested between sets. 'She came in this morning because he finally fell asleep and she didn't know what to do with herself.'

I nodded.

'Yeah.' Marshall did some stretches, and then we did

our second set of pushups. 'I guess you knew she has been followed by this crazy person,' he said, when we were through.

'Yeah, I heard about that,' I said carefully. 'Hard to believe in a town this size, we wouldn't notice someone new.'

Marshall turned an inquiring face to me as we assumed the pushup position for the third and last time. 'That's true,' he said, 'but what other explanation is there? I guess you've thought of something.'

'What if it's her?' I asked.

Marshall gave a derisive snort. 'Yeah, right. She's a nice enough woman but she doesn't have enough grit in her to say boo to a goose. You think she's doing this to herself so she can get a lot of sympathy as Velma Victim? That seems a little far-fetched.'

I shrugged as I stood up and shook my arms out to relieve the ache. 'Who else could it be?' I really wanted to know what Marshall was thinking.

'I hadn't given it a thought,' he said. 'Ah . . . , Cliff, but he'd hardly want to stab himself in the back, and he's nuts about Tamsin. Okay, not him . . . well, what about the new police detective? The tall black woman?'

'She worked on Tamsin's case when Tamsin lived in Ohio,' I said. 'If Stokes stabbed Cliff, believe me, he'd be dead.'

I was serious, but Marshall laughed as though I were joking.

'There was the other new cop, the patrolman, but he's dead now, too,' Marshall said, thinking out loud. 'Oh, there's Jack! He's new in town.'

'Ha-ha-ha,' I said, my voice showing clearly how unfunny I found this.

'And there's the guy that's started dating my ex.'

'I thought Thea was getting married.'

'Me, too. But he got to know her a little too well.'

'And now she's dating someone else?'

'Sure. You know Thea. She's nothing if not flexible, when it comes to men.'

I disliked Thea intensely. She gave women a bad name.

'Who's the guy?'

'The new mortician at the funeral home.'

'Oh, that's right up Thea's alley,' I said. 'I bet she loves that.'

Marshall laughed again, but less happily. This time he knew I was serious, and he agreed with me. Thea had a cruel and macabre streak, and making love in a funeral home would suit her sexual playbook, if all I'd heard were true. 'But he and Thea were in Branson when Saralynn Kleinhoff was killed,' Marshall said.

So I'd developed and eliminated a suspect in the space of five minutes. I was sure all these crimes had been committed by one person. Anything else would have been too much of a coincidence.

Not that I didn't believe in coincidence. I did. But I thought it would be stretching, in this case, to even entertain it as a possibility.

Jack's car was in the driveway when I got home. I was very glad to see it there.

He was cooking something when I went into the kitchen, something that smelled good.

'Bacon sandwiches for lunch. I have tomatoes picked right off the vine,' he told me, his voice unmistakably smug.

I don't eat much bacon, since it's not good for you, but a

bacon and fresh tomato sandwich was just too good to pass up.

'Where'd you get 'em?' There were at least six tomatoes on the kitchen counter. Two were green.

'From Aunt Betty,' he said. 'Can we have fried green tomatoes tonight?'

Two fried things in one day was really a lot, but I nodded. I stood behind him, watching him cook.

'Hold still,' I said.

'What are you going to do?'

'Pretend to stab you.'

'I guess that wasn't the answer I was wanting to hear.' But Jack obligingly stood still.

I raised my hand above my head as though it held a knife pointing downward. My hand whizzed through the air, and I mentally marked the point at which the blade would have grazed Jack's back.

'Hmmm.'

'Can I help?' Jack asked. He picked some of the bacon out of the skillet with some small tongs, and put the bacon to drain on a pad of paper towels. I got out the small cutting board and a knife, and began to slice a tomato.

'Let me stab you again,' I said, and this time, with the knife in hand, I held it straight out in front of me. The wound Carrie had described simply couldn't be made, if the knife was held like this.

While Jack put ice in two glasses, I explained what I was doing.

'Okay, let me try.' He turned me around, and taking the precaution of using a dull table knife, he began to experiment. 'A graze at the top, a true stab at the bottom, going from the left side of the back to the right.' he said. 'So I think you're right, it would have to be an overhand blow.'

'An overhand blow from someone much shorter, right?' I put our plates on the table and folded a paper napkin beside each plate. Jack got out the bread and mayonnaise, my mother's homemade. 'Cliff's a little taller than you, huh?' Jack nodded, as he used a fork to put tomato slices on his bread. 'Maybe six feet?'

Jack said, 'Just barely.'

I could think of no one involved in the episodes who was short, besides a couple of the women in the group, and Tamsin herself. 'Maybe Tamsin did it by accident? And they were too embarrassed to say it?'

Jack even looked good to me when he chewed, which is one of the more unattractive activities for a human being. He swallowed. 'She could have mistaken Cliff for someone else, I guess, but there's a streetlight practically in front of their house. He was attacked in the driveway, right? So how, in good light and in a place where she would expect him to be, could she knife him by accident?'

'There's only one other new person in town,' I said, not able to think of any rebuttal. I told Jack about my conversation with Marshall, about Thea's new lover. Jack said, 'I've met him. He runs in the evening.'

'Joel McCorkindale does, too.' I tried to make something of that. Joel ran, Talbot ran, Joel's wife was in the support group, and she was short. That didn't add up to anything. This made as little sense as one of those logic problems the first time you read it through. 'If Mary has a poodle, and Mary is taller than Sarah and Brenda, and Brenda's dog is brown, read the following statements to figure out who has the dachshund.' Besides, Sandy McCorkindale might be half nuts, but I simply could not picture her catching a squirrel and hanging it in a tree. It was actually easier to imagine Sandy stabbing someone.

We ate in silence, enjoying our first summer BLT. While we washed the dishes, I asked Jack what would happen next.

'I don't know. Stalking's just not that common a crime, and I have no big backlog of experience with it. When I first started my apprenticeship, Roy was handling a case a little like this. The woman couldn't get the police to take her seriously, because the intruder wasn't doing anything to her.'

'Intruder?'

'Yeah, he was actually coming into her apartment while she was gone, sifting through her stuff. Leaving her presents.'

I made a face. Disgusting and scary.

'I agree.' Jack looked grim as he scrubbed the skillet. 'Finally, she scratched up enough money to pay for around-the-clock surveillance. The spot-checking we were doing just wasn't effective. But it didn't take long after that. We caught him jacking off on her underwear the second day. It was her apartment manager. It was a tough case to take to court, because he had a legal key.'

'Did you win?'

'Yes. But of course she had to move, and she found she couldn't stay in the city even after she'd moved. So he got a slap on the wrist, and her life was changed dramatically.'

Gee, that sounded familiar. I had only heard stories like that about a million times. I sighed, and asked Jack what he planned for that afternoon.

'First, I'm hitting the computer to see what background Alicia Stokes has. Then, we're going over to Tamsin's house and look at their driveway. Then, at some point, I plan on us having a serious session in the bedroom, there.'

I got caught between a smile and a frown. 'Why are you looking into this?' I asked.

'Because it's got you going crazy, and I can't have that. I like you happy. We started this whole thing so you wouldn't have nightmares any more, and I hate it that this has turned into something that makes you feel even more angry.'

It surprised me that Jack saw me as perpetually angry.

It was true, but I hadn't wanted him to know that.

So I was being a deceiver, something I despised.

'It's not you,' I said.

'I know that.'

'I love you.'

'I know that.'

'Does it really bother you?'

'It worries me, sometimes. If it keeps on eating at you, some day it might include me.'

'I can't see that happening.'

'I wish I couldn't.'

I looked down, unable to meet his eyes. Maybe he was right. He'd taken a big chance. 'Thanks for helping, Jack.'

'We'll get this solved,' he said.

'Do we have to do those things in the order listed?'

'Why, no, I guess not.'

'Could we reverse the order?'

'I bet we could.' He grinned. The scar crinkled, and his hazel eyes narrowed, the crow's feet at their corners spreading until the smile affected his whole face.

I took a deep breath. 'I'll beat you to the bed,' I said, and got a head start.

It ended up being a tie.

Later that afternoon, Jack had to confess he was coming up empty. Alicia had no previous record. She had good credit and paid her taxes on time. Her income was not great, but adequate for the time and place. She had once been married, was now divorced. She had never been named as the mother of a child. She had never served in the armed forces.

I decided to mow the lawn that afternoon, while Jack was busy on the computer. It was easy to think while I was mowing, and I liked the look of the small yard when it was even and trim. I even used the weedeater and then swept away the clipped grass from my sidewalk. During all this work, I thought and thought, and I could not come up with any clearer understanding of the vicious cycle surrounding Tamsin Lynd. I must have been looking at it wrong, but I couldn't seem to find a new perspective.

Jack came outside when the sun was making deep shadows. I lay on the newly cut grass, disregarding the likelihood of fire ant bites and the certainty of grass stains, and stared up into the vast blueness. My backyard is very small and runs into the slope up to the railroad tracks, and it's overlooked by the second-floor windows of the apartment building next door and by Carlton's rear window, but it does give the illusion of privacy. Carlton was gone, anyway, because I'd seen him pull out in his car, and the apartment on the end closest to me was vacant at the moment. So maybe we really were unobserved.

Jack stretched in the grass beside me. His hair was loose, had been since our session in the bedroom, and I knew we'd have to pick the grass bits out of it before we went to bed. But there was nothing I would rather do.

It was hot, and quiet, and the smell of the grass was sharp in our noses.

'Let's review,' Jack said, his voice slow and sleepy.

'Okay.' I sounded just about as peppy as he did.

'Tamsin moves to Shakespeare because she's been stalked at her previous home in Cleveland.'

'Right.'

'A detective on that case, not the primary, but one assigned to do some of the legwork, is a young detective named Alicia Stokes.'

'Check.' I closed my eyes against the relentless blue.

'Alicia Stokes becomes so fascinated by the case, so obsessed, that when Tamsin Lynd and her husband, Cliff Eggers, move to Shakespeare, eventually Alicia finds herself compelled to follow.'

' "Compelled to follow". I like that.' I turned on my side and raised myself up on my right elbow. 'Also, within a matter of months, a true crime writer whose real name is Gerry McClanahan signs on with the city police in Shakespeare. He's a real policeman, so this doesn't seem fraudulent to him. His secret life as a writer isn't known to anyone . . . anyone we're aware of.'

'Gerry, aka Gibson Banks, knows not only about Tamsin and Cliff, but also about the obsessed policewoman. He's come to watch the showdown.'

I nodded.

'And, once again, things start happening to Tamsin Lynd . . . and tangentially, to Cliff.'

'Tangentially. I love it when you use big words.' I bent over to kiss Jack's forehead. He wiggled closer to me.

'Expeditious. Arraignment. Consequence. Territorial . . .' Jack smiled, his eyes closed against the glow of the sky, and I leaned over to kiss him again, this time not on the forehead.

'So, she gets phone calls,' he resumed. 'We happen by when they find the dead squirrel.'

'Then Saralynn Kleinhoff is killed – and put on display – and put in Tamsin's office. While Tamsin is still in the building. But Janet, who interrupts the killer, is not murdered, but rendered unconscious.'

'Then, the writer who is planning to do a book on both the stalking and the detective who can't stop stalking the stalker, so to speak, is murdered while he watches the stalkee.'

'That's one way to put it.'

'Then Tamsin's husband, her last stronghold, falls into a boobytrap. Shortly thereafter, he's attacked in their own driveway.'

'And that's where we are now.' I lay down with my head on Jack's chest, my arm thrown over him. I closed my eyes, too, and felt the sun kiss my cheek. I knew in a minute I'd be uncomfortable and itchy, but this moment was idyllic.

'And though we figure the stalker also has to be someone who's new in town, the only other new person is a strange, possibly perverted, but apparently guiltless mortician.'

'That's it in a nutshell.'

'And we're nowhere.'

'Well, it's not you and it's not me.'

'Oh, good, just about ten thousand more people to go.' Sure enough, I was beginning to get itchy. I sat up and started to brush off the cut grass. I thought about packing up Gerry McClanahan's house, the life he'd left behind him. His awards and accomplishments, his ties with people in small worlds and big worlds, his notes of projects yet to come, projects that now would never be completed unless his estate hired someone to finish the work he'd started.

The notes. All those notes. I wished now I'd had a chance to read them before the police gathered them up. Gerry McClanahan, after all, had been a trained detective with lots of experience. What had he concluded about the stalking of

Tamsin Lynd? All I could remember was that he'd called it a fascinating case. That wasn't a help.

'What are you thinking so hard about?' Jack asked. He was propped up on his elbows.

I explained my line of thought to him.

'Fascinating,' he said, 'he called it fascinating?'

'Yeah. And he said, "This is a case turned upside down. No one will forget this one." '

'Turned upside down.'

I nodded. 'So let's see,' I said, mostly to myself. 'If a case is upside down . . . the victim is the perpetrator? That would mean Tamsin has been responsible for the whole thing.'

'Or it could mean that whoever is guilty looks innocent.'

'Whoever loves Tamsin actually hates her.'

That gave us both a jolt. We looked at each other. 'Who loves Tamsin?' Jack asked, almost in a whisper.

'Cliff loves Tamsin.'

After a wide-eyed moment, we both shook our heads in disbelief.

'Nah,' I said. 'Did you see how he cried when he picked her up in the parking lot after Saralynn was murdered? And the gash on his leg after he fell through the step?'

'Let's go look at their driveway,' Jack said.

We walked, because it was beautiful, and because it might make the visit look less rehearsed. But we need not have been concerned about that; no one was home at the house on Compton Street.

Up the driveway we went, as though we'd been invited. We gave a perfunctory knock to the front door, and then turned away to enact the attack of the night before.

'You be Cliff,' I told Jack. 'Remember, your leg is still sore from going through the steps.' Jack pretended to emerge from the house. He limped down the front steps, and walked slowly over to where the couple parked their cars. Jack got his keys out, as someone naturally would if they expected to drive off. Then he stopped. I came up behind him as quietly as possible, but the driveway was loose gravel. Even the grass strip running between the driveway and the hedge was full of the stuff.

'I can hear you coming a mile away,' he said over his shoulder. 'No way anyone snuck up on Cliff.'

Of course, if you heard someone coming up behind you when you were outside, you'd turn around to look. Anyone would. You wouldn't just keep on with what you were doing.

But I raised my hand, again pantomiming the knifing. This time, I crouched a little until I approximated Tamsin's height. I made an awkward swing, and was very close to the wound area as Carrie had described it to me. But the angle was all wrong, straight down instead of left-to-right. 'That didn't work,' I told Jack, almost cheerfully.

'You know, and I know, that when someone's coming up behind you, you're going to turn around to see what they want.' Jack's face was getting grimmer and grimmer as he spoke. 'And if the stabber was really determined he'd stick around and try again.'

Jack turned his back to me again. He bent his hand up behind his back as far as he could bend it. He had a pocketknife clenched in his right fist, with the end pointing down. Jack made a chopping, downward motion. The point of the knife grazed his rump in an arc from left to right. If he hadn't been careful, it would've gouged the flesh of his right hip.

It was exactly as Carrie had described the wound.

'Oh, no, Jack.' I felt almost as though I was going to cry, and I couldn't say why.

'It might not be that way,' Jack said. 'But it looks like it to me.'

'So what'd he do with it?' I asked. 'Put it in his pocket?'

'They'd find it at the hospital,' Jack said. He pantomimed the self-mutilation again, he put out a hand to rest on an imaginary car, and with the other he pitched his pocketknife into the depths of the hedge. Then we both got down on our hands and knees and searched, very carefully.

Jack found a splotch of dried blood in the bed of old leaves below the hedge, right after I'd retrieved his knife.

'Of course, his attacker could've thrown it in here and retrieved it later. It didn't have to be Cliff that did the tossing and retrieving,' Jack said.

I nodded. I felt about twenty years older, all in a flash. This was betrayal on a grand scale. And on an incredibly mean scale, too.

'Do you think Claude has figured this out?' Jack and I strode down the sidewalk. Jack had thrust his hands in his pockets and he was scowling. 'Or do you think he's been too distracted by the upheaval in his department?'

We stopped at the next corner. Tamsin was at the stop sign facing us, and through the windshield of her car I could tell she was looking haggard. The plump and assured woman I'd met a few weeks earlier had simply vanished.

We'd finished our little experiment just in time. She waved us through the intersection, and tried to summon up a smile for us, but it failed. We nodded and kept on walking. I felt like a traitor to her. First I thought she'd been persecuting herself, and now I suspected her husband was her tormentor.

'We have to go talk to Claude,' I said.

Jack nodded unenthusiastically. Neither of us is happy in a police station. Since my ordeal, I'd become shy of the police, who were first to initiate me into the range of human reactions to my victimization that I now knew so well. And Jack is still ostracized by some cops for his involvement in the scandal that led to his leaving the force in Memphis.

Claude was in and willing to see us. I had half hoped he'd be outfighting crime or swamped in paperwork.

We went into his office. Claude looked puzzled, but glad to see us, a reaction so far off base that I came pretty close to turning around and leaving. But conscience demanded that we take the wooden chairs in front of Claude's old desk and state our business.

I glanced at Jack, took a deep breath, and launched in to our theory.

Claude said, when he was sure I'd finished, 'That's pretty interesting stuff, there. What do you have to prove it?'

My heart sank. 'You haven't found any evidence to point to Cliff, or Tamsin . . . or anyone else?'

'You mean, in general? Or in the death of Saralynn Kleinhoff? In the murder of my police officer? Let's just take Saralynn's murder. Let's see,' Claude rumbled, scooting lower in his chair and crossing his ankles. 'Got to be someone that had a key to the health center. That's forty present and past employees, plus their families.'

I hadn't even thought of that.

'Got to be someone who doesn't mind getting their hands messy. Well, who knows? My grandmother, the most finicky woman on God's green earth, could butcher a chicken as fast as you can say Jack Robinson,' Claude continued. 'Got to be someone with a personal dislike of Tamsin Lynd. Mental health workers get all kinds of enemies, right? And as for thinking it has to be the same person here as was stalking her in Illinois – well, why? Could be a copycat. Doesn't have to be someone who followed her down here. As far as hanging the squirrel, anyone could've done that at any time. You could tie up the squirrel ahead of time and take it over there, get it strung on the branch in a minute or less.'

This wasn't going the way I'd hoped. Jack was looking pretty bleak, too.

'Then, Gerry. Now that I know about Gerry, I can understand a lot of things about him better. But that doesn't stop me from being mad at him for deceiving me, and I'll bet a lot of other people were mad at him, too. Just because he told you that he was watching Tamsin's house doesn't mean that was why he was killed. And Cliff is the only one giving Tamsin an alibi for that one; he says she was in the shower. Well, maybe she was and maybe she wasn't.'

I closed my eyes and wished I were somewhere else.

'About this scenario you two have worked out – you may be right. May be. But if Cliff did stab himself, that doesn't necessarily mean he killed Saralynn and Gerry. That doesn't mean he's been terrorizing his own wife. We have no proof either way.'

'No forensic evidence?' Jack was leaning forward in his chair.

'There were fibers on Saralynn that came from a pair of slacks a lot like the ones Cliff was wearing that day. Khaki Dockers. Everyone's got a pair of those. And Cliff readily told us that he'd been in there earlier in the day, when he'd brought Tamsin her lunch. Fibers could've been left there then.'

'Say we're right,' Jack said. 'Say that the one behind everything is Cliff. What do you think he'll do next?'

My eyes flicked to Claude, who was thinking the matter over.

'If he follows his pattern, he'll quit. They'll move. It'll start all over again.'

Jack nodded.

Claude continued, his face looking as seamed and careworn as that of a man ten years older. 'But he's escalated and escalated. From nasty pranks, to small deaths like the squirrel, to human deaths like Saralynn's and Gerry's. What could be left? Next time, I reckon he'll try to kill her.'

With regret, I agreed.

Chapter Thirteen

'We might as well not have gone to Claude,' I said to Jack.

We were on our way home from Body Time the next morning when I reopened the subject.

'Yeah.' He stared straight ahead, his face like a thundercloud and his posture just as aggressive as mine. 'We can't just wait for her to be killed.'

'What else can we do? We can't stay outside her house for days or weeks. We can't follow her everywhere she goes, or kill Cliff before he kills her.'

Jack looked at me sidelong, and I could see the idea of taking Cliff out appealed to him. 'We can't,' I said, in the voice my fifth grade teacher had used when she recited the Golden Rule to us every morning. 'We are not going to get in trouble with the law again.'

When we got home, at least part of our problem was solved. There was a message on the answering machine from Tamsin. Even her voice sounded quavery. 'Lily, this is Tamsin. I just can't get up the energy to do any housework, and the place is a wreck. If you're feeling better – only if you're well enough – I would really appreciate hearing from you.'

I called her back right away. 'This is Lily,' I said.

'Oh. Oh, Lily! Can you come to help me clean house today? I don't know if I can go in to work this week . . . and I'm definitely staying home today. I'm so shaken up.'

'I think I can come over,' I told her. After all, it was Sunday morning, when I never scheduled anything so I could have a break from work. But I'd definitely had enough down time this week.

'Oh, thank God!'

We talked a little more – well, she did – and I hung up. Jack, standing beside me for the whole conversation, was sunk in thought. We looked at each other for a second or two.

'Do you have to go over there?' He ran a hand through his hair to push it over his shoulders.

'Yes. I owe her.'

'Do you think Cliff's there?'

'She didn't say.'

'I don't know about this, Lily. I hate for you to be anywhere close to the woman. I feel sorry for her, but she's a human lightning rod.'

I wasn't too enthusiastic about Tamsin's request myself. 'Maybe she really wants me over there to clean. But I'm thinking maybe she needs company, and doesn't know anyone well enough to just ask for it.'

'So, you're going to go?' Jack was still reluctant.

'Yes, but I'll call you when I get there. If you don't hear from me, come over to see how everything's going. I don't know if I could take a lot of weeping.' At odd moments, the loss of the baby still struck me with a peculiar pain.

'You won't forget to call?' Jack touched my hair.

'No, I won't forget.'

I showered and changed, so it was about ten when I left my house, ten o'clock on a hot and peaceful Sunday morning. Shakespeare was at its best. The church parking lots were full. A little towheaded boy was in his driveway operating a remote-control car. Everything looked absolutely normal on Tamsin's street. Both the cars were parked in the drive, and I wedged in behind them.

I wasn't too pleased that Cliff was home, but I had only suspicion, after all. Lugging my cleaning-material caddy, I went up the front steps and knocked. With professional eyes I examined the porch; it needed to be swept, if not hosed down.

Tamsin came to the door immediately. She looked as awful as she had the day before. Her hair was straggly and dirty, her cutoff jeans and truncated sweatshirt were anything but pristine, and she was free of makeup and jewelry.

'Thank you for coming,' she said, in a limp voice. 'I just can't stand for everything to be so dirty, with people dropping by all the time. I can't ever tell who'll be seeing my house, with the police coming in all the time.'

'Cliff home?' The litter of the big edition of the paper and a couple of stained coffee mugs in the living room were like a tableau called 'Sunday morning'.

'Yes, he's in the small den back there where we keep the TV.' This living room, decorated in inexpensive American comfortable, did not contain a television or music system. Shelves hung on the wall held little china statues of wide-eyed children.

'Aren't they darling? I love those things,' Tamsin said, following my gaze. 'My folks started giving me one a year when I was little. Then, Cliff took over.'

Despite her dishevelment, Tamsin seemed calm and in control. I felt encouraged. Maybe this wouldn't be too bad. As soon as she explained the program, I'd call Jack. 'Where do you want me to start?' I stood before her with raised eyebrows, just waiting for her word.

'How about in there?' Tamsin pointed to the hall leading

to the back of the house, and I preceded her down the dark corridor.

'In here?' I asked, and turned the knob of the door at the end.

'Yep,' she said, and I just had time to turn the knob and push the door open, all the while thinking she was sounding so cheerful. I was met with a burst of sunlight, and the sight of Cliff Eggers bound and gagged with duct tape and lying on the floor.

Then she did something horrible to me, something that made every atom in my body surge, and I fell down beside him.

I had some seconds of complete disorientation. Or maybe I lost minutes. My legs had no bones in them. Talking was simply impossible, even if I'd been able to formulate a sentence. My mouth was open and I was drooling. I felt wet at my crotch; I had wet my pants. When I became aware that I was still thinking, that my thoughts could form patterns and make sense, my first clear concept was that I should avoid having that – whatever it was – done to me again, no matter what the cost. My wandering gaze happened to meet Cliff's desperate brown eyes, and I slowly became anchored in the here and now, as unpleasant as that was.

I was still alive. That was the important thing. And I hadn't called Jack, so I figured he'd be coming sooner or later – unless Tamsin had done something while I was mentally out of the room, something to fool Jack, too.

Of course, I felt like the biggest idiot.

Cliff's eyes stared into mine. He was scared shitless. I didn't blame him. But I was just as glad the duct tape across his mouth made talking impossible. I didn't need anyone else's fear. I had plenty of my own.

'What you gonna do?' I asked Tamsin, after tremendous effort. It was the first sentence that managed to make it out of my lips. She was holding something in her right hand, a black narrow shape, and I finally recognized it as a stun gun. I took a deep breath of sheer bitterness. Oh, gosh, who had told her where to buy one? Could it have been me? It would have been hard for me to be more angry with myself than I was at this moment, or more sickened by the human race.

'If you're not outraged by what he's done to me, I'm going to have to do it myself,' Tamsin said. 'Then, I don't know what I'll do about you.'

'Why?' Though that was probably a pointless question.

Oddly, she looked like she was thinking of answering me.

'I just realized the past few days. At first, it just didn't seem possible. That someone living with me, someone sleeping with me, someone who took my dresses to the cleaners, was trying to drive me crazy. The first stuff, the stuff in Cleveland, even that was Cliff.' Instead of looking at me, she was staring off into space, and I swear she had the most disillusioned, heartbroken expression. I would have felt sorry for her, if she hadn't just disabled and humiliated me. 'I figured out just this week that after I lost our baby, Cliff was out to kill me. He thought I did things to kill the baby. And he knew I had a lot of insurance – one big policy through work and another on my own. He thought, in my profession, getting killed wouldn't be so strange. He was doing my transcripts for me, then. In fact, that's where we met, at that clinic.' The narrow black device swung in her hand like a television remote control. 'So Cliff transcribed my sessions with a patient who had potential for great violence, one who actually might think of killing me. I think Cliff planned to beat me to death.' She got right in my face to confide this. If I'd had the energy, the hair would have been lifting on my neck. 'He could count on the investigators going through my patients, finding – this man – and arresting him.'

'And?' If I didn't try to say too much, it came out okay. My legs were slowly feeling a little more functional. Cliff was moving a little more. She'd bound his hands in front, which wasn't too competent. He was picking at the duct tape across his mouth.

'We moved once, in the Cleveland area, after I found a snake nailed to the door. Moving didn't help. Then, as I've come to realize these past few days, Cliff stretched his fun out a little too long. Charles, my patient, died in a bar fight. Cliff had to stop. Of course, I didn't put two and two together then.' Her face became blank, her eyes opaque. 'I really thought Cliff suggested this move to Shakespeare because he was concerned about me. He gave up his business and everything to move south with me, and I believed we would be happy here. I didn't put Charles's death together with the end of the persecution, the end of the horrible messages on the answering machine. But Cliff told me just a few minutes ago that the police up there did make the connection, did mention – to *Cliff* – the possibility of my stalker being Charles. They would've wondered if the calls had kept coming. So here we are, and we get settled, and I think everything is going so good, and I start getting the calls again. The house is entered. There's . . . poop . . . smeared on the door.'

Cliff had succeeded in ungagging himself. 'Lily,' he said in a weak voice 'don't let her kill me.'

I didn't even glance at him. 'Yeah?' I said to Tamsin, to encourage her to talk. The longer she talked, the more time I had to recover.

'So we decided the police had been wrong. That

someone else had followed me down here. It still didn't occur to me to suspect the most obvious person.' She shook her head at her own naïveté. 'We figured – that is, I figured, and Cliff pretended to – that since the calls only came when Cliff was gone, that meant the guy was watching me, knew when I was alone. That made it more scary. Notes slid under the door, notes in my clothes – oh, God!' She shuddered and wept.

My sympathy would have been deeper if I hadn't been sitting there in wet pants.

'Lily,' Cliff said, 'I didn't do those things. I love my wife . . . even though she planted the stake in the step for me to get hurt on. If you'll just let me go, we can work this out.' He was plucking awkwardly at the duct tape around his wrists, but that was going to be much harder.

I said, 'Tamsin, why'd you call me here?'

'Because you can kill him.'

I shook my head.

'You can kill him,' she repeated persuasively. 'You killed a man before. This one deserves it, too. Think of what he's done to me. He shouldn't live!' Her face grew crafty. 'What if he gets off and does this to someone else? I know from our therapy group that you have a sense of justice.'

Unhampered by the rules of law, she meant.

'You could kill him for me. We'd all be safer.'

She had condensed Cliff into every man who'd hurt a woman.

'Please do this for me! My mind is too fragile, too delicate, to sustain killing him.' She made it sound like her mind was made out of old lace. 'I just don't have the guts, the determination. I need you to do this favor for another woman.' The empty hand touched her chest. 'Help your sister out.'

'You – stunned me.'

'I was afraid you'd run away before I could talk to you if I didn't do something,' she told me, and her voice was so reasonable that I winced. 'I know you, from the group. You wouldn't sit and listen to me unless I made you. Would you? Just think about it, Lily. You have to understand this. I loved him more than anyone else in the world. He took everything away from me. I think he did something to make me lose the baby. I don't believe in anything any more.'

And she should have made him unconscious, because he was eyeing me frantically, shaking his head to deny what she was telling me. 'Lily, Tamsin has just lost her mind. Don't cater to her when she's clearly off her rocker. I love my wife, and I've done everything I can to help her through this. Please don't let her do something worse than this.' I noticed he was making progress on loosening the duct tape binding his wrists. It was difficult, but he was managing. The next time I wanted to secure someone, I wouldn't call Tamsin to do the securing.

Tamsin went on enumerating her wrongs. Since I was still too weak to move, I had plenty of time to think. I thought it was pretty lucky their baby hadn't been born, whatever had caused the miscarriage. What if what Tamsin was telling me wasn't true? She was deeply disturbed. She might be mistaken, and she might just be a liar. What if she just wanted an excuse to kill Cliff, with a reasonable chance of an acquittal, or at the most a light sentence? Pretending he'd confessed his long persecution of her, pretending he'd told her he'd killed Saralynn and Gerry McClanahan, would provide an excellent story to tell a jury.

Especially with a witness like me.

She could have no serious hope that I would take the bait

and do Cliff in, but she could provide a good case for herself if I was there to witness her frenzy and her anguish, even if she had to immobilize me to make me watch it. I was pretty sure Tamsin was not quite as crazy as she was making out; I was pretty sure she was making a case for temporary insanity.

But I wasn't *completely* sure.

The only certainty I had was that I hated Tamsin, my counselor, who was twisting what she'd extracted from our therapy sessions to serve her own ends: my disregard for the letter of the law, my strong sense of justice. She'd ignored other things about me that were just as important, like my absolute and total hatred of people who made me feel helpless, my loathing of being physically unclean, and my dislike of being bested.

'What happened in your office when Saralynn was killed?' I asked. My speech was better, too.

'I swear to God, exactly what I told the police,' Tamsin said.

'You knew I was there,' Cliff said, his voice ragged. 'You knew someone was killing Saralynn. And you hid. I wondered the whole time, does she even care enough to come out? If she'll come out, if she'll be brave, I won't finish . . . and she yelled for you, Tamsin. You heard her. And you stayed shut in that conference room, doing nothing.'

'Lily, he's trying to take you in just like he took me!' She was all but wailing, rocking back and forth, the stun gun still in her hand.

'You knew she was being killed,' Cliff repeated, 'and you knew it was me.'

Tamsin was breathing like she'd been running, and she was pale and sweating.

'I hear what you're saying,' I said, unable to stop myself from registering that Tamsin wasn't the only one who had had a sad disillusionment here.

I was feeling stronger by the minute. I was going to take that stun gun away from her if I had to beat her senseless to do it. In fact, that was starting to sound very appealing.

'I'll help you out, Tamsin,' I said, staring into Cliff's eyes. I noticed, as I pulled myself up to my knees, that Cliff had made great progress unwrapping his wrists. In a minute, he would be much more of a factor than he was right now. I gripped the arm of a couch, and pushed myself up. I thought my muscles would all work. Upright had never felt so good.

Cliff began rolling around on the open floor like a giant bowling pin. He had given up plucking subtly at his wrist bindings. His fingers were tearing at the last wraparound of the silver tape, yanking so hard they sometimes broke his skin.

Tamsin, standing in the open doorway, looked absolutely crazed. 'Kill him, Lily!' she shrieked. 'Kill him kill him kill him!'

They were both using up valuable oxygen, as far as I was concerned. While Tamsin had been enumerating her woes earlier, I'd been learning the room. A sofa and an armchair divided by a small table, a television on an oak stand, and my cleaning caddy; and in it, my cell phone. It was awfully close to Tamsin, too close, I'd decided. I wouldn't willingly get within range of that stun gun again. Somewhat closer, there was a telephone on the table between the couch and the chair.

I snatched up the phone and hit nine one one before Cliff crashed into me from behind. I went sprawling on the couch, rapping my nose sharply on the edge of the wooden arm. Suddenly there was blood everywhere, and a blinding pain.

I scrambled up as quickly as the pain permitted. Tamsin was shrieking and darting at Cliff with the stun gun, only to dodge away when he got near enough to kick at her. Seeing Cliff still rolling on the floor, his hands still bound, I realized that he was looking for something to roll up against, to provide stability so he might be able to struggle upright. I brought back my foot and kicked him as hard as I could, just as he ripped his bonds apart. I didn't have time to choose, but my foot connected with his lower back. The jolt ran all the way up to my face and made my nose hurt even more. He bellowed in pain, and I very nearly joined him.

'That's it, Lily! Kick the son of a bitch!' yelled Tamsin, delighted. She actually had her arms up in the air in a cheerleader gesture. No way she could get the stun gun down in time. I hoped fervently that I'd recovered enough strength to finish this. I took two strides, drew back my fist and hit her in the pit of her stomach as hard as I've ever hit anyone in my life. To my intense pleasure, Tamsin finally shut up. I stood swaying on my feet, watching her gag.

The moment of silence was as refreshing as a cool shower, but it ended when Jack dashed in. He stood in the doorway panting, his face dripping with sweat. 'You didn't call. How are you? Your nose is broken.' I nodded. He surveyed the floor, and looked at me. 'Well, which one of them did it?'

'Hell if I know,' I said, and called the police.

Because he is a good and merciful man, Claude let Alicia Stokes interview Tamsin. 'If you're smart,' he told Alicia in his deep, rumbly voice, 'you'll learn more about being a cop in the next two hours than you have in the last year.' Jack and I were sitting in the designated waiting chairs as they came through on their way to the interview rooms. Alicia gave me a long, thoughtful look as she went into one interview room.

Claude was in charge of Cliff, whom the hospital had treated and released.

The only part I had left to play was that of incidental victim. My misery and my trembling muscles were the byproduct of the secret war between Tamsin and Cliff. They were victims of each other; at least, that's how I figured it. How a man and a woman who both set out to do good, at least by their choices of professions, could have gone so far into the red zone of human torment is not something I care to understand.

I had gone to the hospital to have a nose X ray, and then home to shower, before I was due at the police station. I was still shaky and felt very much like some other person who bore only a distant relationship to Lily Bard. Jack made it clear I wasn't going anywhere without him. I gave him no argument when he said he was going to drive me to the police station.

I was feeling much more like myself by the time Alicia and Claude sat down with me to go over what Tamsin had said before Jack came in like the cavalry. From the direction their questions took, I pieced together the public line they would take in their prosecution.

Claude believed that most of what Tamsin had said was true. But he thought that Tamsin must have realized Cliff's intentions earlier than she alleged. In fact, he thought the move to Shakespeare had been conceived by Tamsin, who believed a small town's less experienced and sophisticated police department would not be able to solve any crimes committed on its turf, provided the criminal was clever. Well, as Claude put it, the hell with her.

On one level, their marriage had proceeded at a predictable pace. They made love, worked, fought sometimes, and each made their own plans. On another level, they were engaged in a life-and-death struggle.

'I don't know what happened in their early marriage, but Cliff's deep problems with his wife seem to have started because of the miscarriage. Tamsin seemed to enjoy the sympathy it earned her, to a real suspicious extent,' Claude said, recrossing his ankles. His feet were propped up on the edge of his desk in his favorite pose.

'Tamsin said she thought he wanted to collect on her insurance money, too,' I said.

Claude shook his head. 'I just don't see money as an important part of this, and I guess it's the first time I ever said that.'

I shrugged.

'But somehow, at some point, he decided to make a game out of retaliation. Tamsin was fun to scare. She had more education than Cliff, more pretensions; he enjoyed getting the edge back.'

'Cliff upped the ante when he killed Saralynn,' Alicia Stokes said. She'd been sweating. Her skin gleamed like highly polished mahogany. 'Tamsin admitted to herself, then, that she suspected her husband. Maybe his footsteps in the hall were too familiar for her to block the knowledge from herself.'

'She told you that?' I asked.

Stokes nodded, slowly and deliberately. 'Yes, she figured Cliff had access to her keys to the building, knew its layout and her routine, and also knew she was meeting a new group member early.'

'Janet's appearance was a real shock.' The chief of police resumed his part of the narrative. After all these months of silent struggle, talking must have been a relief to both Tamsin and Cliff. I would have called a lawyer, myself, and clammed up, but that was not as much a stretch for me as for most people. 'And the fact that Tamsin stayed in the conference room. I think he'd looked forward to her reaction to finding the body; he'd planned on at least listening to the sound effects from out in the lobby. But she stayed low, and he had to leave. He knew the members of the group would be arriving soon. He went out the front door and to his car, which he'd parked at Shakespeare Pharmacy about half a block away. He didn't think anyone would particularly remember his car at the pharmacy, and he was right. Then he showed up at the health center. He expected his wife to completely collapse. But she bore up under it pretty well. Cliff's reaction, in the parking lot, you remember how upset he seemed? He really was.'

'What about Gerry McClanahan?' Jack took another drink from his plastic foam cup of station-house coffee. He'd be up all night. I would be too, unless the pills Carrie had given me packed a true wallop. I had had many painful things happen to me, but the broken nose ranked right up there in the top three. I had tomorrow to look forward to, when Jack said my face would be even more arresting. But at least I was clean and dry, and the soiled clothes were in the washer back at the house.

I was putting my money on Gerry having pegged Cliff as the stalker, but as it turned out I was half wrong.

Claude had just finished reading Gerry McClanahan's notes about the odd behavior of his neighbors. In fact, when Jack's call had come into the station, Claude and Alicia had been discussing what they could prove, and who would be charged with what. Tamsin's mental collapse had settled some of their questions.

As the surveillance log showed, Gerry had noticed Cliff going to the toolshed at what Gerry considered odd times. The writer had thought it was strange that Cliff always emerged empty-handed. Gerry had sneaked over to check out the shed once or twice when Cliff and Tamsin were both gone. He'd seen an animal cage, but didn't question its presence until the dead squirrel was found hanging from the tree. After reading the police report on the incident, Gerry had retrieved the squirrel corpse from the garbage where Jack had put it. Then he'd stolen the cage (I'd later seen it in Gerry's house after his death), which contained plenty of squirrel hairs. Gerry planned to get a lab to test the creature's DNA.

Claude didn't know if such a test was possible, or if it was, if the results would be admissible in court. But from Claude's voice I could tell he admired Gerry's tenacity and his willingness to put his money where his mouth was.

The page of Gerry's log I'd found had noted that Cliff went to the toolshed the night before we'd found the poor squirrel murdered.

Gerry had planned to return the cage so Cliff wouldn't get suspicious. But before he could act, he witnessed something even stranger. He'd seen Tamsin sabotaging her own back steps. The worm had turned.

Gerry had been completely gripped in the drama he saw unfolding before him. He'd acted like a writer instead of a cop, and when Cliff had noticed the missing cage and followed the faint traces of footsteps in the damp yard, he'd come across Gerry. Maybe Gerry had already been out in his backyard, filling out his log; maybe Cliff had knocked on Gerry's back door and demanded an explanation or created some excuse to get Gerry outside. And he'd killed him. Later, reasoning that two stabbings would throw the police off even more than one, he'd staged the clumsy attempt on himself. A hastily arranged mistake, that self-stabbing; Tamsin could not have had any doubt after that, no matter how much she had blinded herself to the truth.

'But she backed Cliff up,' Jack said incredulously. 'When he said he'd never seen the knife before, the one in Gerry's throat. Surely she recognized it? And Cliff had called me, to have me back in Shakespeare so maybe I'd get blamed for Gerry's death.'

'The world would've been a better place if those two had never met,' Claude said.

'Uh-huh, you got that right,' Alicia said, trying to cover her yawn with her hand.

'As for you, Detective Stokes, we need to have a private conference. Cliff Eggers has told me he recognized you from Cleveland. I have reason to believe you've been far more aware and involved in this case than you saw fit to tell me. According to you, Tamsin's case was one you'd heard about while you were on the Cleveland force, not one you'd worked on.'

Alicia suddenly looked wide awake.

'Well, Lily and I will be going home now,' Jack said. He held out his hand, and I took it gratefully. He gave me a gentle pull to help me up. Having help was such a luxury. I hoped I never would grow to take it for granted. At least I could be sure that Jack and I would never become like Cliff and Tamsin. Our hard times and aggressive impulses had been flashed to the world. Everyone knew what we were capable of. We didn't have to prove ourselves in any secret way.

Claude clapped Jack on the shoulder, just when Jack was

almost out of the room. Claude said, 'By the way, a little bird told me you married this woman.' He was not smiling and he did not look happy. Something pretty old-fashioned and definitely paternalistic had surfaced in Claude. 'You better treat her right.'

'I'll do my best,' Jack said.

'He hasn't done too bad the first three months,' I said.

Claude began smiling at us. Behind him, I saw Stokes was sitting in the old office chair with her mouth hanging open. 'When are you planning on letting the rest of the world in on this?' Claude asked.

'It's seeping out gradually,' I said. 'We just wanted to get used to the fact ourselves, first.'

'Was my wife the first to know?' Claude still sounded proud saying 'my wife'.

'Yes, my wife told your wife,' Jack said, grinning like an idiot.

As the door began to close behind us, we heard Claude open a conversation with his detective. 'You want to tell me who you're really working for, Stokes?' he began, and then the door thudded into place.

Though the next day was Monday, Jack and I lay in bed late. My face was swollen and bruised and I looked like hell. I still felt a bit weak from the stun gun, which the police had regarded with great respect. They'd charged Tamsin with use of a prohibited weapon, in addition to all the other charges. I wondered if Sneaky Pete would get into trouble, but I couldn't summon up enough energy to get really worked up about it.

'How could two people who are supposed to love each other get so crossed up?' Jack asked. 'They could have just gotten a divorce, like other couples.'

'They must have enjoyed their little war, somehow. Perfectly matching pathologies.' I'd been thinking of getting up and changing our sheets, but it was so nice to have a reason to lie in bed, so pleasant to have Jack beside me. I was sure I would get used to that pleasure, in time; waking up beside Jack would become routine. I'd begin to notice the little things that irritate any spouse. But because of the tenor of my life, I appreciated the simple fact of love. So did Jack.

I couldn't help but feel convinced that if Tamsin and Cliff had deserved each other, so did Jack and I. Gazing up at my white ceiling in my clean bedroom, I pictured a panorama of centuries of mating: of men and women looking for the perfect match, and finding pairings that were at best convenient – at worst, the product of one twisted psyche calling to another equally perverse.

I had been a child of love. My parents were lucky in their marriage, and I had been the beneficiary of that luck. After I'd been forced into a different kind of mating, I'd changed irrevocably into someone my former self would hardly have recognized. It seemed to me that now I had a chance to change back. I wondered if that was really possible.

But I am not a woman who can sit and think theoretically for long stretches of time, and I am not a woman who can change philosophy easily. In fact, I floated away from that vista of pairings and sank back into myself on the bed with a distinct feeling of relief.

'Today,' I said, 'we're going to clean the gutters.'

Acknowledgments

My thanks to Laura Lippman, Phil Gates, Susan McBride, and Officer Kelly Blair, who all were kind enough to answer more or less peculiar questions.

There's more than one story in Shakespeare . . .

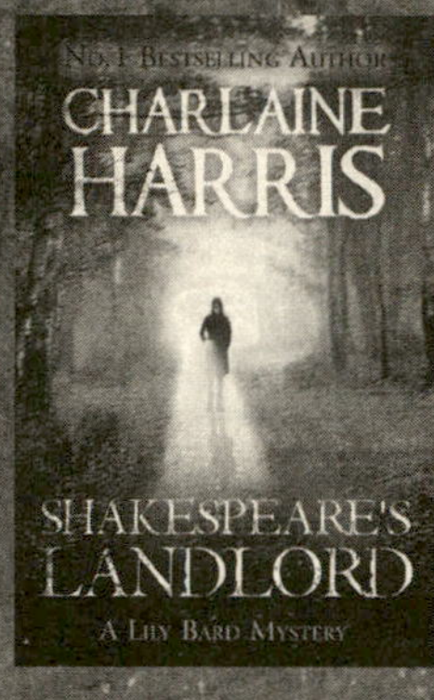

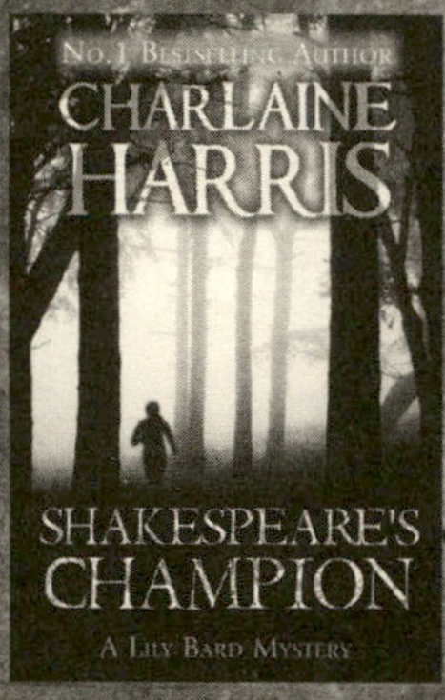

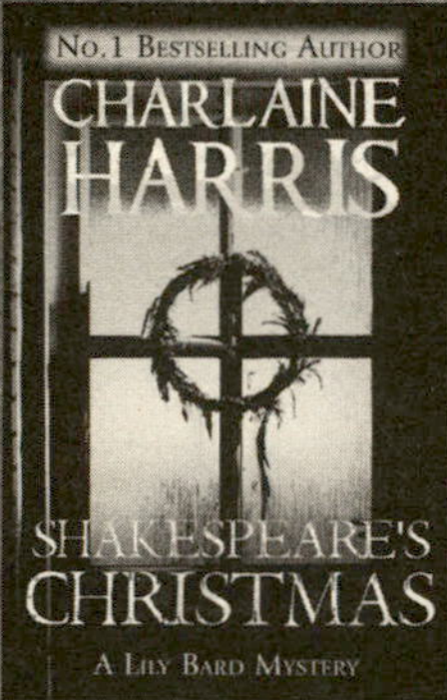

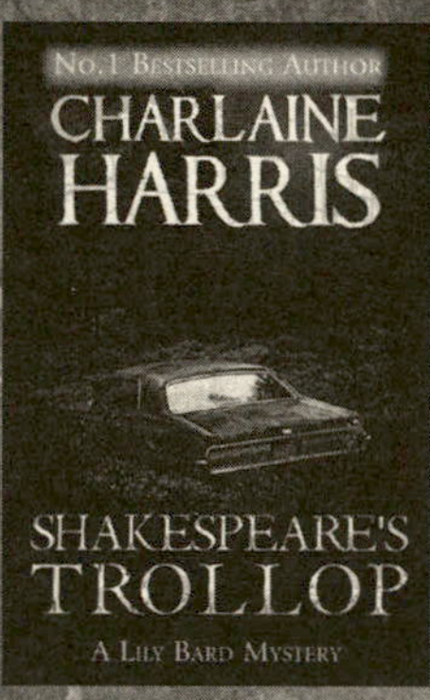

THE LILY BARD MYSTERIES

MORE CHARLAINE
MORE MURDER